Skinny Women Are Perfect

a novel

T.Richard

iUniverse, Inc.
Bloomington

SKINNY WOMEN ARE PERFECT
A NOVEL

iUniverse books may be ordered through booksellers or by contacting:

iUniverse
1663 Liberty Drive
Bloomington, IN 47403
www.iuniverse.com
1-800-Authors (1-800-288-4677)

ISBN: 978-1-4759-7912-1 (sc)
ISBN: 978-1-4759-7913-8 (hc)
ISBN: 978-1-4759-7914-5 (e)

Library of Congress Control Number: 2013904058

Printed in the United States of America

iUniverse rev. date: 5/15/2013

Dedicated to the Richard in T.Richard

Thank you for being the best part of me and making sure
I know the real definition of beauty.

For Mum, you always see the beauty in me.

With love.

One – *The Four Chicas*

"Hey, Vista." Vernon greeted me over the phone in a playful tone as I sat at my desk, expecting a call from a business client. My brother knew I hated anyone calling me that.

I responded with a tinge of irritation. "What do you want?" And as he should have expected, the conversation was brief.

"Just saying hi. You sound really busy," Vernon commented, the playfulness in his voice now tempered.

"Yes, Vernon, I'm waiting on a call," I said, not letting up on my irritation.

"Oh come on, Rory, you know I love that name." He sounded as if he were feigning sincerity.

"And you know I don't. Good-bye Vernon; I'll call you later," I said as I hung up without allowing for any rebuttal or finding out exactly the purpose of his call.

Vista Aurora Glazer is what's written on my birth certificate. Vista? I was convinced that my name was inspired by my mother's drug-induced spells at the hospital. She said she wanted to name me only after meeting me, so go figure—she met me when coming off her epidural and Demerol high. I hated my name, and so I went by Rory Carter.

"Carter" is thanks to my adorable husband, Michael Carter. He has that "get along with everyone" personality in a subtle, charming way. They say there is no real Prince Charming, but to the naysayers: you haven't met Mr. Michael Carter. I really could go on and on about him, and his butt cheeks get their own rave reviews!

I stand about five feet six inches, and currently my weight fluctuates between 150 and 155 pounds. I am thirty-one years old, with a twin brother who is seven minutes older than me. He has to live with the name Vernon Golin Glazer! You have to really wonder what my parents were thinking with our names.

It would be different if we were stinking rich, and then our names would be distinguished by default. Instead we were middle class, and our names, as our middle-school classmates put it, were "stupid!" Vernon's was okay, but of me they would ask, "Why did your parents name you Vista? What the hell does that even mean?" The great thing about some of those loudmouthed classmates was that they weren't particularly the smartest, so they really couldn't come up with any rhymes to make the name worse. They just hated my name, and that's where it started and ended—with the name.

My size was a different story. Those were my extremely heavy, awkward, and self-deprecatingly insecure days. Where I got my heavy build from is still a mystery. My mother was model perfect, and the pictures prove that she has been, at every age. My dad had a solid athletic build and has never been heavy. Vernon was a spitting image of my father in every sense, so with his natural athletic build and ability, he has been on one athletic team or another right from elementary school—and along with that came swooning from the opposite sex.

I was a spitting image of me.

I never knew I was "fat pig," "big chunk," or "Michelin tire," until I got to middle school. At home, I wasn't fat. I was just Rory with a healthy appetite. Regardless of a seemingly healthy home life, the name calling, teasing, and pranks eventually took their toll on me emotionally. Once before gym class, someone took my gym shorts and poured honey in the pockets. Not long after I got them on, while I was still in the girls' locker room, it started oozing out. A handful of classmates exclaimed that fat was literally evaporating from my body. I didn't cry on the outside because I couldn't give them the satisfaction, but I was wailing on the inside. The teacher stood by the door and yelled, "You can sit out of class and clean yourself up."

I grew to like nothing about how I looked except for my face and my hair. My dark, full hair hung perfectly, never a strand out of place. But all the beautiful hair in the world didn't make any of my classmates see me as beautiful. Seeing that the only girls Vernon and the other jocks hung out with were about half my size, only made it worse. The solution seemed obvious to me: to be considered attractive by anyone, I had to lose weight. I buried my feelings deep inside, pasted a smile on my face, and determined to become one of the pretty, thin girls.

The plan was simple: less food, more physical activities by joining sports and dance teams, aerobics with exercise tapes, weekly check on the scale, and I should reach my goal of being this beautiful, skinny girl. The monkey wrench in my plan was my mother, who wasn't having any of it. "You can't skimp on meals," she'd say. At the dinner table, she glared at me as I pushed the food around my plate.

"If you don't want that," Vernon said, reaching over and spooning mashed potatoes off my plate, "I'll take it."

It took two weeks, but finally my mom had had enough. "Rory, I don't know what's going on with you, but if you're going to just play with your food, then just don't eat," she said in a stern tone. And so it began. I flirted with starvation and skipped some meals altogether. But since she hadn't linked my eating habits to my poor body image, she also started cooking different meals for me to accommodate what she thought was my changing palette.

Thanks to Mom, in less than a month of embarking on phase one of my master plan to become beautifully thin, it crashed before it even started. Her savory dishes made only for me, were near impossible to resist without intense scrutiny. Phase two was also a failure, thanks again to Mom. The ever-involved mother that she was, this time she questioned my involvement in the added extracurricular activities which now included being part of two dance teams.

"Why are you trying to kill yourself?" she asked.

"I really like all of them and couldn't choose," I lied.

"That's not true," she pressed, the suspicion audible in her voice.

How do you tell your mom that you just want to be as beautiful as she is? That no matter how much you tried to explain it, she wouldn't understand? How do you tell your mom all the names you get called in school, when you know that hearing them would hurt her? Everyone talks about how gorgeous my mom is, and she has never been my size, so in my head there was no way she could relate.

I was careful in my approach of the subject with her; I knew it was important to her that I never saw myself as different. For example, whenever we went shopping, she bought me the same chic styles that she wore, only my size was bigger. Whatever didn't quite fit right, my mom made sure a seamstress fit it to my size. I remember how bad it felt to have one of those conversations with my mom when I had barely hit my teenage years.

"I really don't know how to talk to you about it, Mom," I said.

"About what?" she asked.

"Well … I just need to be skinny," I said with blunt resignation.

"You *need* to be skinny?" she asked, in a confused tone.

"Yes, Mom. Look around. People like you are the attractive ones," I responded quietly.

I know she didn't really know what to say, and as I continued to share some of my experiences in school with her, I felt bad that I was making my mom go through listening to this. I knew there was nothing she could do, but with the tears that were welling up in the corners of her eyes, I also knew she would spend plenty of time worrying about it all. I now felt selfish for telling her any of it.

"You know there's nothing wrong with you, right?" she eventually said. I didn't respond, but nodded, knowing she was right but feeling she was so wrong. She hugged me. It was tight and I felt the helplessness right through her chest.

For days after our talk, my mother would make me cards that offered sentiments of how beautiful and special she thought I was. One was inscribed, "Beauty is in the eye of the beholder. I am the one beholding you, and you are the most beautiful thing I see." Although corny, that was probably one of my favorites. For my remaining two years of high school, as consistently as she could, she continued with the sentiments, which sometimes came in the form of cards, an uplifting voice message, and little notes in my notebook that I would find days later. It meant the world that I had my mother in my corner, but no amount of cards could stop me from getting on that scale every time I took a restroom break, hoping that even an ounce of fat had been shed from my body.

With every phase of my weight-loss plan annulled by the end of high school, my next plan was to get away from all the people I knew in Caldwell, New Jersey. As caring as my mom was, I needed to be away from her prying eyes as she now constantly looked over my shoulder to make sure I wasn't dabbling in any more crazy weight-loss plans. I know, I know—she was a caring mother who wanted to make sure her daughter didn't become anorexic or bulimic, and I have always been thankful for that, but the teenage me thought that I might have had a chance of working toward being beautifully skinny without Mom's constant voice in my head. Yeah, she thought I was "perfect the way you are"; however, I wasn't living in her world 24–7 but in the outside world that *did* judge me as entirely unperfect the way I looked. My mother wasn't in denial about my physical reality; she just couldn't accept that it was a big deal to me. To her, I wasn't overweight but full-figured. What she *may* have been in denial about is the fact that in high school, no one was going around delicately referring to someone as full-figured. No, you were simply fat!

That last year of high school, I was a college-searching machine. The initial motivation was to get away from my small world in Caldwell, but the process of my college search soon became a fulfilling goal all its own. It became an exploration into worlds that were beyond me, and fantasies of meeting people who weren't going to judge me from the minute they saw me. My flights of fancy fueled my college search, and it excited me. My mom was rooting for two nearby universities and hoping that New York City was the farthest I would go. To appease her, I checked them out, but my plan was to move farther out. I applied everywhere that had a great arts department, even as far as Singapore.

We weren't yet sure what my key artistic talent was; I could sketch almost anything, and I loved photography and painting. I had taught myself almost every graphic and design software program available and was good at it, designing logos and overall identities for anyone who asked. The problem was that I didn't quite prefer any one of those talents over another. I was hoping college would challenge me into selecting one or two of them to focus on, and thereby build my career.

My top two choices were Hardford University in Washington, DC, and Boulvare Institute of Art, in Atlanta, Georgia. I visited both with my mom and Vernon, finally turning down BIA because it didn't have a well-developed graphic arts curriculum. Hardford it was.

I walked into Hardford's arts building, and it was a true dream. Each wing in the building fed into each of my artistic interests, saying to me, *If you can't figure it out here, you won't figure it out anywhere.* The college offered me a full academic scholarship for my first year. I had the opportunity to reapply for the same scholarship yearly as long as I maintained a minimum 3.75 grade point average.

I was excited to be moving to DC, totally excited. It was far enough from home to provide me the distance that I craved but close enough to make my mother happy.

During our last summer at home, the closeness Vernon and I shared grew from the whole twin thing to being friends as well. We were each leaving home at the end of the summer, and Vernon decided to teach me how to drive even though I wasn't being sent to college with a car. My father had taught Vernon, and I still can't put my finger on why I wasn't privy to those lessons; in all fairness, I also hadn't been too eager to learn. Vernon taught me how to work both my dad's stick shift as well as my mother's automatic. In those six weeks that we went driving, we got to know each other.

When it came up in conversation, I filled him in on some of the details of the teasing about my weight. Although we had never discussed it before and he had not let on if he had suspected anything, I just knew he had to have known something. Every now and then, out of the blue, he would ask if everything was okay. I had always said it was.

"You never really said anything to me, Rory," he said.

"Vernon! As if you didn't know what was going on? I didn't have to say anything to you."

"Okay, maybe I suspected one thing or another every now and then, but honestly, Rory, the way I see it, if I defended you against that crap, that would have meant I was agreeing that there was something wrong with you," he explained. I knew it—he *had* known something. *What the fuck!* I thought to myself.

"Also, it toughens you up for when no one's there to defend you," he continued.

Tough love, just like my dad, but did it have to be so tough? As I sat there in the driver's seat, my emotions were mixed. My feelings fluctuated between a sense of incredulity that he truly believed he did me a favor and a brewing anger. Anger at him, and even though *he* wasn't there at the time, anger at my father. Vernon definitely got that ability to dismiss another's emotions from my father, so I had to blame my father for that. Perhaps he had even talked about it with my father, because those words surely sounded crafted by my father and not Vernon.

Anger was winning. The tears that were welling up in my eyes weren't from sadness, but that anger that now coupled itself with a feeling of abandonment. I did not feel like explaining to Vernon why saying something at the time of his suspicion would have meant the world to me. Still maintaining a steady sight of the road, Vernon glanced over in my direction, trying to read my silence. Not once did I look at Vernon, because I am sure the tears would have fallen, and I wasn't in the mental state to explain to him exactly what those tears meant. I tried to appreciate his line of thinking for not defending me, I really did, but no matter how much I tried to understand it, I still wished he had stood up for me.

On a clear Saturday early afternoon, driver's license in hand and only two bags in tow, and accompanied by Vernon and my mom, I was college bound. The excitement that filled me was only matched by the crippling fear that this experience that I had craved so much wouldn't in fact be my saving grace. We rented a sport utility vehicle, and Vernon and I took turns driving.

L Street in DC was busy, and with butterflies beginning to flutter in my stomach, I prayed the traffic would extend even further. I could see Hardford U ahead of us, and all of a sudden, I felt that I wasn't quite ready to make this journey. Located in Washington, DC, it wasn't an enclosed campus. Although the campus spanned several buildings throughout the city, the main campus primarily lined L Street and the admissions building sat at the intersection of L Street and Hardford Road, marking the official start of the institution.

Panicking internally, I thought about roommates and classmates and teammates. *What will they think about me? Will they like me? Will we get along? Will I be the biggest girl in my residence hall?* I was sick to my stomach, but I couldn't procrastinate. We were there. I picked up everything that I would need for registration; got my key cards for my room, residence hall, and mailbox; and said a quick prayer that I'd be the first person in my room. My prayer was answered.

The building I was assigned to was called The Ship, and it had absolutely nothing to do with the shape or a painting on the building that summoned thoughts of the sea. It was so named because it housed all scholarship recipients.

Our suites were set up as mini apartments, with four people to a suite. An average-sized room was on each side of the apartment, with the living room and kitchen serving as the median dividers. Each bedroom was equipped with its own full bathroom.

Vernon and I started moving in my belongings while my mom stayed in the room. She was going to get me hated by my roommates on my first day. By the time Vernon and I were back in the room, she had started interior designing my room. It explained what was in the enormous bag that she had brought along with her. I had assumed it was just one of her travel bags.

"Mom, you do know she has to share this room with someone, right?" asked Vernon.

"I know, I'm helping them spice it up," she said in defense.

"What if *her* mom walks in here and starts doing exactly the same thing, with absolutely no consultation from the two people who will actually be living here?" continued Vernon. Although she reluctantly stopped, I knew she wouldn't give up that easily.

It took Vernon and me only two trips to the car before all my stuff was in my new room; two suitcases, my computer, and my exercise bike were all I had. The room had two separate walk-in closets and two dressers. I wanted to be considerate and wait for the others to get there before I started setting up, but Mom was impatient at not being able to start decorating, and she insisted we start setting up my closet. Vernon left to go and check both of them into their hotel rooms for the weekend.

Left alone with Mom, she started ranting, "This can't be all the stuff you brought down here, Rory! This is nothing. We are going shopping before I leave."

"This is really all I need Mom, seriously." Although I appreciated her desire to leave me fully prepared as she viewed it, I didn't know all that I would need yet, so I was beginning to feel as if she was being a bit overbearing.

"No it isn't," said an unfamiliar voice coming from the doorway to my room. I turned to see a well-toned model entering the room. She was picture-perfect thin. Vernon had left the main door to the suite open, and there was so much movement going on through the entire floor that we hadn't heard her come in.

"Sierra Snowden," she said, introducing herself with an outstretched arm. "You don't mind us being roommates, do you?" she asked. She looked nice enough.

"Nope, my name's Rory, and this is my mom, Katherine Glazer."

"Call me Kathy," my mom said. She looked around Sierra. "You're not here by yourself are you?" my mother asked.

"Oh no, my two older brothers are on their way with my van-load of stuff." She looked at my meager belongings. "You've got to be kidding me." She lightly chuckled. "All your stuff could fit into one of my suitcases."

"We're definitely going shopping before I leave," my mother assured her.

Sierra's brothers finally made their first trip up to the room, and they weren't happy.

"Damn, this shit is heavy!" one of them exclaimed as they set one of Sierra's trunks on the floor.

"If I knew there were stairs involved, I swear I wouldn't have put all her stuff in the truck," the other brother chimed in.

The first brother, who now noticed they had company, added, "Sorry about that. I'm Shane."

"I'm Sean," the other brother greeted.

My mom didn't seem to care about the cursing. Gingerly looking past the brothers, she was looking to see if there were any parents in the background. Not seeing anyone, she started showing Sierra her thoughts for interior-designing the room and asked if she minded her setting the place up.

"You seem really passionate about decorating this place," said Sierra with no real emotional attachment to my mom's desire to decorate the room.

"Don't you think these walls are entirely too bland?" offered my mom.

"Hey, as long as I don't have to pay for any of it, you can have at it." It was clear that Sierra, like myself, could not care less what the walls looked like right now. I was more concerned about the people I would be rooming with; a nicely decorated room wasn't going to ease my mind about that.

Sierra was about three inches taller than me, and she was gorgeous. She had naturally dirty-blonde hair, which at that time she wore shoulder length in no particular style. If I could imagine a near-perfect hourglass shape on a slender frame, it was her. She had brown eyes and baby pink lips; there were no rosy cheeks to match the lips, but sculpted high cheekbones and perfectly arched eyebrows to complement a perpetual picture-ready look. Her long, full eyelashes, also gave her face a sultry sweetness that added to her beauty. On that summer Saturday in mid-August, she had on light blue fitted pants with a shirtdress. She topped it off with a three-quarter-length light denim jean vest and a tattered newsboy cap.

Her style was what I came to call bohemian-chic. Unabashedly looking me over, she expressed how much she loved my style. I hesitated with providing my grateful response, believing she was simply being polite. It was the first time an age-mate had given me an image-related compliment. Like many before her, she stared at my hair. She actually came over and ran her hand through my hair. I didn't know how to take this whole moment and found it all a bit awkward. She asked, "What do you use on your hair?" My hair almost always looked as if I had just had a good wash and a professional blow-drying at the salon. That was never the case.

My mom laughed, offering, "Everyone asks Rory that, and I don't get it." My mom knew that I used nothing more than generic products in my hair.

Sierra got on my bike to ride while her brothers did all her moving-in. By the time her brothers got all her stuff in and tried to figure out how to wall-mount her television, I was done organizing my stuff neatly into my closet and dresser. I looked up and around to see the guys sweating profusely. Sierra kept talking and riding. I wasn't listening to her and couldn't tell if she was talking to me anyway, so I didn't feel bad about walking out of the room to the kitchen area to get them something to drink.

"We don't have any ice, but my mom got some bottled water and apple juice," I called out to her brothers. Shane and Sean joined me in the kitchen, effectively leaving my mother as Sierra's only audience. Without answering to a preference, Sean took a bottled water out of my hand with a "Thanks." He uncapped it and gulped down the water in what seemed like only three swallows. "Care for another?" I asked with a raised eyebrow. Shane, Sean, and I chuckled as Shane took the bottle of apple juice and much less dramatically, quenched his thirst. I stood there in the kitchen, enjoying their company.

I noticed that while all the movement was going on around her, Sierra had cycled over five miles on my bike—and in half the time it would have taken me. Although she was breaking a sweat, she wasn't out of breath.

"Track scholarship?" I asked.

"Yep." She grinned. "You don't know what it means that you have a bike in here," she continued excitedly. "This way I can continue with my own training even when I am not training with the team."

"This way, you guys can team up on your workouts," my

mother chimed in. I shot her an ungrateful look while I mouthed, "I'm sure she has to practice with the team, Mom."

"I had thought about bringing in some exercise machine," she continued, "but I didn't know if my roommate would mind the noise." Sierra hopped off the bike finally, heaving a contented sigh. "This is great."

"Oh, great." The exasperated whisper escaped my lips. Now I had a roommate who was going to be a workout nut, so even if I tried my hardest, I would never measure up to doing enough at my workouts. Just great.

Sierra only got off the bike after her brothers had finished successfully mounting the television, even though they had continuously asked her to get off as they wanted to get back to Frederick, Maryland. Shane looked at his watch for the second time in less than thirty seconds. "Sierra, do you not care about having your car with you at school?"

"What time do they close?" Sierra queried with no sense of urgency. She didn't even acknowledge that clearly her brothers wanted to depart immediately so that they could return home in good time and she could pick up her car that was currently in the shop.

Just then, Vernon showed up—right on time for our planned dinner outing that evening. Sierra asked to come along with us. *Didn't they have to leave?* I wanted to spend this time with my mom and brother, alone. Hoping she would take the cue to leave with her brothers, I said, "I'm sure your brothers are hungry too, Sierra."

"So why don't we take two cars?" she asked by way of actually inviting herself and her brothers. My approach had backfired. We all headed out to dinner at an independently owned steakhouse in downtown DC.

Although I was curious about Sierra's background, I would have picked another time to hear about it, but through several mouthfuls, she chose that dinner to share. They had lost their mother when Sierra was ten years old, and their father kind of disappeared afterward. They had been staying at their maternal grandmother's house shortly after the death, and he never came back for them. They knew exactly where he was, and unsolicited promises from him that he'd be coming back, eventually gave way to them getting sporadic financial assistance from him.

As awkwardly as Sierra had journeyed into her past, she reverted back to her plans for that weekend. It was a torturous dinner for me that I was happy so see end. Sierra left with her brothers to get her car, and she would be returning later that night. I looked forward to being by myself, but my excitement at finally getting some alone time was short-lived. Once we were back in the car, my mom instructed Vernon to locate the nearest mall to get a few things that she insisted I had forgotten.

I had *forgotten* a lot of stuff, it seemed. We were out till about 1 a.m. and returned with a fully loaded vehicle. Thankfully, Mom was ready to fall out, so Vernon took them back to their hotel. I couldn't remember being so happy to be alone in my own space. I took a shower and settled in. In our focus to get all my newly acquired possessions into the suite, I hadn't noticed that another one of my roommates had moved in. However, it was now two o'clock Sunday morning, and Sierra—who unfortunately for me was back—very ungraciously let me know, "We've got another bitch in the house." Her tone wasn't mean-spirited, but the Sierra who walked into our room in the wee hours of the morning was a slightly different personality from the one I met earlier that day. This one sounded crass, rude, and a bit of a bitch herself. The "new bitch" in the house wasn't actually there, and I was thankful because how the hell would she have taken to such an introduction?

I really hated that Sierra was back. I just wanted to go to bed, but Sierra started talking about nothing that was meaningful to me, and she continued until four in the morning. I barely said two words through her soliloquy, but I still couldn't go to sleep until she shut the hell up. So many times the silence command was on the tip of my tongue, but instead I retreated right back to that Caldwell High School girl who just couldn't speak up for herself as she should.

Sunday morning, I made myself get up at nine. It was customary for Mom to find a Catholic church for us to go to whatever city we found ourselves in, and this Sunday was no different. She had left a message really early in the morning that St. Joseph's was less than a mile from Hardford U and had a service at ten thirty that we just weren't going to be late for. My mom was late for everything under the sun—oh, but not church. I have since come to realize that my mother believed that going to church late was an unforgivable sin all by itself. Today I really needed her to be late, or forget about it all together, but my better judgment knew they would be at the dorm promptly at ten.

I needed a little bit of noise to jolt me into really staying awake as opposed to rolling over under the sheets and slipping back into comfortable unconsciousness. I turned on the television to *CNN Headline News*, and before I could fully acclimate myself to the idea of being awake against my earthly wish, I heard, "What the fuck is that? Can you turn that shit off! I'm trying to sleep." Turning the volume down slightly, all I could think was, *No, this girl couldn't be serious, not after she kept me up the whole night.* I proceeded to fully curse her out—in my head.

I got into the shower, knowing that whatever tone the conversation was going to take, I still couldn't engage it. I locked the door. This morning shower was more for my mental state than a need to freshen up for the day. This was one of the moments that my anxiety was making me feel quite conscious of my weight, and for whatever reason, my weight always seemed to drop a pound or two right after a shower. I *needed* that shower. I turned the showerhead off and stood in the tub as I whisked the water off my body. The anticipation of seeing a lesser number on that scale was already lessening my anxiety. I climbed out of the shower and stepped directly onto the glass body scale. There it was; it read out the numbers two pounds lighter. A smile relaxed my facial muscles and sent the same relaxation signals through my whole being. My anxiety-reducing shower had taken about fifteen minutes, and I was dressed in another fifteen.

When I walked back into the room, Sierra was up. "You're headed to church? Man, I wish I had gotten up a little earlier. I would have gone with you. Thanks for getting me up though; I have so much stuff to do today and need an early start." All this she said with an "I just got out of bed" smile on her face.

I stood there for a couple of seconds with an utterly confused look on my face, debating a response. I was fully convinced that I was sharing my room with a schizophrenic, bipolar, foul-mouthed, bohemian, track-running, freak of nature! I got that timely phone call from my mother right at that second, letting me know they were turning into The Ship's parking lot. I hurriedly told them that I would meet them downstairs. "Say hi to your mom and have a good service. Say a prayer for me," Sierra called out as I was leaving. Sure. I bolted, having given no response.

I was going to definitely say a prayer that she would find a reason to permanently vacate the room because she would meet with the coach, and he would prefer that all the members of the track team stay together—that would be the prayer I would be saying in church that day. That, together with praying that the new girl who had moved in was nothing like this human being that I was so unfortunate to be rooming with. Sierra had seemed so different the day before.

"Hey, babe," my mom greeted. "You look good."

"Thanks, Mom," I responded, hopeful that a longer conversation would not ensue. It didn't.

It was only day one, and I felt I was in for an interesting ride rooming with Sierra. I was silent and in deep thought throughout the very short drive to church. Did I make a mistake wanting to leave Caldwell so badly, just to land in DC with someone who I was sure at this very moment, was certifiable? We got to church with ten minutes to spare before the bells started chiming, signaling the start of service.

After a more psychological than spiritual reprieve at church,

I got back to the dorm. A person who would have nailed the position as store manager at a high fashion boutique, greeted me at the door. It was roommate number two. There was a brand name on every part of her—a multiple billboard of sorts—that included the sunglasses she wore on top of her head, even though no sunlight beamed through the living space where she stood.

"You must be Rory," she said.

"I am. You must have met Sierra."

"Yes, very briefly, earlier on. I'm Bailey Irish Kennedy Johnson. Call me BJ." The accent was somewhere from the west, and the whole time she was talking, all I was trying to do was place where she was from. And I also couldn't help but notice how skinny she was. Not as slender as Sierra, but out of the three of us, I was still holding on strong to the "biggest girl in the suite" title. *The last roommate's got to be bigger than these two,* I thought, sighing internally.

We both stood there. I know *I* was contemplating whether or not to engage in the obligatory banter expected of two who had just met, in order to provide each other with those little tidbits needed later in building a relationship; maybe she was contemplating it too. I launched into it. "I'm from Caldwell, New Jersey, and got here yesterday. My mom and brother just left, actually."

"Oh come here; I do hugs," she said, almost relieved that I had decided to engage the obligation. "I didn't know if you would be welcoming," she said very honestly. I smiled.

She explained her reaction. "I did it the other way around earlier on with Sierra. I hugged her as I introduced myself, and she really didn't like that." This time I chuckled, wishing I could offer this new girl some comfort words regarding Sierra, but I couldn't.

"My family's from San Diego, California, but I've spent most of my life in Scottsdale, Arizona," said BJ, thankfully taking the lead of our introductory repartee. "And before you say it, yes I know there aren't that many of us, but there are a few black people in Scottsdale."

I wasn't going to say it—I knew very little about the whole state of Arizona, so I kept quiet. I liked this girl because, unlike me, she said what was on her mind. And unlike Sierra, the expression of her thoughts wasn't intrusive. She may have sensed that I wasn't particularly aligned with the current line of conversation, and she changed the focus to her need to get situated. "I need help with my room," she admitted, motioning toward her room.

"How the heck did you get all this stuff here from Arizona? This is a lot of stuff to put on a plane," I couldn't help exclaiming. Still lined up in the small hallway leading to her room were three Louis Vuitton luggage bags, and in the room were two more Louis Vuitton garment bags, a Tumi backpack, and about five more high-end bags whose brand names I wasn't familiar with.

"Oh my friend and I decided to make a road trip out of it and drove down here in a rented truck. And I need to find a way to get all my stuff into this room and out of the way before the last girl gets here," she replied.

I helped. She took that moment to fill me in on details about her favorite pastime: cooking. From the sounds of it alone, she was a good cook, and I was getting hungry just listening to her. I didn't have to say much, and simply aided her in emptying all her bags. I placed the contents in neat piles on her bed, and she organized them into her dresser and closet. Without breaking a single step while organizing her clothes into the closet, she shared about her desire to open her own restaurant someday. The dreamy excitement in her voice was endearing.

She wanted my opinion of her take on the traditional staple of macaroni and cheese, only the pasta base in hers would be rigatoni or penne. She would bake in six different types of cheese, including cream cheese. "Maybe I'll make some tonight," she suggested.

I wanted to provide an emphatic approval to that suggestion, but I thought it would be the expected reaction from the fat girl, so instead I said, "I don't even know where any of the grocery stores are around here."

"Trust me, I'll find one," BJ assured herself.

As we were packing up items to fill up trashcans, our last suite mate arrived. Dressed in gray sweats, all-black sneakers, and a high-collared, short-sleeved, pink polo shirt, this skinny little unassuming girl walked in, almost engulfed by the camper backpack strapped to her. She wasn't taller than five feet I guessed, treating her to a friendly once over.

"Hi," came from her lips, almost as a whisper.

"Hi, I'm Rory," I greeted. *Another skinny one,* I thought, with a knowing smile on my face. I did not move in to hug her, as I was afraid I'd crush her. "Petite" suited this new girl perfectly.

"I'm BJ. You're rooming with me. You are so lucky you didn't walk in here twenty minutes ago. We just cleared all my stuff off your bed," BJ confessed.

"Oh, that's okay." The new girl just smiled.

"So what's your name; where are you from?" BJ asked her.

"Oh, sorry, I'm Neekoo Rahul, and my background is Japanese, Spanish, and Indian. I live in DC, so if you guys aren't from here, I can definitely take you around." Her voice was soft, and she seemed shy. I wished that I had waited to pick roommates. It was now clear to me that Sierra and BJ were the more vocal ones, so I felt those two would be a better match with each other, unlike Neekoo and I who could get drowned by their strong personalities.

"And you guys?" Neekoo inquired. "Where are you from?"

"I'm from Caldwell, New Jersey," I responded, beginning to feel like a broken record. *We should have waited until we all got together in one space and did all the introductions at once,* I thought. To her quizzed look, I added that Caldwell was about thirty-five minutes or so outside of New York City. I don't think that helped, so I stopped talking.

"I'm from the west coast, and I can't wait to see the rest of the world!" said BJ as she now ripped off her pants and was standing in her gold boyshort panties and rummaging through her middle drawer. I was hoping that she was looking for another pair of pants, so I reminded her, "You folded some of your pants in the very bottom drawer and the top of your closet."

"Thanks, girl. I was looking in the drawer that I keep my pants in at home," she said, taking out a pair of wine-colored velour lounge pants. BJ continued, "Like, can you imagine traveling the world? That's why I came here to the east coast for school. I have never left the west coast, and as much as I really love it there, I just needed to see what else was out there, you know." BJ hadn't stopped talking, and I wondered how that was going to work with Neekoo, who as of yet spoke so few words.

I turned to Neekoo, who was still standing by what was now her bed and asked, "Would you like us to help you get some of your stuff in here, or is that all you have?"

"I have more. Thanks. That would really be nice."

She finally relieved herself of her backpack, and the three of us headed downstairs. I thought to warn her as we were walking out to her car. "By the way, Sierra's our last roommate. She's on the track team, and she's from Frederick, Maryland."

"Oh, that's not far from here," said Neekoo.

"And that thing is abrasive as hell!" BJ added to the rundown of our last roommate.

The second we got Neekoo's last bag into the room, BJ offered to cook dinner for all of us. She left the suite in search of a grocery store, and we offered to tag along, but she said not to bother because she was hoping not to be gone long. Neekoo started unpacking, and I went to my room. The door to my room closed behind me. I leaned against the wall, and all my thoughts started racing. I was trying to resist taking an anxiety-reducing shower just to check my weight, but the thought was overpowering me. I tried to reassure myself of my own confidence, but seeing the girls I was spending the next few years with on this "coming into adulthood" journey, the sinking realization that I was the biggest person in the house gave me an anxious, very self-conscious feeling.

Were they reincarnations of the girls I had spent my middle school to high school years trying to socially and psychologically ignore because of their intentional and unintentional verbal revelations of their low tolerance of unskinny people? I didn't want to be referred to as the subject of a conversation where the response went something like, "Of course I like fat people; my roommate's fat," almost as if befriending that person was a favor. *Why the hell do I have to deal with this crap?*, was my ending thought as I walked into the restroom, deciding to skip the shower, but needing to get a quick check of my weight on the bathroom scale. I needed to get out of my own head. We hadn't had any real interactions yet, and they might not be as shallow as their delicately perfect shapes potentially portrayed them to be. I hadn't eaten much all day. Why was I heavier now than I was in the morning? *Maybe I should have taken that shower* was my thought as my mobile phone rang.

"Hey college girl, you okay?" It was Vernon. I smiled. It was as if someone had filled him in on the conversation I was having in my head, and he was just picking up where I needed him.

"You know you're one of the best people I know, and if anyone can make this work, it's you," he reassured me. He continued without me responding, "Don't let that girl get to you. Just be Rory." Then he followed with, "She's cute, you got a number for her yet?" I was thinking, *Jabs and all, where was this brother when we were in high school?*

"Vernon! I am not doing your girl scouting for you!"

"Just kidding." He chuckled. "Just remember that you don't need anyone to defend you. Your interaction with people and them seeing the real you will do that for you when needed. Okay? … Okay, Rory?" he repeated, to make sure I was still there. I was. "Okay, that's all I called for. I've got to run." His words weren't lost on me.

"Give Mom a hug for me, and say hi to Dad. Let's catch up later tomorrow. Love you," I said.

"Love you too. Don't forget that number," and with laughter in his voice, he hung up before I could say another word.

In my mind, I turned on the shower, but I turned it off again. I was feeling better about myself, thanks to Vernon's confidence boosting. My father did not call me to see if I was moved in. I did not call him.

Later, Neeko, BJ, and I were sitting in front of BJ's television in the living room. We ate dinner together, watching old episodes of *Golden Girls*. BJ hadn't found all the ingredients she needed for her macaroni and cheese, but the chicken Alfredo dish gave promise that we were in for some mouthwatering meals. She had spiced up the chicken with a variety of crushed peppers, adding a contrasting yet pleasant accompaniment to the creamy Alfredo sauce. Neekoo, the smallest of us all, chewed every bite with a slow, deliberate pace. I now consciously slowed down my pace. We weren't halfway through dinner before we were greeted very loudly with, "Hey, chicas! Damn! Looks like you guys have made yourselves at home without me."

Sierra was home.

"There's a plate in the microwave for you if you're hungry," offered BJ.

"There better be!" Although her tone was unthreatening thanks to the lightness in her voice, the words were easy to misconstrue. Before she said a word, I felt that BJ was going to respond more to Sierra's words and not her tone. That's exactly what happened.

"Now you do realize I didn't have to do any of that, since it's not like anyone knew where the hell you were or anything." And as expected, BJ's tone matched Sierra's energy but with a slightly more irritating bite. This incidental exchange now had me curious about exactly how their first meeting went. It was clear from BJ's earlier statements that she wasn't a fan of Sierra's. These two were going to butt heads during our stay here—it seemed inevitable.

"Hey, chica, I was just kidding. Sorry. Damn, you guys can't bruise that easily, man." Sierra made it clear that she wasn't trying to start a fight. "I don't mean anything by it. I'm going to have to toughen you up a bit," she added, dumping her stuff in the short hallway as she walked into the kitchen. BJ, already turned toward Sierra's direction, motioned as if to respond but decided against it. I was glad for that.

"Who cooked, anyway?" asked Sierra.

"That would be BJ," I answered.

The nice tone of Sierra's came back with, "It really smells good, thanks." She reached into the microwave and then changed her mind. "Nah, I'll get lazy and not shower later on, and I stink, so I've got to jump into the shower first." She was really talking to herself, and with that she walked into our room to head into the shower.

"Okay, me and that girl are going to have some problems," said BJ even before the shower started. Neekoo's voice held a reassuring tone within her question, "She can't be that way all the time, can she?"

"We haven't been here that long, but I can honestly say she wasn't this way yesterday, well not the whole day," I said.

"The key to what you said was "not the whole day," meaning it's a freaking toss-up!" said BJ in a slightly mocking tone that drew chuckles out of all three of us.

"That's okay. If she's like that all the time, we can vote to toss her out, or at least the half of her that's a continuous bitch," Neekoo said through a bite of her garlic bread. There was nothing about what she said that was laugh-out-loud funny, but that's exactly what BJ and I did. We must have had the same thought, but we weren't expecting anything like that to come from Neekoo. It was a pleasant surprise.

Sierra joined us shortly after her shower; she looked refreshed and ready to make friends. She was the only one to ask about how we wanted to manage common activities. "Okay chicas, how do we want to do this? We have things we all have to use, and I know I'd rather not have to buy all the books for all my classes if I don't have to." She got a friendly reaction from all three of us with that last comment, as we chimed in our agreement.

I also added, "We do have at least one year of taking the same classes. Sierra's right, we can at least share some textbooks if we need to."

The next question, Sierra really directed toward BJ as her gaze went in BJ's direction. "Are we flying solo? Or we're going to divvy up some stuff?" I felt this was the best Sierra could give in showing BJ that not only was her bark worse than her bite, but also that she didn't want to force herself on any of us.

BJ didn't answer Sierra's question directly, but instead offered how she saw what her contribution would be. "I love to cook, and actually I hate cooking for one person, so we might decide to skip cafeteria meals every weekend or something. No, no, skip that. What I will do is cook at least one meal a day, just in case any of us miss school cafeteria times. Is that good with everyone? You guys can simply tell me what you feel like eating and what your preferences are, and I can try to accommodate it."

"So we can each contribute money on a weekly or monthly basis for the groceries, and take it from there," Sierra interjected.

Neekoo took out a little notepad—one that was clearly never too far from her, as it was very well inscribed. She ruffled through pages covered with black, blue, pink, red, green, and purple ink until she found a blank page. I didn't know exactly what needed to be written down yet, but she started jotting notes anyway. Neekoo was clearly the most quiet of all four of us, but even she seemed quite comfortable in her skinny frame. I shifted slightly in my seat, wearing a smile that was a facade to shield any of my current thoughts from reflecting on my face. Nothing we were talking about had to do with weight, but sitting there that evening amidst those three perfect frames, it seemed clear that I didn't belong there.

Maybe in an effort to allay any of her own anxieties, or because she really didn't feel like going to bed for the next few hours, Sierra orchestrated a four-hour girl-talk by simply asking the question, "Is anyone nervous about tomorrow?"

I was thinking it. It was on the tip of my tongue to emote about my fears of being judged by the skinny girls in my classes. But my suite mates were skinny girls. Wouldn't that be insulting to them? The conversation I was having in my own head was frustrating me. I still wore my facade-smile as I tuned back into the ongoing conversation, and my thoughts vomited out as words before I could control it. "They couldn't have had any fat friends like me in high school."

I prayed that it hadn't been audible, and thankfully Sierra and BJ kept talking. Neekoo, however, who was seated closest to me asked, "What did you say?"

"Oh nothing, I was just talking to myself," I quickly responded. Neekoo's left palm patted my knee. I couldn't tell if she had actually heard what I said and was simply seeking confirmation, or was instinctively being empathetic. BJ looked over at Neekoo and then at me, and I didn't know what the look meant. Had she heard me after all?

Now I felt like crap, and I wanted to just go to my room, but I stayed. We fell asleep in the living room. Sierra was curled against BJ's back on the floor, and Neekoo and I were on the couch. We were an interesting set.

TWO – *When sleep escapes you*

"Rory! We need to get together tonight," Sierra called out through the phone in an unusually cheery tone.

"You do know it's not even seven yet," I mumbled back, while yawning.

Even though I was sleepy and her tone seemed light, I knew Sierra must have been serious. Since our days in college, the only time Sierra started off any conversation with my name was when it was something serious, otherwise it was "chica."

"Is it anything you can talk about over the phone?" I asked.

"Vista!" She *never* called me Vista.

"All right, Sierra—when and where? And it can't be before eight tonight," I said in a sluggish but aware voice.

"How's nine at my place then?" Sierra asked.

Covering the mouthpiece, I nudged Michael, who responded with, "Yeah, I've got Bella tonight," before I could even ask. As he turned over to give me a little push in bed, he added with a smile, "We don't need you. Sierra can have you for the night."

I gave him a kiss on the forehead and then went back to Sierra. "Okay, nine tonight. You're sure it can wait that long?" I asked, wondering if I had been insensitive by insisting on a later meeting without knowing the urgency of the matter.

"Sure, that's fine. I just wanted to make sure I got on your schedule today," she responded in a reassuring tone. "Thanks, chica, I love you."

"Love you too, Sierra," I said and hung up the phone.

As I was contemplating getting out of bed and heading into the office, Michael said, "Whatever's up with Sierra must be serious. She called you Vista."

I nestled closer into my husband, not wanting to get up yet, and said, "I wonder what it is."

"She better not be discussing any of her patients with you again."

"Oh stop. I know it's probably wrong, but she only tells me because she knows I won't tell anyone, not even you! And you've been dying to know what her patients tell her during their sessions," I said cheekily.

"She's a good therapist, but I think she's overdue for some therapy herself." I didn't respond to that comment.

Our attempt at a desired lie-in together that Tuesday morning successfully ended with Isabella Michele Carter bumbling into our room, demanding that Daddy come into her bathroom to inspect as she brushed her teeth. Our lovely three-year-old daughter had developed this habit of making her father inspect her teeth after she brushed them, after which she gave him a morning kiss to start his day. It was never Mommy. It was one of the special things she shared with Michael, and he always obliged.

I sprawled out in our king-sized bed, loving having all the space to myself. I smiled, thinking about groggy Michael getting up to *work* for his morning kiss with Isabella—it was cute. The two partners in crime shared a beautiful relationship; it was the one I wished I had with my father, so I was delighted that she had it with hers. As I listened to the water running in the bathroom, my thoughts trailed back to wondering what Sierra wanted to discuss with me. In our adulthood, my feelings had grown into being protective of Sierra. She had given no inkling of the forthcoming subject matter.

Initially, rooming with Sierra had me playing the game of "try to catch up on sleep," and I was losing. In the first year, our class schedules were the same, so we were mostly in and out of our suite at the same time; that left Sierra's track and social schedules. She trained with her team from six to eight in the morning and then again from five to seven in the evening. Athletes also had to keep a mandatory study hour from eight to nine at night and supposedly had a curfew afterward. Sierra kept that entire schedule, but the curfew.

Within first semester freshman year, "Sierra" was a name almost everyone, professor or student, knew. The cliché "either you love her or hate her" applied here. The professors loved her! And that included the ones that most of us didn't care for. Most students who lived in The Ship had the same professors, and those professors were notoriously tough. Their classroom doors closed within two minutes after they walked in; papers turned in five minutes after class started were considered late; and they prided themselves in dishing out the least numbers of A's each semester. Why did they love Sierra?

Her smarts came from her questioning everything; most people read and then questioned what they read, but Sierra did it the other way round. She would sit in class and listen to the instructors and soak everything in and ask the most engaging questions that made it seem as if she had actually read the material beforehand. The instructors appreciated the ensuing engagement even when she vehemently disagreed with them. I felt that her tone was sometimes disrespectful or disruptive, but the teachers never heard that. They heard a critical thinker.

Her work was top-notch, and her ability to analyze what to many of us were the toughest concepts and theories into clear, concise, fluid ideas was intellectual art. So most days, Sierra's mandatory study hall hour was spent helping others, and afterward, she did her own thing. Her *thing* was to party almost every evening of the week. Normally she would start anywhere from ten to eleven thirty at night and stay out till three in the morning. Sometimes she would simply come back in to take a quick shower and head right back out toward practice where she would easily be the first student checking in. It was an unbelievable schedule to keep, but she did it. This schedule was no secret to any of her coaches. Initially the head coach tried to get her to change, but after numerous losing battles with her, he gave up.

Sierra was no easy person to fight with, and Coach Peters eventually conceded, since she was never late to any of her team trainings, attended study hour, and had the highest grade point average on both the men's and women's track teams combined. He didn't like having to concede, but there was no real reason to keep requiring her to keep curfew. However, any track member who felt they could follow suit with Sierra was sorely mistaken, as the results weren't the same; a drop below a 2.8 grade point average got them kicked off the team and out of a scholarship. Sierra was in a class all her own.

I was convinced that Sierra feared sleep. On some nights, I peeked through my sheets as Sierra came home in the wee hours of the morning, and she was never drunk. Not that I wanted Sierra to drink, but what was the point of the nightly escapades? Sometimes she seemed sleepy, but if I wasn't obviously awake and open to a chat, she would sit in her bed, turn the television on, mute the volume, and just sit there. No one saw but me—this was the quiet, contemplative, reserved, unobtrusive Sierra. Her outlet of choice I would find out, was talking it out, although that was quite sporadic. One of those mornings that she came in at around two o'clock and I was still up, we talked until it was time for her to go to practice. Point of correction: she talked, and I mostly listened.

Sierra started, without providing any initial context, "I have always wondered what my mom was like before she met my dad. Whether she smiled more, laughed more, relaxed more. I remember her smiling on my tenth birthday. She was so happy. She had planned this little get-together for me and a couple of my friends. Our menu for the party was chocolate ice cream, ice cream cake, carrot cake, my favorite sour cream and onion potato chips, sweets, multi-flavored popsicles, and ginger ale. I loved it! She played all the games with us: Twister, our dance competition, dress-up, and even the games we made up. I always remember that day because of how she threw herself into it, as if she needed it a lot more than we did. My dad got home later on that evening, and everything changed."

Sierra's monologue continued without her having yet looked at me. "What you have to understand is that Stewart Snowden was no father, but I had to call him dad. He was a functioning alcoholic. Every day before he got home from work, he would go drinking at his favorite bar, and when he got home, we all hated it. To hear the sound of your dad's key turning in the door and know that it sucked the life out of you wasn't a good feeling. Although my mother and brothers tried to shield it from me, there was no hiding it."

Initially I had been lying in my bed, an indifferent audience of one to Sierra's story, but at this moment, my eyes were glued on her as I had been reeled into her story. The Sierra that lay across from me was no ordinary eighteen year old. The maturity was thick in her voice and she seemed only a distant semblance of the inconsiderate roommate we were all learning to tolerate.

She continued, still not having even glanced in my direction, "Stewart Snowden was an angry drunk, a very angry drunk. If he got home and the dishes were still in the sink, he yelled at my mom; if the bed wasn't made in their bedroom, he yelled; if he stumbled on *anything* while trying to get to wherever the hell he was trying to get to in the house, he yelled. It's a horrible routine to get used to, but my eldest brother, Shane, knew exactly when the yelling would escalate to beating, and he would hover around any room my mother was in because he knew very soon, she would become a punching bag. He often used his body as a shield. Stewart Snowden never beat up on either of them enough to break any bones, but their torsos bore the scars. I wondered why she didn't ever call anyone, why didn't she leave?" Sierra stopped talking for about thirty seconds.

The pause felt awkward. I knew the question had to be a rhetorical one, but all the same, I wasn't sure if this was her reaching out for an answer. I didn't move, but bore an expression on my face that betrayed my lack of direction on how to respond. I was thinking, willing myself to come up with something, and come up with it fast.

Just as I was about to offer what I was sure would be a less-than-poignant answer to her question, Sierra continued. She shifted slightly in her bed, then continued, "The night of my birthday, my friends had left about an hour before he got home. Almost immediately when that doorknob turned, the smile that had lighted her face for so many hours, disappeared. His booming, strong voice made it known that he was upset about something, and as usual, no one knew why. My mother took my hand and led me to my room. I didn't argue. Less than five minutes later, Sean came into my room, trying to distract me from the noise. He got us to play video games and turned the volume up loud enough till we could barely hear my father's voice. We were both competitive, but I had no chance of winning against a fourteen-year-old who spent no less than two hours a day playing a variety of video games. By the time I was done losing that day, my mother was also done.

"About thirty minutes had gone by when Shane knocked on my door. 'Sierra, Mom wants to see you,' he said in a low voice. Normally after the episodes, my mom waited until she thought I was asleep, and then she would come into my room and sleep on the floor next to my bed, and as quietly as she came in, she would leave before I woke up the next morning. She didn't know it, but I never slept. I would watch her sometimes cry herself to sleep, sometimes get up and give me a kiss on my cheek numerous times, and then finally fall asleep on the floor. It was her safe place to be after her episodes, and I was glad she chose my room, so I watched over her in my own way.

"That night, Shane and Sean left my room, and my mom came in to see me. My mom was beautiful. I can't even begin to describe her. My grandmother says that I continue to remind her of my mom and that I'm a dead ringer for her, but I don't think so. Nina Sierra Snowden is the most beautiful woman I have ever seen, and I am not just saying that because she was my mom."

This time when Sierra stopped speaking, it wasn't as awkward. For the first time since she started talking, she also got up from her bed. She could have reached over the bed, but instead she walked around to the other side and bent toward the top drawer of her bedside table. She reached for a slightly worn, leather-bound journal and pulled it out. Between the pages, she retrieved a four-by-six black-and-white picture of her mom.

Her only acknowledgment of someone else in the room was when she placed the picture next to me and resumed her crucifix-like pose, lying in her bed. She did not immediately begin talking, but stared at the ceiling. Sierra had not overstated the likeness she shared with her mother or how drop-dead gorgeous her mother was. The lady in the picture that I held in my hand was absolutely beautiful. In this picture she was smiling; her smile was piercing, and it made me smile as a tear trickled down my face. She seemed like a carefree spirit, as her long dirty-blonde hair fell loose around her ears. She nestled a child that had to be Sierra, against her chest, holding Sierra's head to her cheek. Her grandmother was right; the woman in the picture could have been Sierra holding her own child. Whereas Sierra was a bit more athletic in physical appearance, her mother was soft and very feminine, but they both had that same frame. I wondered how someone so beautiful, so seemingly perfect and caring could have suffered so much in the hands of someone who loved her. That is what brought the tears to my eyes.

Sierra must have decided that she had given me enough time to deliberate on the picture. She continued her soliloquy, and this time there was some emotion in her voice. There was a forlorn lightness in her tone that betrayed emotions of despair. "She looked like an angel and acted like one too, and that's why I have to believe there had to be a time when my dad was a better man and once worthy of her. That night, when she came into my room, if it wasn't for her tearstained eyes and puffy cheeks and the muffled screams that Sean and I had heard through the loudness of our games, there was no real evidence of the ordeal that she had just gone through.

'You enjoyed your birthday, right?' she asked, as she came over and sat down at the foot of my bed.

'I had a good time, Mom, thanks.'

"I smiled, but tears were running down my cheeks, even though I wasn't exactly crying. Without addressing anything she had just gone through, she sat directly across from me and held my hands in hers, and then she looked straight at me. With tears welling up in her eyes, she said, 'Always remember that you are the better version of me. The second half of me is who you are, who you will become; the stronger, vocal part of me. That's why I didn't give you my first name. Don't ever change who you are, okay? Don't ever change that.'

'I'll never change that, Mom, never,' I promised her. At ten, I wanted to do more, but didn't know what, so this was my chance. I spoke those words with determination in my voice, convincing myself it would make things better.

"She hugged me really tight, and moving to a hum in her head, she rocked us side to side. With a kiss on my forehead, she reminded me, 'You have to go to bed now; the birthday girl still has to go to school tomorrow,' and she left my room."

At this point in Sierra's story, I was able to clearly visualize that ten-year-old girl. Every mean thing she had said, every erratic behavior that Sierra had exhibited since we became roommates, became irrelevant. Her face was soft, her eyes wide, and I could see her heart now beating a little heavier through her chest as she still lay there telling her story.

"About fifteen minutes after she left, I saw her shadow hovering near my closed door, and I knew she was waiting for me to fall asleep, so although I wasn't sleepy, I turned off my lights. She waited about another fifteen minutes and then came back into my room with a pillow and bedspread, and after a kiss on my right cheek, she retired to the floor and cried herself to sleep. I wanted to scream my tears out, but couldn't. I didn't want her to leave. I could not let her know that I wasn't asleep and that I wasn't going to sleep a wink until morning.

"She left my room around seven in the morning. This time, she didn't take her pillow and spread with her. Instead, she folded both and pushed them under my bed. She stood over me almost as if she had just entered my room, and she woke me up with kisses and hugs. My mind was occupied with plans on how to run away with my mother. I was a silly little girl. That plan wouldn't have worked; she couldn't leave my brothers behind," Sierra mused with the first smile she had worn on her face since she started talking.

Sierra broke into a slight chuckle as she recalled her moments with her mother that morning after her tenth birthday. "I pretended as if I was just being woken up from sleep."

'I know, I know,' my mom said, sitting on my bed giving me a hug. 'If it wasn't a school day, I'd let you sleep in.' Of course, my slight reluctance with getting out of bed right then was because it was at that moment that I was beginning to feel really sleepy.

'I'm going downstairs to make you eggs and crabmeat with some toast.' She knew how much I loved that; no one else in our house ate their eggs like that, just her and me. I was ready for school by seven-thirty, and she and I sat to eat our breakfast together as we waited on Shane and Sean to join us. My father was the first to join us. He came to the dining room table, ruffled my hair as his good-morning greeting, and gave my mom a kiss on her cheek.

'How did everyone sleep?' he asked as he got himself a bowl of cereal. My mom had already started a pot of coffee, so he poured himself a cup. Almost in sync, and without prompting from my father, my mother got up to get him his flavored creamer from the fridge. 'Thanks, honey,' he responded, and the two sat down to continue breakfast. Entering our house that morning, no one would have guessed our dirty little secret."

I was sitting cross-legged on my bed and listening to Sierra, and it was all beginning to make sense; how natural it was for her to switch through emotions and express herself in those moments, and see that as normal. I made a mental note to share some of this with Neekoo and BJ, as I knew that having some of this background information would explain some of Sierra's behavior from being so jarring at times. I was still thinking about which parts of Sierra's story would be appropriate to share with the girls, when I tuned back into Sierra, who was sharing the internal thoughts that she was having on that day.

"I have always wondered though, that maybe, just maybe if someone had come knocking, forcing my dad to admit that he had a drinking problem, things might have changed. Instead, my mother was married to two men: the one who loved her during the day when he wasn't intoxicated and who made attempts to make her happy, and then there was that guy who mostly came out at night that hated her.

"That morning at the breakfast table, I looked at my mom. I looked into her eyes and wanted to know what she felt, what she was thinking, how she was resolving herself into the person who had to respond in kind as a caring wife this morning. What I saw in her eyes that morning, even though it was only for a split second, scared me—she was empty.

"Shane and Sean came down just in time to drink some juice, since it was time for my mom to take us to school before heading down to the photography gallery where she worked as a manager and photographer. She needed Shane's help. 'I have to stay a little late at the gallery today, Shane. Can you stay with Sean and Sierra after track practice?' asked my mom. Shane nodded his head without looking my mom's way. That was typical.

"Every morning after the episodes, Shane, who was fifteen at the time, was never the same. Shane had asked my mom on one such drive to school, 'Why don't you just leave? Don't worry about us, I can take care of the two of them, but you need to leave.' It was the plea and frustration of a son who loved his mother so much he was willing to sacrifice himself as possibly the next punching bag. The plea of a son who knew the only way he could protect her if she stayed was using his body as a shield. My mom's response was always, 'I'm not going anywhere Shane, but I do love you dearly.'

"Even at fifteen, fourteen, and ten, we still gave Mom a kiss on the cheek right in front of the steps at school. We said good-bye, and with 'I love yous' exchanged, she drove off. For the first time, the three of us all stood there as we watched her car drive out of sight. Normally, I was the only one who stayed behind to see my mom drive into the distance. Sean went up the stairs to the building of their school, and Shane walked me over to my school, which was joined to theirs by a bridge.

"It was a short day at school for me. About noon, the teacher told me that I had to go into the principal's office. The principal walked me over to Shane and Sean's building to meet at their principal's office; when I got there, there was an officer waiting to see us. He told us that he was instructed to bring us home.

"Sean asked, 'Is everything okay?' I wanted to know specifically, 'Is everything okay with my mom?' To all our inquiries, the officer answered, 'I just have to get you guys home, okay? I'm sorry, but that's all I know.' I knew he was lying.

"We got home. The officer who had brought us stayed with us. He assured us that our dad would be joining us soon. That was the first hint that whatever had happened involved Mom and not Dad. The second hint was seeing my mom's gallery assistant, Ms. Lydia, pulling into the driveway about five minutes after we got home. She was not doing a good job of holding back tears.

Shane hadn't sat down since we entered the house, and in a clearly upset tone, he addressed the officer again. 'You have got to tell us what has happened to our mom. Was there a car accident or something?'

"Ms. Lydia said in a soft, teary voice, 'Shane, Sean … it's your mom.' Shane's voice was steady when he asked her, 'What happened?'

"I was in tears. I did not have to be told; something in me knew my mother was dead the second Ms. Lydia called my brothers' names. It was a feeling that was indescribable. I wanted to scream, but nothing would come out of my mouth; yet in my own head, I heard myself screaming to the point that it was deafening. I was not paying attention to anything around me; I just wanted to get away from everyone. It seemed to take me forever to get up from where I was sitting, because my body felt as if I was pulling it through quicksand. I finally got up. My exit from the living room happened in seconds, but it felt like forever. When I got to my room, I pulled out the pillow and bedspread that my mom had shoved underneath my bed, and taking in her scent, I cried into the pillow as I hugged it tight. Left in that exact position, I may have suffocated myself. Shane found me in the same position on the floor, curled up in a ball and crying, when he came into my room a few minutes later. He pulled me away from the pillow and hugged me.

"While I had run to my room, Ms. Lydia gave Shane and Sean the details. That morning, Ms. Lydia was running a bit late and got to the gallery with only fifteen minutes to spare before the doors opened for business. My mother had been there for about an hour. What they suspected was that she took the pills almost as soon as she got into the gallery. She was found in her back office on the couch with a picture of me and my brothers and a note clutched in her right hand.

"When Ms. Lydia arrived, she had just enough time to do a final walk-through of the gallery to make sure everything was ready for their ten o'clock opening. Before she disarmed the front door alarm, she went back to my mom's office. When Ms. Lydia saw her, she first called out my mom's name, but when there was no response, she then proceeded to shake her. The picture and note fell out of my mother's hand. Though panicking, Ms. Lydia managed to dial 911. The paramedics arrived at the same time as the officers and tried to revive my mom, but she was pronounced dead at the scene and transported to the morgue. Ms. Lydia had asked to be the one to tell us.

"When Shane left the little crowd that was gathered in the living room, he came to my room to check on me. He handed me the letter that the officers had found on my mother in the gallery. It was a short note and addressed to Shane. He sat on my bed with his head in his hands, and tears streaming. The letter read,

> Shane,
>
> You are my hero, my protector, my strength. I am sorry, I am so sorry for what you have gone through and for what you might have to go through. I am sorry that I can't be there for you, but I don't even belong to me anymore. I have been nonexistent for a while, and I can no longer do that. I know you will take care of Sean and Sierra better than I can, but let them take care of you too.
>
> I love you,
> Mom

"I don't know what I could have said at ten years old to console my brother, or if at that age I could console myself, but after reading the letter, I just hugged him. Shane was still sitting at the edge of the bed and with emptiness said, 'We should probably go back downstairs.' I didn't want to leave my room, but I got up, while still clutching my mother's pillow. A paper fell out of the pillow when I got up, and Shane bent to pick it up. 'It's for you, from Mom,' Shane said in a slightly confused tone. I was surprised that the entire time I held on to the pillow, I hadn't noticed the now curled-up piece of paper."

That piece of paper had been nicely preserved in the same diary where Sierra kept her mother's picture. She had kept the letter neatly folded in a plastic wrap. Sierra reached back for her diary, which was now sitting on the large bedside table that separated our two beds, and she gently removed the letter. After Sierra noted that her mother had placed the pillow and spread under her bed, I felt that something bad was going to happen in Sierra's story, but nothing prepared me to take in her mother's suicide. I didn't know this woman, but looking at the picture that was still on my bed, I couldn't imagine her life ending that way. The pain that drove her to act in such finality was unimaginable. Sierra handed me the letter, which I read in silence. The entire time that I was reading, Sierra was still lying on her bed with her arms behind her head, looking up at the ceiling, but now she couldn't hold back the tears trickling down the sides of her face. She closed her eyes, but she didn't wipe the tears away.

> Dear Sierra,
>
> If only you knew how much just the thought of you puts a smile on my face. Seeing you ignore your brothers even when they are right makes me laugh! You are going to do it your way, even when your way fails. You have to listen to them though, because they are the best for you. Shane loves you dearly and will not stand to see you hurt. Sean listens to everything you say, and I mean everything. Remember that time you were much younger and he wanted your banana, and you very seriously told him that you had gotten yours from some patch of ground in the backyard? I saw him go back out there and dig for a banana. Can you believe that? I am sure he thought it was

> ridiculous even as he dug, but if you said it, he gave it the chance to be true. Please never lie to him; he trusts everything you say, even more than he trusts Dad and me.
>
> I am sorry that I have treated you as if you have no eyes and ears, and that I never mentioned anything to you. You are stronger than me, bolder than me, smarter than me, and you will always be that way. I smile, knowing that you are the better version of me, and will always be. I will always be proud of you, always love you, always be your biggest fan, cheering you on—don't ever forget that.
>
> I love you, Sierra
> Mom

I felt that the letter Sierra's mom had written to her was a bit mature for a ten-year-old to fully digest, especially in comparison to the letter she wrote to Shane. However, I couldn't help but feel that her mom wasn't just writing this to that ten-year-old girl, but for the future Sierra who would need those words and apply them more actively, years later. Seeing the tears trickling down her face, I wanted to say something to her. I was mulling over in my head what the right words would be, but Sierra had only stopped long enough to give me time to read the letter. She hadn't finished her story.

Without wiping the tears that were drying on her face, Sierra continued talking. "Almost the second after I finished reading my letter, the front door unlocked, and we heard my father come in, wondering what was going on. It was a simultaneous act: the officer going toward my father to start explaining what happened, and Shane rushing out of my room and barreling toward my dad. Shane pushed my father so hard that it caught my father off guard. The police officer moved in to hold Shane back, and Shane exploded with, 'You killed her! You made her do this.'

"Shane managed to slip out of the officer's grip, continued yelling at my dad, and with balled-up fists, he hit my father in full-on rage. The officer struggled to get Shane off my dad, but my father let Shane get it out, not once defending himself. My father still didn't know the details, but he attempted to embrace Shane in consolation. That one gesture curtailed Shane's rage. He recoiled, walked out the front door, and slammed it behind him. Ms. Lydia went after him. As the officers got my father caught up on what was going on, Sean joined me in my room and we both just sat there. We had cried so much that in that moment, we didn't really have any more tears. None of us cared to see or know my father's reaction to the news of my mother's death, but Sean and I heard his outcry clearly: 'No, no, no!' That was all my father could keep saying in disbelief.

"At ten, you understand what suicide is; at least I did. I understood that I would never see my mother again, and it was in that moment, sitting in my room with Sean a few feet away from me, that I realized that I hated my dad.

"The next few hours were a haze. Ms. Lydia stayed downstairs with my dad to help make the initial arrangements that were necessary. My brothers and myself stayed away from my dad. For the first time, it wasn't my mother's call to dinner that I heard, but my eldest brother. Shane, with a very quiet knock on the door, opened it and asked Sean and me to *please* come down to dinner. It was a quiet plea, knowing that if all of us had the choice, including him, we would have stayed on the floor of my room and just sat there. We got up in solidarity for Shane and dragged ourselves to the kitchen.

"It was a simple dinner, all with me in mind. My mother had often made the dish for me when I just didn't feel like eating anything else. It was macaroni mixed with cream cheese and chopped, boiled eggs. Shane had cooked. My father tried to help, but Shane didn't want any of it. 'What would you like us to cook?' my father asked Shane. He was ignored. When my father saw Shane reach for the jar of macaroni, my father reached for a saucepan and filled it with water. Shane put the jar of macaroni back. My father asked, 'Are you going to make something else?' Shane responded by walking out of the kitchen; he went and sat hunched over in the living room. My father turned off the stove and went to sit at the dining room table, and Shane went back into the kitchen to begin cooking again. This time, my father didn't attempt to help again, or even talk to Shane, but simply hovered around the kitchen; he did not know what to do or how to be. When Shane was almost done cooking, my father proceeded to set the table.

"It came from a good place, but I couldn't eat. At a table that sat eight, Shane, Sean, and I sat on one side and my dad joined us at one end. He blessed the food and in my head, as young as I was, I asked what right he had to pray when he had caused my mother's death. He asked for someone to pass him a glass for some ginger ale, and again, in my head, I asked what right he had to ask any of us to do anything. I couldn't stop thinking that way, and with every attempt at conversation he made, I just kept thinking, *how could he*? *How could he?!* The thought overpowered me.

"My father was the only one who was able to eat. Not even Shane, who I knew was trying so hard to keep a facade for my sake, could take a single forkful to his mouth. I was sitting closest to my dad, and probably as a sign of solace, my dad moved to pat my left hand, which I quickly withdrew. I burst into tears. I didn't care how he took it, but my tears were those of despair. How could I be left alone with this human being? If not for him, I would have my mother. I would have my heart.

"He motioned as if to hug me, and I froze. Shane came over. 'Come on,' he said. I followed him to the kitchen, where we started washing the dishes together; Sean joined us. I wanted nothing to do with my father at that moment, and thankfully Shane knew it. Left alone at the dining room table, it was the first time I heard him cry. He sat there without saying a word and sobbed with his hands to his face and shoulders shaking. When we first heard him, we stopped for a second and looked at each other, but none of us went to him.

"The following week was hell for us. But looking back, it had to be worse for my father, who knew and felt that the three of us fully blamed him for my mother's death. During those first few days after she died, I don't think I spoke more than two words to him. Once I heard his key in the lock, I stayed in my room, as did my brothers. Noticeably, Stewart Snowden didn't drink that entire week. It only took the woman he loved, committing suicide. I didn't allow myself to feel sorry for him. He deserved our silence; he deserved his loneliness.

"We hadn't gone back to school yet, and our principal had called, saying we should take all the time we needed. Ms. Lydia visited every day, and so did the assistant principal of Shane and Sean's school, who came by with our work every day. She was also one of their school counselors and believed that our work would provide a temporary mental distraction from our mother's death. She was right. It helped.

"My mother's mom, Iris Satchel, refused to step foot in our house and refused to speak a single word to Stewart Snowden. The funeral was fully orchestrated by Grandma Iris and had flowers everywhere. She was determined that everyone would remember how beautiful, how delicate, how precious my mother was. There was no part for our father in the whole ceremony, only his attendance, which Grandma Iris didn't even care for. Shane spoke on behalf of the kids and had all three of us up there with him. I can't remember everything he said, but I knew he ended by saying that we were always going to carry her in our hearts and would live up to everything she dreamed for us. People couldn't stop crying when we were up there, and neither could we.

"The reception was held at Grandma Iris's house, and she held my hand the entire time. At the end of the night when my dad was ready to take us home, she held me so tight. Nothing was different when we got home. We went to our rooms as usual. Then, as they had done each night since she died, Shane and Sean came into my room and did their homework till they thought I was asleep. Just like with my mom, I never slept. I only pretended so that it would give them peace of mind.

"Saturday morning after the funeral, Grandma Iris was on the phone; she wanted us to come and spend the weekend at her house. Shane was the one who passed on the message. He came into my room, telling me to pack one of my book bags with clothes and to take my other book bag for school. Grandma Iris thought it would be a good idea for us to go back to school the following Monday. Stewart Snowden dropped us off, and that was the last time I saw him for a considerable length of time."

I was now sitting cross-legged on the floor at the foot of my bed, facing my roommate who had just bared her soul. I had wiped away the tears that freely flowed down my face at different times of her story, but I could taste the salt from the tears on my lips. Sierra had shifted around on her bad a couple of times, but now she was back in her main position, with arms behind her head, looking up at the ceiling with a tear-stained face. Realizing that indeed this wasn't a pause in her story, I moved forward and leaned against her bed with my elbows and forearms resting next to her torso. I had felt it since she started her story, but now I was sure about this feeling that swelled within me and knew it would never leave me. I looked at her tenderly as I now felt a genuine love for her, and told her so. "You know I love you, Sierra."

Sierra smiled and said quietly, "I know." She gently tousled the top of my hair and repeated it, "I know." Sierra leaned forward and hugged me tight as I reciprocated while rubbing her back. That night was the beginning of two things. The first was a genuine closeness between Sierra and me; I became her confidant and supporter, making it impossible for me to ever see any of her brash antics as malicious. On a more self-serving note, my internal vision of the *beautifully skinny, perfect woman* started to wane.

Recalling the moment that Sierra started engaging me for therapeutic catharsis, I just knew within me that whatever she had to tell me later that night was something serious. But right now, I loved the idea of indulging my lazy side this morning. I started watching each minute go by. It seemed like only a second ago that it was 9:45 in the morning and now the clock read 10:18! Isabella ran into the room, chased by Michael.

"You're taking her this morning, right?" asked Michael, not really needing to remind me that it was my day to have Isabella with me. Isabella wasn't in school yet, and if we could keep her homeschooled, we would because Michael was sure we would do a much better job educating her. I wasn't fully sold on that idea yet. We took turns: I had her most days of the week, and Michael mostly took her when I couldn't. We each owned our own business, which was great for setting our own schedules, but bad for wanting to homeschool our daughter.

I owned The Look, an image-branding agency that specialized in providing corporate businesses with different aspects of an image as it related to their advertising campaigns. We took care of all of it: providing the models for any of the shoots that they needed for their commercials; conceptualizing and executing their commercials; logo, graphic design, and photography needs. I had eight fulltime employees, all of whom I used as models, but who also doubled as the designers, photographers, and agents. It was a unique idea that many had said wouldn't work, but one of my visions for the agency was to dismantle the image of the "dumb model" in my own way, so I forged ahead. I remember the first model call I had. It was a week long, and I had Sierra, Neekoo, and BJ join me for the model call.

The first day was typical—mostly girls who really needed to pack on at least ten more pounds showed up. I was annoyed. I wanted those girls, but not just them; I needed every type of woman walking through my doors. After that first night's experience and my obvious disappointment, Sierra badgered me into explaining exactly what I wanted. Initially the notice asked for models with an artistic flair, seeking a full-time job. Sierra and BJ rightfully pointed out that I was getting exactly what I had asked for. Although the general idea had always been there, it was that night that my vision really took hold. We redesigned our notices to include *"New agency seeking models of all looks and sizes, preferably with a college degree and arts background, seeking full-time job."*

Days two, three, four, and five brought exactly what I wanted. By the end of the week, I had eight models: three of them were graphic designers, another three were artists, and two of them were photographers. I was excited, and we went to work immediately. I had three clients that I had already lined up and only four weeks to deliver a comprehensive and integrated media branding package, a national ad campaign, and a media tour. My team was excited, but I was nervous as I had taken out a sizeable loan to finance my vision.

That was five years ago, and the sky truly was our limit. Outside of the eight who made up our core team, The Look also served as the representative agency for a roster of thirty models, about ten photographers, and fifteen graphic designers. We were listed as one of the best places to work in Washington, DC, for the past three years in a row. We had to be doing something right; of the team that started with me, only one had left us—a young woman who got married and relocated with her husband to California.

We were housed in a three-level building that looked like a row house but with no adjoining homes. Michael found the building for me and handled the entire purchase, which became mine at a steal since surprisingly, the building was abandoned. Although it was in a relatively busy part of northwest Washington, DC, it hadn't been a desired location for prior businesses because there was nothing directly surrounding it; it worked perfectly for us.

Michael had initially hired an architect to handle the entire rehabilitation, wanting very little input from me. His reason was that he wanted it to be a surprise for me; I wasn't having any of it. I got my mother involved on the project, and we designed what we felt was a spectacular workspace. Each level of the building incorporated the original exposed stone wall, and that was the busiest part of the décor. The theme we used was the landscape of an open-floor art gallery. The first level was a large reception area with floor-to-ceiling paintings from local artists. The second level had five offices lining one side of the building and opposite the exposed stone wall. The third level and largest space had four more offices as well as open space for photo-shoot setups.

The morning the workers were done, even though I knew what everything looked like, Michael made me have a ribbon-cutting with him, Sierra, BJ, Neekoo, Vernon, and my mom in attendance.

"Michael, you know this is corny." I smiled as we walked into the building for a light reception.

"With all the work I put into this? This ribbon-cutting is for me, not you. You thought it was for you?" he teased me and gave me a kiss on my forehead. The warm feeling that crept through my being reminded me that I couldn't have had a better partner in life.

Michael was a financial planner—the best. I thought I was good with money, but watching him in action was a different story. He was determined that we would become millionaires before we were forty, and he was slowly but surely executing his plan. I had wanted to eventually own my own business someday down the line after a few jobs, but Michael, my darling husband, gave me no choice but to own my own business shortly after college. I have never regretted the decision. The amount of trust I had built with Michael in what seemed like a short time, still scared me. If he told me to clean out my savings for a venture, I would, and I wouldn't look back once, even if the venture failed.

What he did with money wasn't taught in any textbooks.

He saw what the rest of us didn't or couldn't. After his first degree in college, the third largest financial planning firm in the country snatched him up, and he blew their minds. While there, he also managed to attain his master's in business administration in eighteen months. The level of respect he garnered from the key executives was I thought, uncommon. So much so that when the time came that he put in his resignation, they flew him to the headquarters in New York for a "sit down." The "sit down" was a proposition; he could resign, but they needed him to stay on as a consultant on a part-time basis. He had to have been worth it, as his salary became his consulting fee to buy face time in the office if they needed it, twice a week.

My husband had it going on! I remember when he called me from New York to ask me what I thought about the offer before he gave an answer. In between excited screams, I said, "If you don't take that deal, I will hurt you when you get here!" What it meant for me was that I would get to see my guy more, and that took care of what he had hated about the job. As the highly sought-after financial advisor, it had meant less face time with me, and then Isabella. So thanks to a company that rightfully thought the world of him, Michael was able to start Carter Financial Advising.

"Okay Mamee, we're going to be late for work, so *we* are going to make breakfast, and you have to be ready to eat it when we are done." With bossy Isabella's declaration, I got up and into the shower. We said good-bye to Michael, who was staying at the home office today. His home office was our soundproofed basement with a separate personal driveway and its own entrance, and it pretty much ran quite separately from our home, down to a designated mailbox. It was his dream office, and I was happy to see him indulge in it, because he deserved it.

Isabella was at that age where she wanted to look just like mommy, and I have to admit that I loved it, and I did to her exactly what my mom did to me. This morning, I was in jeans, a pink polo shirt, a black cardigan, and black open-toed heels; Isabella was in a cute little jean skirt, pink polo shirt, and her little brown-leather gladiator sandals. We got into my car and made our supposed-to-be-short commute from one end of northwest Washington, DC, to the other.

"Okay, so you know the picture that I didn't finish coloring for Daddy yesterday?" she asked in a very grown-up voice. I smiled back at her. "Yes."

"Okay, so that's what I want to start working on when we get to our office." She started everything with "okay, so," and that was the case regardless of whether it was a question, statement, or comment that she was making. We were trying to break her out of that habit and having absolutely no success.

People still reacted when she said it, but I smiled when during her stories to people, she would talk about "our office," because in her defense, when you walked onto the third floor of The Look and into my office, all you had to do was look to the right and there was her little desk. A contractor friend of Michael's replicated my desk for Isabella in a smaller frame, complete with her own desk set and desk nameplate. She looked like her own little boss when she got behind her desk to get "her work" done.

I could only hope that one day, she would realize how lucky she was. My office was her classroom with eight brilliant instructors! When Isabella came in with me, she normally started her day in my office, writing a schedule that I dictated to her, albeit in images and references and not actual complete sentences. She would then translate this into whatever made sense to her and start with her workbook, getting the assignments done on her schedule. When she got tired of this, any one of the team members would normally come in and redirect her learning artistically during their downtime, engaging her in anything from photography to graphic design. My three-year-old was even playing around with Adobe Illustrator, even though I'm sure she had no clue of what she was really doing. We had initially set a television period for her, but canceled it since she didn't have much interest in television.

This morning, Isabella toted her little bag into The Look and *we* went to work.

THREE—*Prescription Plus*

"Chicaaaaa!" greeted Sierra. She was excited. "Come here," she motioned and wrapped me up in a warm, tight hug after she opened the door to her townhouse.

"Are you having your regular orange peel green tea?" she asked me as we walked the short landing and into the kitchen.

"Sure. And a snack with that?" I requested.

I took a seat at one of the bar stools at the kitchen table as Sierra prepared us some tea. Her kitchen was a little too masculine for me. All the appliances were stainless steel, and almost everything else was black and white. Even her countertop was black granite. It was a beautiful kitchen, just a bit harsh, but it worked for her. In the middle of her deep mahogany kitchen table, there was a beautiful floral arrangement in a crystal vase—the only feminine element in the space. Her favorite flower was the white lily, and every time I had visited any home Sierra had lived in, she almost always had an arrangement that included those somewhere in her house. In tonight's arrangement were white lilies interspersed with pink and red roses.

It was now nine fifteen at night, and instead of her getting to the reason I had been summoned over, Sierra delved into a case she was treating—a suicidal teenager.

"She's a sixteen-year-old girl whose mother hadn't known the depth of her daughter's state of pain until she noticed fresh and old body scars from self-inflicted cutting," said Sierra as she started with the narration. We were seating ourselves at the kitchen table as she talked, and I reached over to get some honey for my tea from the cabinet next to the range.

I grimaced at the act of this teenager and said, "I have never been able to understand it and probably never will. And having such a feverishly low tolerance for pain, I couldn't imagine how each razor-slice on any part of my body could bring about mental relief. There had to be a resounding depth of pain and turmoil consuming her that rationalized cutting as an act of relief." Sierra was probably going to give me the full version anyway, but my expression solidified the need for it.

Holding a cup of tea that still hadn't been sipped on, Sierra was critical with her words and tone. "This girl is the stereotypical perfect girl; one who has seemingly no reason to be unhappy. Her parents are very successful professionals who provide their children with everything they need and almost all of their wants. The mother had always known that her last child needed a little more attention, and once the girl even told her mother that she was scared of her own thoughts."

"What was the response to that?" I asked. "She was scared of her own thoughts?" I repeated, more so thinking out loud.

"Her mother had immediately cut back on her work hours and external responsibilities. By the time they came knocking on my door, the mother had gone through every phase of self-blame, self-doubt, and mental abuse that a loving mother can self-inflict: How could she not have seen this? What had she left out? Had she tried to buy her daughter's love instead of being there? Was she too focused on her career? Had they expected of their child what she wasn't equipped to offer? Had they shown any preferences to the other children even if indirectly?"

"That sounds unbearable," I interjected sympathetically.

"Yeah, the mother had blamed herself for everything, and that was my first suggestion to her—stop it. I needed the mother to begin cleansing herself of the mental anguish she was drowning in," Sierra said shaking her head.

Then in a moment of silence from her story, and without any warning, Sierra said, "Come on, I need to show you something." As we walked up the stairs to her bedroom, she continued with, "Ignore the mess."

It's a habit she's kept since college, with absolutely no explanation. Literally everything else will be in its place—for the most part anyway—but when it came to her bed, I could literally count how many times I had seen it made. Her laptop, notepad, loose papers, her most recently worn clothes, and a much worn throw pillow were often on her bed.

Heading directly to her bathroom, with her back toward me, she said in a subdued voice, "Listen, I don't really know how to tell you, so I have to show you," and she opened her medicine cabinet. There were five rows in the cabinet, and on two rows were bottles and bottles of prescription drugs. I was confused. I couldn't pronounce half of the names and some of the bottles were empty, but the dates went as far back as three years. I stood there frozen and confused, with a handful of the bottles in my hand and a distraught look on my face. What did this mean? But I think I knew what it meant, and the thought was giving me a migraine. Sierra started opening up a couple more drawers in the restroom, where there were more bottles. I was shown more bottles in the drawer of her nightstand, and having traveled back downstairs to the kitchen, there were even more bottles in a cute little box marked "special recipes" in her pantry.

First I had both my hands over my nose and mouth, and then I just started rubbing my head. I turned to Sierra and said, "You're not really running your own pharmacy, right?" It was a lame attempt at a joke.

She smiled. "Nah, that would be a much better explanation,

right?" She stood beside me, and I could feel the energy from her. When she spoke next, her voice was low. "I think I might be dependent on prescription pills, because—"

"Might? Sierra, you have over a hundred bottles in your house," I interrupted her in an unnaturally calm and deliberate tone. "And have you just never thrown *any* of the bottles away?" I followed up, as an afterthought.

"It's nothing to get alarmed about. I do have it under control; I just needed someone to know, just in case," was her bionic woman response. My voice stayed calm, and I was already feeling this was a battle I was going to lose.

I asked, "Just in case? There are hundreds of pills in this house. What exactly do you think you have under control here?"

"Hundreds of *bottles*—not pills, bottles," she corrected with a cautionary index finger.

I picked up a couple of the empty bottles and, waving them in front her, I corrected her with, "Sierra, they had pills in them. Again, what exactly do you have under control?"

She backed out of her master bathroom into her bedroom, moving away from me with, "I don't think I feel like dealing with this right now."

"I'm here now, Sierra, let's deal with this now." My statement was driven out of fear, and I quickly glanced at her, hoping that she hadn't sensed it. Could I handle whatever all of this really meant? I was also internally annoyed that Sierra had started my visit with telling me about a patient of hers when this was the real reason I had been asked over; I would have rather she told me *this* first. She probably needed to engage in the initial diversion, but I really didn't care about that teenager right now. I stood there confused, trying to take it all in.

Sierra was a natural on the track; the long graceful legs had to add to it. When she ran, it wasn't speed. From the time the gun went off to the time she hit the finish line, it was an air glide. When one foot guided that leg into the air, her reach traveled back to the other leg to follow suit, and it was a continuous leg-air symphony until the music stopped.

Neekoo and I were in attendance that day. Sierra had four races: the hundred meter, two hundred, four hundred, and four hundred relay race. Neekoo and I were close enough to the track to talk to Sierra during her warm-ups, and we held on to her stuff for her. She never drank water between her races, but instead, she poured it on her body to regulate her temperature. Drinking water in between races upset her stomach and made her cramp up, so she always waited until all her races were done. The hundred-meter sprint was a breeze, and she came in first place with a time of eleven seconds. The two hundred and four hundred races were as effortless as the first, but not so for the four hundred relay.

The time lapse between her last two races was about thirty-five minutes, and like she had done hundreds of times before, she spent the first five minutes after the four-hundred-meter race cooling down, ten minutes or so stretching, and another ten minutes as downtime, talking to us and icing one of her legs. We didn't think to ask Sierra why she was icing her leg, since we had seen her do this several times before. Normally when she did that, she waited until all her races were done, using the ice pack to relieve some soreness. As the call for the relay came up, she shed the layers, and after some very light stretching, she walked toward the track lines. She was taking the first lap. Then I saw it. It was a slight stiffness in her left leg. It didn't hamper her movement, and almost as a reflex reaction, she stretched her left leg with a heel raise and then bent down to her mark. The gun went off, and so did Sierra, straight into her air glide—only this time it was different.

When her right leg came down in one of her strides, for the very first time, you saw pain in her face when her left leg followed suit. She was no longer gliding; her pace became slower. She was in third place, quickly falling to fifth, and if she fell back four more spots, she would be dead last. Placement however became a nonissue when, forcing herself to forge ahead, her left leg landed in what was visibly an awkward and painful position. Her whole body crashed down right after her leg. The severity to the naked eye was unmistakable as the paramedics ran to her with Coach Peterson in tow. Neekoo and I were not far behind, but we were held back.

Within what must have been two minutes but seemed like a lifetime, the paramedics had an oxygen mask on Sierra, and had put her on a stretcher. Her left leg was quite swollen, and I was guessing that a bone was broken. The paramedics were calling out different instructions to each other, and called out that there was probable bone fracture and internal bleeding. With enough space in the ambulance for Neekoo to ride with Sierra, Assistant Coach Johnson drove three of Sierra's teammates and me to the emergency room, right behind the ambulance. I called BJ on the way to the hospital and filled her in on what happened; after a typical BJ dramatic outburst, she was supposed to be on her way immediately.

We had been sitting in the waiting room for about forty-five minutes when the attending doctor came out to update us on Sierra's condition. It was more like a debriefing as opposed to an update, as we were asked more questions. "Has Sierra been complaining about shin splints?"

"No, but that doesn't mean anything," Neekoo responded.

"She's not the complaining type," one of her teammates added.

The attending was one of those who could benefit from patient sensitivity training. When we were responding to him, he was looking through Sierra's chart, flipping through and studying the same pages over and over again.

He looked up. "It would appear that she had been experiencing shin splints for a while and instead of laying off training for a considerable amount of time, she probably aggravated the area by not allowing any complete healing to occur."

Still not really addressing anyone in particular but seemingly all of us at once, he continued to deliver his diagnosis in a matter-of-fact tone. "There were several hairline fractures in her right tibia that clearly set the stage for that bone breaking in about four places." Finally, some emotion was present in his tone in the form of condescension when he said, "I am shocked that she was able to run three of her races earlier. Was anyone even paying attention to any strain that she was showing?" He finished with, "She should have been pulled from any of the races. Right now, she's going to have to stop training competitively."

They were moving Sierra into surgery to insert titanium rods in her tibia. Then she would be transferred into a recovery room. I left a message for BJ, telling her she didn't have to come over right away. Assistant Coach Johnson and the three teammates joked with Sierra as she was being taken away. "We thought you were made of steel before. You'll truly be the bionic woman now." This made all of us chuckle through Sierra's challenging time.

The nurse who stayed behind advised, "She will be gone for a few hours and probably won't be back in the room for another five hours or so. You may want to come back then." All of us chose to leave and come back later.

I called BJ as we were heading to the car. "Hey, where are you?"

"Well, I *was* on my way there, but I got your message," said BJ.

"Yeah, you didn't need to come, because they were wheeling her to surgery at the time and she won't be in her room for a few hours," I quickly explained.

"I don't want anyone thinking I didn't care or anything," BJ continued in a slightly defensive tone. I laughed, knowing that Sierra and BJ's love-hate relationship would have Sierra playfully accusing BJ of not caring, yet not meaning a single word of it.

"I'm just going to grab an overnight bag for her and whatever else she may need for a few days. We'll see you shortly."

"See you soon," said BJ, and we both hung up the phone.

"What happened?" was the question we were greeted with when Neekoo and I walked into the room. BJ was cooking. We filled BJ in, on the details of the day's event. With one hand slowly stirring a pot of simmering homemade wild mushroom soup and the other holding a glass of water, BJ turned to Neekoo. "You okay?"

"Sure," Neekoo responded, slumping down to the kitchen floor and into a cross-legged yoga position. "Yeah, I'm good," Neekoo said again, talking to no one in particular.

By the end of our freshman year, we had grown comfortable in our positions with each other. We were all close, but BJ took on an almost motherly responsibility for Neekoo, facilitating the two of them getting a little closer than Neekoo was with Sierra and me. It was now early junior year, and our relationship definitions were the same. Sierra had grown on all of us. Sierra and BJ had their great days, and then there were days that they went for each other's necks. I was generally close with all my roommates, but I was more understanding and tolerant of Sierra the most thanks to the different moments that she opened up to me in our room.

I went to the room Sierra and I shared to place a call to Sierra's brothers and update them on her condition and to grab a few of the things that she would need. Neekoo and I headed back to the hospital about three hours after we had left, and BJ said she would join us later and bring some food for Sierra. We were in the waiting room for another hour or so before the nurse came out to let us know that Sierra was back in her room. Sierra's brother Sean was with us by this time, and all three of us went back to her room. It was weird seeing Sierra in this vulnerable state.

"Sheeawwn," Sierra slurred. "You are two," she said, with a half smile on her face. Her eyes were only open in slits.

"They gave you the good stuff," Sean joked with Sierra, standing next to her bed and bending over so that he was more in focus. He reached for her hand and held it, then she rolled her head to the left and fell asleep. This was pretty much her state of being for that night—she would rouse out of her sleep, say something that made no sense, and drift right back into sleep. Sierra was in her own room and had quite a bit of space, so when we asked if we could stay the night with her, the nurse didn't fuss—she even brought us a cot. Neekoo slept in the chaise lounge chair that was already in the room, and I slept in the cot. BJ joined us later that night but didn't spend the night. She brought the food that she had cooked for Sierra, but Sierra was never lucid enough to eat any of it. Sean gladly helped himself to the food and left with BJ at around one in the morning.

Her second day in the hospital, Sierra was awake longer and was able to have more lucid conversations. I had long believed that Sierra ran because she was effortlessly good at it, and as an escape—I had wanted to escape my own body for not acting right for me and remaining slim. I understood escape. I was sure that in relation to her mother's passing, Sierra wanted to escape her own mind. I had believed it was something she was entirely passionate about not because of the competition, but because it momentarily freed her mind. Nonetheless, Sierra was quite agreeable when the doctor warned against her continuing to run competitively and in that one moment, Sierra's career of running ended. Neekoo and others thought the meds had something to do with her reception of the news, but I wasn't convinced.

There was no shortage of pills for Sierra. She popped them consistently during her recovery, and none of us said anything. After all, she had just been through a harrowing accident and surgery, and she needed those pills. I know she was taking codeine and oxycodone as part of her regimen, and later a sleep aid was added. The pain from the accident had further kept her up through the nights. Initially, the intake of the pills was heavy; she would take her entire daily dose in the morning, doubling her daily intake, which caused the physician to up her medication instead of suggesting alternative pain management.

If I ever suspected that she had a drug problem, I hadn't mentioned anything to Sierra because every time *I* felt she was taking too many, a doctor would prescribe more to her. They were the experts, they knew better, so my suspicions were fleeting at best. Still, as the one who shared a room with her, I should have been the one to notice, at least so I now thought.

Sitting there in Sierra's kitchen, I tried not to be riddled with guilt. Were our days in college with all those prescription pills the start of her dependency? I tried not to blame myself for not having noticed or suspected. I asked so many questions: Was she seeing someone about this problem? When did the actual dependency start? Had it affected her work? Was it affecting any other part of her life? As expected, she didn't directly answer any of the questions. The battle lost, and with teary eyes of frustration, I carefully said, "Chica …"

Sierra smiled when I called her that. That term of endearment was primarily hers for the rest of us, with the rest of us using it sparingly. This was one of those times when it was my way of letting her know how much I loved her.

"Tell me what you want me to do, and I'll do it. Anything."

Head down and with hands in her hair holding on to her head, she started with a long, soft, and raspy sigh. Then as she had done with me in college when she revealed who she really was, she proceeded to let a little more out and launched into a monologue.

"After my mom's passing, as required by our school and persistence from my grandmother, my brothers and I were required to see psychiatrists and therapists. I don't know, but I think that because of my age, they must have thought that my feelings would come spewing out. What they didn't know was that the only person I had ever really confided in was my mother; I couldn't replace her with anyone at that moment.

"So for a very long period, the sessions were utterly useless. The sessions were an hour long, and the therapist did the talking; I think her name was Diane Holster. She always sat next to me in her office, and I didn't like that. I also remember the hard wooden chairs being so uncomfortable. When she was talking, I was wondering how long it would take for my butt cheeks to become devoid of feeling.

"'Hi Sierra,' Holster greeted in a sad, pitying voice the first time we met.

"'Hi,' I responded with no emotion.

"Holster asked, 'Are you enjoying being back in school?' (I didn't care). 'How are you feeling?' (How exactly should I feel?). 'Are you doing well at your grandmother's?' (What did she expect?). I hated the round of questions she asked. I had all those thoughts in my head and did not respond out loud to her, not once. Instead, I stared at my hands, my shoes, at her desk, her walls. It was such a bland office, I thought; degrees on beige walls were the entirety of any touch of décor in the space.

"My brothers weren't in therapy as long, probably because they talked things out with their respective therapists. I asked myself even then, why I couldn't talk to this lady, but all I could think was, *You are not going to replace my mother.* When my grandmother started showing up with me at my sessions, I don't know how helpful she was—I am sure she thought she was helping. My grandmother chose to be my mouthpiece, answering the therapist's questions with an assertiveness that wasn't questioned. But not even Grandma Iris could voice how I felt: hollow, in pain, and full of despair.

"At one of the sessions, my grandmother revealed to the therapist that I wasn't sleeping, so at ten years old, I was put on sleeping medication. And that is in addition to the antidepressants that I was also being given at about the same time. The pills never worked immediately. Instead of making me sleepy soon after I took them, initially they would keep me up. Later, they would keep me up for a while. I never told anyone that the pills didn't work as they should, because it gave me an excuse to disappear from different activities in which I didn't want to participate. It was a golden reason. All I had to do was present my doctor's note, and I got no flack for laying my head down in class and skipping some altogether.

"No one saw anything wrong with this except Sean. He brought it up with my grandmother, but bless her heart, all she could do was hope that I wouldn't need them for much longer. 'Sierra, make sure you aren't taking those pills all the time,' she had advised. I loved my grandma and stopped. However, with the goal of trying to get me to open up, I was made to visit physician after physician, and no one really tried anything different, so I stayed on a variety of antidepressants and sleeping pills for a while."

Sierra finally addressed me directly. "I know you probably have thought that I pursued the path of being a therapist because of what happened with my mother. I could always see that in your eyes as you signaled approval, hoping that the whole process of studying psychology and gaining my certification would actually help me sort out the loss of my mom. I also know that you now believe that in fact none of that has happened, and that as I continue to listen to other people's issues, I probably need to see someone myself, and maybe you're right."

I chuckled slightly, and before I could stop myself, the sarcastic thought in my head came out. "That's the blessing and curse with you, Sierra. You have all the answers; I can't even say anything to you."

"Well, am I wrong?" Sierra asked pointedly. "Well?" I just sighed; she was right.

"I have successfully shielded most of it from everyone, and I am slowly admitting that I have a dependency on prescription pills—but it's under control."

"How exactly are you defining 'under control'?" I asked, trying to get her to hear the delusion in that statement.

"Oh give me some credit, Rory. I've been around addiction.

I know when it's out of control. I don't have the affinity to being addicted to anything, because when I need to stop anything, I do. I don't take the pills all the time." I had this confused look on my face as I shook my head; she ignored my expression.

"How–e–ver," she stretched the word out as if the next few words would help it all make sense. "As much as I have chosen to see myself as unaddicted, I can't shake the fact that no matter how long I stay away from taking the pills—and I have stayed away from them for years at a time—I still come back to them. I have taken a variety of pills, albeit on an irregular basis, since I was ten, which technically would have made me drug dependent before I was even a teenager. Can you believe that? Oh gosh, I don't want to do the math." This was followed by a nervous chuckle.

Doing the math in my head, I wondered if she could really hear herself. I immediately thought, *This girl needs an intervention.* And as soon as I had that thought, I had visions of every which way the intervention would go terribly wrong.

Sierra started rationalizing it all. "Popping the pills at parties didn't bother me; it made me able to tolerate people more. In fact, that goes way back to college when I would hang out with those guys till the wee hours of the morning, and since I couldn't have cared less about being there with them, the pills made me even like them. It made my harsh comments less incessant, and made me treat people a little nicer, because as you know, I am not in the habit of sparing anyone's feelings—"

I went and sat right in front of Sierra and shook her knees. "Sierra, stop for a second; stop for one second, please."

"No, I've got to get this out," was her reply to my attempt to get her to stop rationalizing. She continued, "Also, and don't gasp about this, but I was entirely drugged up as we sat in the waiting room during Isabella's birth. But I promise you, I didn't pop any pills during your wedding—I was tempted several times because people were really getting on my nerves, but not once did I take a single pill."

"Sierra." I let out an exasperated sigh as my right palm rubbed my cheek. "Sierra, you can't hear yourself. I know you are trying to apply some logic here, but none of this makes sense."

I felt an intense hot flash overcome me as I realized that nothing I could say at this very moment would make much of a difference. And as much as I wanted them to stop, tears started trickling down my face now. I got emotional because I was afraid of the response I would get from Sierra if I asked her if she felt the need to take pills to even be around *us* sometimes. I wiped the tears from my cheeks.

Sierra was calm as she continued. "It's not just logic." And finally I got to hear why she had told me about the suicidal teenager patient of hers. "Last week, I saw a picture of myself that scared me. Remember the suicidal teenager? On one of her visits last week, the first thing I wanted to do after I asked her a series of warm-up questions was to scream at her when she just sat there and continuously shrugged her shoulders. I really wanted to be me, the Sierra that can get mean, you know? Give her a piece of my mind with regards to how good she had it, and the fact that she had no conceivable reason to be in my fucking office.

"This girl *really* had a good life and was wasting her mom's money by being here and making her mom feel so guilty. My training taught me that all of this wasn't just in her head, and that even if latent, there were some specific reasons that explained her state of mind. I excused myself to the restroom, where I didn't even count the pills I took. Before that day, I hadn't taken any pills in about two months. The rationalization, of course, was simple. If my pills made me indifferent to most of what was going on around me and put me in a good enough mood not to care to be so horrible to people, then I would be a more pleasant therapist to deal with. But this time was terribly different. … I sat back at my chair, ready to be the ever-concerned therapist, and for the first thirty minutes, that's really what happened."

"Then the teenager said, 'Dr. Snowden, I don't know why the bigger girls hate me, but it's not even worth fighting them.'

"'But you *are* fighting. You are fighting yourself,' I responded to her, referring to the recent round of cutting she was inflicting on herself. 'What specifically happened this time that makes you think they hate you?' And that was the last question I remember asking. The next thing that I remember was this young girl tapping me on the shoulder from having fallen asleep while she was talking.

'Dr. Snowden, Dr. Snowden?' the girl called out to me repeatedly.

"I heard one of the calls and raised my slumped head, while wiping off the drool that I felt on the left side of my mouth. A flush of embarrassment came over me as I straightened up and excused myself yet again, this time to cleanse my face.

"When I got back, she asked me if I was okay, if I had had enough sleep and needed to take a nap, because she wouldn't mind if I spent some of *her* time taking a nap. I felt so small when she made the offer, because it was her way of saying she cared that I was 'exhausted,' since that's what she thought. I told her it was okay, but she didn't think it was, so with the tables turned, she became the therapist, as she asked with concern, 'What's your day like Dr. Snowden?'

"For a split second, I thought not to answer her, but I knew that this was our breakthrough moment. If she felt that she was helping me, we could eventually get somewhere with *her* future sessions. As I gave a true rundown of my day, that's when I made the decision that I had to talk to someone about the truth." Sierra looked at me with eyes glassy and a slight grin. "I chose you."

Even though I really didn't know the right reaction to give to the entire revelation that Sierra had just shared, I managed to force a smile at the end of her catharsis. I knew that beyond that sometimes harsh exterior, Sierra truly cared, and the fact that she had probably made a breakthrough with the girl really made her feel good. She related the girl's breakthrough to her own circumstance, and she was telling me about all of it. I took this to mean that she was ready to do something about the problem, so I asked her, "Where do you go from here, Sierra?"

With a sigh, she stood up and walked toward the kitchen to get a glass of water, but answered, "I was hoping you weren't going to ask me that."

"Is that because you know what you should do but won't?"I asked. Sierra laughed and almost choked on a swallow of water. "You know me too well, Rory. I know …" She paused and rephrased that to, "I think I need to get treatment because I have tried stopping on my own with no success. But I don't know, I don't know."

"You don't know if you need to get treatment or if you're ready to get treatment?" I asked. Clearly shutting down, she said with an irritated edge to her voice, "I just don't know, Rory."

With stern determination, I still pressed her. "Can you promise me that if something triggers your desire to use any pills, that you will immediately seek treatment then?"

"I can't promise that, Rory." Sierra shook her head slowly. "I *can* promise that I'll try not to use the pills, but seek treatment? Nah, I can't promise that."

I just sat there and stared at her because I didn't know what else to say, and I didn't want us fighting on this. I needed to figure out what supportive role I would take, and I was lost on exactly what that would be. I was about to get up, but it was Sierra who came over to me, and feeling as if I needed consoling, she motioned to me, "Come here, chica." She gave me one of those heartfelt "I love you, but I can't bring myself to say it right now" hugs.

It was now almost one in the morning. Although I wanted to get home to my husband, I didn't want to leave Sierra alone, so I still hadn't made any move to leave. However, Sierra noticed how late it was and, leaning into the back of the long leather couch that we were now sitting on, said, "I think I've given you enough to worry about for one night." She smiled and looked directly into my eyes. I smiled and creased my eyebrows but didn't say anything immediately. Then I asked, "Do you have any appointments tomorrow?" I didn't hear her response.

The second I asked the question, the irony shook me: a therapist dependent on prescription pills to deal with her issues. I shook my head feverishly. I wanted the thought out of my head. "Yeah, I should probably be heading home," and we said our good-byes, with her making me promise to deliver a kiss for Isabella.

As if he was sensing, listening, or watching for the right moment to reach out to me, I got a call from Michael as I got in my car and drove off from Sierra's. It was now one-thirty in the morning.

"Hey, babe," he said. "You on your way home yet?"

"I don't care what you say, I am sure you have a private investigator following my every move," I said with a dry laugh. This wasn't the second or third time that he had called me right at the opportune time. Moments like this made me wonder how I got so lucky. If two people ever fit like a hand in a glove, it was the two of us. He talked me through my short drive home.

"I let Bella stay up a little longer than usual. She wanted to wait up for you."

"You're going to let that girl do anything she asks of you," I said.

"Look who's talking. Ms. 'She's such a good girl I just can't say no to her,'" Michael mocked me.

"Okay, okay," I conceded. "She also left a kiss for you on your pillow," Michael informed me.

"Aww, see, how can you not do anything she asks of you with gestures like that?" I said.

"Softie! You're probably tearing up a little, aren't you?"

"No, I'm not!" I said with playful defensiveness. But I was tearing up at the corners of my eyes.

"You're still not giving me another one anytime soon," Michael stated. I almost didn't respond, but I couldn't stop myself. "When you figure out how I won't blow up into a whale in the process, then we can talk about it."

"There you go. Don't worry, I'll work on figuring that out. Anyway, how is she?" He was referring to Sierra.

"She's okay," I answered quietly.

He knew that as much as he wanted to ask about the visit with Sierra, this I would prefer to discuss in person. I wanted to see all his nonverbal reactions and read his body language, and I wanted him to read mine. Whenever he read my reactions, he was able to help me with advice that wouldn't have occurred to me. Almost as important was the fact that he knew I needed time to figure out what I wanted to tell him and how I wanted to tell him, and it was beautiful that he could tell it in my voice, listened to it, and always respected it.

I got home, knowing that we weren't going to bed for another hour or so. After the kiss of the day that I never missed from my husband and a good caress of his amazing backside that I loved, I looked in on my daughter, who was peacefully asleep in her bed. I changed into one of his gray sleeveless undershirts, we settled into the seating area of our bedroom with cups of tea, and I started to divulge only some parts of my conversation with Sierra.

The main part that I left out of the retelling was Sierra's motivation for telling me about her drug dependency, which included her therapy session with the girl. It wasn't appropriate for me to talk about it, and I felt Michael could make his deliberations without it.

He wanted to know, "Is she going to see someone professionally about this?"

Sarcastically I said, "Sure." Losing the sarcasm I added, "You know Sierra. She made it clear she's not ready to go yet, and that means she's not going." Michael was silent. "What are you not saying?" I asked. I knew that look—it was the first look that I had gotten from him, the very first time we met.

In college, I continued the somewhat active lifestyle that I had initiated in high school. But when you live with three skinny women who eat whatever they want, whenever they want, and one of them is less physically active than you are and still keeps her perfect figure, you begin to question that maybe it's not all you. That realization was put in play, and so my active lifestyle was refocused from a need to break my body down to the need to feel my body working with me for a desired goal. In the effort to achieve this goal state, I visited the college gym two hours a day, three days a week.

On one such occasion, I had spent forty-five minutes on the treadmill and was going to do my rotation of different muscle toning and strength training machines, and then finally end with fifteen minutes of stretching. I was on the abs crunch machine to target my lower abdomen, working the machine as I had always done. My eyes followed my movement, sometimes down to the ground and other times looking straight ahead. As I came up from one of the curls, there were two large feet in view. My eyes settled on this well-sculpted guy who had chosen to position himself in front of me. From my seated position, he looked over six feet tall. His chestnut brown eyes matched the color of his naturally wavy hair, which was worn in a short, layered cut that was tapered at the sides.

"Hey," he said quietly.

"Hi," I said with hesitation. I didn't appreciate this stranger breaking my routine. With his hand outstretched for a handshake and an introduction, I was forced to take that break.

"I'm Michael," he offered.

"Rory," I replied.

"Uh, I saw you across the gym. You're doing a pretty good job."

That's what his lips said, but there was something in his eyes, something that made me feel that something wasn't right—with me. I am sure I had a quizzical look on my face.

He was nervous; he didn't know where to place his hands and perhaps he was sweating a bit, because he proceeded to gently rub his palms together. He should have been nervous! His first line made him sound like a stalker. Whatever courage he had that led him to stand in front of me, needed to come through for him. I needed him to say exactly what was going on, as I was visibly beginning to seem bothered by this person.

"I w–was watching you," he stuttered. "Don't get upset, but you're k–kind of doing it wrong."

Wow! I thought. *The nerve of him!* But I also thought, *That was bold.* He wasn't being rude, so I tried not to take it that way. Instead I became curious. I gave a creased-lip smile with furrowed eyebrows, all while thinking, *I wonder who he thinks he is or what expertise he has that gives him the right to criticize my style?* He just knew what the smile meant and smiled in return—he had a beautiful smile. He now began to explain what he meant, in the most agreeable way possible.

"I'm not criticizing you or anything, I just thought you might want to know a better way so that you notice some results faster, that's all. I'm on the tennis and basketball teams." I raised my eyebrows with interest. "I know, weird combination, but I did all my workouts wrong until one of my teammates gave me some tips. So when I saw you working the abs machine the way I used to, I felt I had to say something to you."

"Really? Thanks," I said, and I meant it.

"You don't think I'm crazy, do you?" he said with a laugh that still bore a hint of nervousness.

"Not at all," I said. *Not anymore,* I finished in my mind.

"I thought up every possible scenario that this could take, and all of them led to me being a stalker."

I couldn't help it, I burst out with laughter that filled my entire stomach.

"Cool, so you don't think I'm a stalker anymore, right?" He chuckled, and in that moment I appreciated taking the break. He motioned me off the machine. I accidently brushed against him as we switched places, and his abs were rock hard.

"Always make sure your arms are at a ninety-degree angle when you raise the bar, and keep your back straight. Now you try it." We switched places again.

I tried it his way a couple of times, and he approved. "That's looking much better."

"Thank you!" I said with playful indignation. "Any more tips from the expert?"

He dismissed my tone with a slight sideways head nod. "I would stay and show you a few moves, but I'm running late for practice." It was basketball season.

"Thank you?" I said in a form of a question.

"Hey, you let me interrupt your workout flow. So I guess, thank you. Keep it up okay?" and he walked away. That's when I saw what I loved most about his body. He was in a pair of basketball shorts and sleeveless jersey, but he had to be wearing compression shorts underneath the basketball shorts because I know I saw the outlined form of his butt, and it was perfectly sculpted. It freaked me out, but I was definitely attracted to this guy.

I stopped working out for a brief moment. Every fiber in my being stimulated me to briskly walk out to see if I could catch another glimpse of him. Instead, I moved to another machine and continued my workout. The rest of my workout, all I could think of was this guy that I just met. What was wrong with me? I had mixed feelings about the butterflies in my stomach. I played out every minute of our brief exchange over and over again in my mind, and I found myself smiling to myself in the gym. I looked around discreetly to make sure no one was watching me. My smile waned, because I thought maybe I was too fat for someone like him. I moved on to the triceps dip machine to induce an intense burn to distract my current thoughts. It didn't work. I couldn't get him or his body out of my mind.

The next home-court basketball game was in a week. I wasn't going to miss it. I planned to drag one of my roommates with me. I wanted to see this guy play, but more importantly, I wanted to see this guy again, period. My first choice for any sporting event was Sierra, but she wasn't around, and Neekoo also was nowhere to be found. That left BJ, who truly could not care less about sports unless she needed to, so I pretty much dragged her with me.

He was good. His speed and agility were quiet yet exacting. We sat two rows behind courtside because I was hoping he would see me. I thought we made eye contact a few times, but it could have all been in my mind. However, at halftime, I knew. As he was walking back to the locker room, when he was sure our eyes were connected, he raised his hand slowly, probably hoping I wouldn't look away and ignore him. But when I kept his gaze, he smiled and mouthed a "Hi." Clearly blushing, I waved back. *Oh my gosh!* He liked me too. Right after the game, during everyone's commotion over the home team victory, he made his way into the stands to where BJ and I were.

Although he was sweaty, remembering the feel of his abs at the gym, I went in for a hug. "Congratulations." He responded with a tight hug, and feeling his muscles against my chest, my heart leaped.

"Who's your girl?" he asked. I had forgotten all about BJ. I did the introductions. Then he asked for my number, and the rest was magic.

"What do you think I should do or should have done when a friend halfway admits that she's addicted to pills?" I asked Michael, knowing that his look meant that he thought I was doing something wrong.

"That's not it, babe, but you've got to get a little tougher with Sierra."

"What do you mean? Sierra's tough, and either she's going to get treatment on her own or she'll shut me out if I try too hard."

"But from what you've just said, she's clueless when it comes to herself, so you've got to get her to realize that she doesn't have all the answers, especially in that case." I agreed with Michael, but all I could think of was Sierra shutting me out. "I know you don't like to think it, but if she shuts down, she shuts down. She'll come around."

"I know, Michael." I moved from my side of the couch and lay against his chest. "I really didn't know what to say at the time. I just want her to know that I'll be there for her for the long haul, no matter what." Gently rubbing my back, in a low voice he said, "But please remember that you can never replace her mom."

I was quiet. It wasn't the first time that Michael cautioned me against that notion, and I didn't like it. I knew I could never replace her mom. Michael's arm tightened around my back for a deep hug, and I circled my arms around his back, my head against his chest, listening to this strong, clear, and rhythmic heartbeat.

"She's lucky to have you," he said, dropping a kiss on my head.

"And I'm lucky to have you," I replied with a kiss on his arm.

I lay there, entertaining thoughts about the four "chicas." Thanks to Sierra's revelation, a wave of anxiety swelled within me. Although all four of us seemed to talk about everything, I hoped Neekoo and BJ didn't have any such living skeletons that they were holding on to. I quickly cautioned the hypocrite in me who wanted to jump off that couch and get on a scale. I didn't share that with them.

FOUR – *There's something about the color teal*

We were celebrating BJ's birthday on Saturday—her twenty-eighth. She had a lot to celebrate. Shortly after graduation, BJ took the biggest gamble of her life. In college, BJ had been a business administration major with a minor in hospitality management. We all knew that BJ would have her own eatery someday, but that "someday" was within five years after graduation. She started an apprenticeship program a year before we graduated and continued for one more year to complete the program. An additional year of internships ensured that her foundational culinary training was complete. Certifications in hand, BJ took out a loan, cleaned out her savings, and went to work on opening a café-lounge-restaurant-style spot that she called Pink Bailey's. We immediately liked the name, although it wouldn't have mattered if we didn't. From the time she decided that she liked the combination of her favorite color and her first name, she had fallen in love with it and resolved that when she opened her own restaurant, that would be the name. So with a will like no other trumping experience, Pink Bailey's was born.

Everything at Pink Bailey's was pink and brown and "simply beautiful"—that was the sentiment of the guests who had left comment cards and started a weekly blog on the spot. It was even reviewed as one of the best places to visit in Washington, DC.

The atmosphere at Pink Bailey's was, in the words of one blogger, "deliciously inviting, calmly pleasant, and excitingly curious." Not the exact words I would have chosen, but the description was apt. The doors were upholstered in brown suede with pink buttons strategically centered, creating diamond-shaped patterns all over the door. The deep pink paint chosen for the walls had a suede finish to it that complemented the door; rich brown crown molding finished off the accents for the interior. BJ chose a mixture of gallery lights and spotlights for each section and drop-down ceiling lights in gold over each table. Deep mahogany tables came in both circular and rectangular shapes, with high-back chairs upholstered in brown and little pink dots. Each table had a white bed tray—that all four of us were forced to make—with stainless steel handles, normally set in the middle or side of the table. Each tray had condiments and a little cylindrical pink broken-glass-patterned vase that variously held a single flower or shortened brown, pink, and green wooden sticks.

The menu was a textured matte dark brown booklet with pink text, and creative and curious titles. For example, she named the homemade veggie burger, "The Crowning Delight." The names weren't always self-explanatory, but she felt strongly about the menu items becoming conversation pieces. BJ also allowed guests to name at least one dessert bimonthly. The guests loved it. The dessert was something simple like cheesecake, and based on the winning name, BJ added an ingredient that she thought went best with the name and included it on the dessert menu for the following month. Normally the winning guest asked if they could keep a copy of the menu, and BJ obliged. They loved the inclusion, and it was only one of the brilliant ideas that BJ came up with that gave Pink Bailey's almost a religious following and kept it fresh and desired. She even held cooking demonstrations at the restaurant.

We had always joked around that BJ really needed her own

show on television, because we were sure she could easily convince women to fall in love with cooking. Watching her cook was a pleasant sight. Her routine was the same even if she was just making eggs, which come to think of it, never turned out to be "just eggs" when BJ was in the kitchen. No matter what she was wearing, she would almost always change into a tank top and jeans, pull her hair back in a ponytail, and slip into her bedroom slippers. The last step in her preparation process that signaled that she was ready to start cooking, was the music. Her collection was vast, and she would pick a tune that to her, went along with the style of food she was going to prepare.

I was stumped on what to get BJ as a birthday gift. BJ had it all. Really, she had everything. A lot of it she got from guys as gifts, without giving most of them the time of day. Most of the gifts she got had heavy price tags. Like the car she drove, for example—her deep gray, fully customized BMW 745iL. I don't know how she did it, and I really didn't want to know.

The BMW 745iL guy? - His name was Anthony DeLuca, a self-made businessman who owned one of the largest exotic car dealerships in the Washington, DC, metropolitan area, DeLuca Inc. He was a second generation Italian American, and had signature dark features that made him look delectable and distinguished all in one package. BJ started dating him when she was five months shy of her twenty-seventh birthday; he was thirty-seven. She had just decided that she was going to go into business by herself and open Pink Bailey's, and she wanted to celebrate this milestone by buying her first brand-new car.

She walked into DeLuca Inc. in Georgetown dressed in a safari-style teal shirtdress accented with a pink coral belt, pink coral patent open-toed stiletto heels, and a clutch in the same color and style of her shoes. Her attire on that day was so important to her because she wanted to be taken quite seriously when she walked into the dealership. I sat on the floor of BJ's huge dressing room, not knowing why she wanted my opinion on her selection. She didn't really need it. BJ was the most stylish of all of us.

She also didn't want them to question her ability to pay; BJ always passed for younger than her age. Most people gave her three to five years younger than her age at any given time, and in some cases, some guessed her age even seven years younger. She was one of those with a smile that made her look even younger, and most of the time, BJ was smiling.

What she got when she walked into the dealership annoyed her. A middle-aged salesman came to the aid of everyone who walked through the door, inquiring what they were in the market for, but no one came to her. According to BJ, most of the salesmen actually wouldn't make eye contact with her. She strolled around the showroom for about twenty minutes and still, no one came to her assistance. One, as BJ put it, "mistakenly" made eye contact with her and therefore had to ask, "Um hi, has someone helped you?"

Trying not to sound angry and exasperated, she kept it very simple with a, "No," to which he responded, "Let me get someone for you." After another twelve minutes, the same guy came back out and then asked, "What can I help you with?" The smirk she was just sporting was amended into a pursed smile. There was also an intense look emanating from her eyes, and anyone who knew BJ, understood that her nonverbals at that time really communicated, *You're not worth shit!*

BJ asked in a very calm voice, "Can I speak to the owner, please?"

"Do you mean the manager?" asked the sales guy.

"No sir, the owner please," BJ said.

With a disrespectful sigh, he walked away. Sporting an artificial smile, a new guy sauntered up and introduced himself as the general manager for the dealership. "I am told that you need to speak to the owner, but is there something I can help you with?" His entire body language said the opposite of what his lips expressed.

"No, thank you, sir, I do appreciate your desire to help, but I did mean the owner."

With an impatient tone that wasn't being much disguised, he informed her, "Miss, we can't just get you in touch with the owner, especially when you haven't even told us exactly what it is you need to see him about. So if there's anything I can help you with, I would like to know. Otherwise there isn't much I'll be able to do to help you."

Her left leg was kicked to the side with the foot turned outward and her right palm rested on her chest as if to calm her heart. BJ wanted to scream at the guy. Instead, with the same earlier calm which was actually worse than her screaming angry voice, she assured the salesman, "Sir, my sister is Neekoo Rahul, senior staff reporter for the *Beat*." (the *Washington Beat* was the number two newspaper in the district and number four nationally, with its own nationally syndicated newsmagazine show.)

BJ continued before the salesman could mount any response. "I am sure she can get her hands on his information. I am also sure the owner wouldn't be too happy to be hearing from a reporter about the less-than-stellar service received by some of his customers. So I would rather get the information from you, but if you insist, I'll have her make the call."

The general manager excused himself, returning a few minutes later with a card that simply had the name Anthony DeLuca on it and a phone number. Sure that they were still trying to dismiss her with a number that would get her nowhere, she inquired, "Can I have his direct line please?" For a split second, he looked as if he was going to argue, but decided against it and actually penned in a number below the one printed. The two men must have hoped that BJ was going to now exit the showroom, but instead she pulled out her mobile phone and proceeded to dial.

DeLuca's personal assistant picked up the phone. "Hello, how may I help you?" Her first mistake was telling BJ that she was *only* DeLuca's assistant.

"Yes. I asked to speak to Mr. DeLuca please," said BJ, a sharpness entering her tone.

"Sure, I just want to find out how *he* may help you," the assistant responded without matching BJ's sharp tone.

"Well, I am standing in Mr. DeLuca's showroom, and I'd like to speak to him. I don't like the treatment I have received so far, and I am willing to wait for him for as long as that takes, even if it means all day," BJ retorted.

"You won't have to do that," the assistant responded in an ever-pleasant tone. "Hold while I try to get Mr. DeLuca for you on the phone, okay?"

"Thank you," escaped from BJ's lips.

"You are welcome, hold on please," and she transferred the phone to DeLuca within minutes of putting BJ on hold.

Hearing a man's voice on the phone, BJ immediately changed to the friendly "you are going to see things my way" tone she used when she was determined to get what she wanted.

BJ started working her charm. In a much softer voice than she had treated everyone else to, she said, "I really like your name. DeLuca, that's Italian?" You could almost hear him smile through the phone, "Well, thank you."

Quickly, she continued, "I'm Bailey Johnson. I'm standing in your showroom because I came to buy a car. I've been mistreated, and because of that, you and I need to meet."

Perhaps he was taken by BJ or he was simply being a good businessman. Either way, he apologized. "I regret that you've had that kind of experience in my shop. Let me make it up to you."

"And what exactly does 'make it up to you' mean?" asked BJ with a slight chuckle.

"We can both decide what that means when I get there" was his response.

"Let's hope you don't regret that," BJ said, teasing.

"I'm sure I won't. Now if you don't mind waiting for about

forty minutes, I'll be over there to at least start by being your personal salesperson." BJ didn't mind waiting. He got attendants in the showroom to set her up in the sales team's conference room and provide her with lunch. She did not eat the lunch.

Within thirty minutes of the call, Mr. DeLuca introduced himself to BJ, and there was no mistaking that he thought she was attractive. It was in the approving glint in his eyes when he set eyes on her. BJ's eyes went down to his shoes first; his were black square-toed shoes with a nice weave pattern on the sides. His tailored gray pants fell comfortably against the leather. The attire was finished off with a teal dress shirt and black sweater over it with no tie. In classic BJ style, she worked her charm in a way that not too many guys had been able to resist. She caught him off guard with, "Wow, anyone would think we were a couple, based on our complementary dress style, and the teal looks really nice on you too." His smile was that of a guy who had just felt his ego stroked, and BJ knew it. Her anger from earlier was all but melted away.

They spent less than five minutes on the discussion of why BJ had walked into his dealership that midmorning, as they went on to cover those usual topics that two adults engage in when there is an interest toward dating. As an offer of apology for not being treated as she should have been when she came in, DeLuca asked to take her out a few times in any of the cars in the showroom, to help her make up her mind about the one she would get. She agreed to this, and with a date set for that Saturday, that's how BJ and DeLuca started dating.

He had called her earlier in the day to make sure that she wasn't canceling on him—something BJ never did. Somewhere in that conversation, BJ—really talking to herself, but doing it out loud—had muttered, "Damn, I don't really have anything to wear." They continued their conversation without any response being made to her utterance, but hours before they were supposed to meet, BJ got a call from DeLuca's driver, asking her where she was because the boss had sent him to get her. Even though slightly confused, BJ didn't think much of it and told him where she was.

The driver showed up within thirty minutes of the call. "Ms. Johnson, I've been instructed to take you to any store of your choice to get something to wear," he said once she was in the car.

"Thank you," was all BJ said, with a warm smile. Her smile was for DeLuca, who wasn't there to see it. It was all going to be on DeLuca's dime. BJ took out her phone and thumbed through to his number, then changed her mind about calling. Someone else might have called him then and there out of excitement, to thank him, but BJ didn't. She had always felt that if she let any guy know that his charm was working on her, he would have the upper hand, and that's not something she was going to consciously let happen.

DeLuca hadn't told her where they were going, so she played it safe and went looking for a short cocktail dress. She found an adorable ivory and gray sleeveless number that she matched with grey stiletto heels accented with rhinestones, and a clutch. She also picked up a teal cropped jacket that accented the outfit, just in case she'd need it. Then she selected some diamond stud earrings and a tight-fitted diamond tennis bracelet. Before leaving the boutique, she finished her shopping with a purchase of a gray-checkered newsboy cap. It was bold—very bold. Only BJ would dare do something like that regardless of what impression it would leave on a guy.

DeLuca was at BJ's door at around five o'clock for their date. Her hair was pulled back in a bun, and she only had light makeup on, but as always, she was effortlessly gorgeous.

"I did well," DeLuca said, referring to her outfit.

"How do you figure that? Picking it out is tougher than paying for it," BJ said with a playful matter-of-fact tone.

"We did well?" DeLuca responded. BJ smiled and leaned up to give him a hug. He kissed her on the cheek and said, "You are a tough one. Tough, but gorgeous." BJ responded with a coy smile and stepping into his chauffeured car, they proceeded on their date. He did not tell her where they were headed, and she did not ask.

They arrived at an airstrip, where DeLuca had them flown to his Florida home for the evening. They had dinner at his mini mansion, with a spread to satisfy any palate, made by his personal cook. She said the conversation was one of the best she had had with a guy, and that for the first time that she could think of, she had been entirely genuine and wasn't putting on a flirting act. They later went to a jazz lounge with a live band, where he mostly watched her dance.

When the night was over, DeLuca showed her to the guest room, where there were some nightclothes for her at the end of the bed, as well as an entire outfit for the next day. BJ asked no questions. DeLuca went to his room, and that ended their first date, which BJ has since described as her best moments with a guy. For the first time with a man, she wanted to make the first move and go into his room, but didn't. She lay in the bed, hoping he would come in. He didn't.

After breakfast the next morning, they headed back to DC where the three of us were waiting for BJ to fill us in with all the details on this guy that we all thought was a keeper.

Pink Bailey's was opening two days late, and DeLuca was supportive in every way, offering more than anyone would ask of a fairly recent acquaintance. Neekoo had made sure that there was enough buzz in the press about the opening, and Sierra and I had pitched in to help with set up and design whenever called upon. I also was responsible for the guest list for the opening, which tripled when BJ met DeLuca and he found out about her restaurant opening.

In the whirlwind of dating a guy who provided her with a chauffeur and car to wherever she needed to go and the opening of Pink Bailey's, the thought of getting her car had conveniently taken a backseat. She was comfortably getting used to being chauffeured everywhere, and therefore being able to get more done in the backseat. However, on her twenty-seventh birthday, at precisely eight thirty the morning of September 3, DeLuca personally delivered the customized dark gray 745iL to BJ. He knocked on the door and announced himself. And with a kiss, he wished her happy birthday. She offered him a light breakfast, during which he informed her that he would be acting as her chauffeur that day to mark her birthday. She laughed. When he assured her that indeed he was serious, she finished getting ready and they were out the door.

The floor mats were the tell—the gray mats with the initials *BJ* embroidered in teal got that excitement out of her that she had rarely showed any guy.

"No, you're kidding me!" she exclaimed.

"Yes, it's all yours," he assured her.

She fell silent, looking at him, and then the car. Whatever his reason was, even if it was simply the fact that that was a color they both had on when they first met, it was good enough. The little accents in the car that were in teal brought a smile to her face. He went around and opened the driver's door for her, handing her the key. "All the paperwork is in the glove compartment, but you do have to take me to my office, since I don't have a car on me."

She kissed him, and with a hug she whispered, "Thank you," in his ear. It was a tight hug. In the moment of that hug, she felt what could be love, and definitely fear.

As she drove him to work that morning, one would have sworn that they were indeed a perfect couple. He asked her what her plans were for the day. They hadn't really talked about what she wanted to do for her birthday. She said, "You know, I have to see what the girls want to do, since we try and spend a part of our birthdays together."

"Do you know when you might be making it back home then?"

"Not sure, but probably after ten," she answered, not really knowing what we were going to end up doing.

"Just give a quick buzz when you get in, okay? So that we can spend a couple of minutes celebrating your birthday."

"I will," BJ promised. She dropped him off, and with a kiss, she was on her way to Pink Bailey's.

It had to be within seconds that they had left each other; I got an unexpected call from DeLuca. "Good morning, Rory, how are you?"

"Hey! I'm good. What's going on?"

"I was wondering if you had a key to Bailey's place, and you could let me in around one this afternoon," he asked.

"I have a key, but I will have to get it to you instead, because we should be taking BJ out for the day and I won't be able to let you in," I informed him. Although they had been dating a short while, I was rooting for DeLuca as *the* keeper. The sappy romantic in me was hoping that he wanted the key so that he could get her place ready to propose. That thought excited me, and I didn't ask him why he wanted the key. All he offered, as an explanation, was that he wanted to surprise her. Surprise her! Imagine my surprise when I found out that he had already gotten her a car. What other surprise could there be but a diamond ring?! As soon as I got off the phone with him, I got a call from BJ. I heard the excitement in her voice, but she wouldn't tell me what she was excited about. She simply said, "You've got to see it!" Had he proposed already?

We were meeting at Pink Bailey's. I dashed to DeLuca's to drop off BJ's key and was able to get back into my office around eleven thirty. It was just enough time to place reminder calls to Neekoo and Sierra, put Cynthia Knox (my next-in-command) in charge of The Look while I was gone, and try to beat traffic down to Pink Bailey's so I would not be late myself. I got there in time to meet Neekoo, and we waited another fifteen minutes for Sierra, who was running a little late because of a patient. Lunch was light, with a lot of laughter; BJ had a lot of jokes on all of us being older than her, even though we were talking about only eighteen months difference between her and Neekoo, who was the oldest.

In BJ's world of fashion, accessories ruled, so what we had done was create a little booklet in pink and brown and mapped out connectivity points to a few accessory stores and boutiques between Washington, DC, and Alexandria, Virginia. We were going to visit as many of them as we could for BJ to indulge in whatever she wanted, on our dime. Corny as we were, we had actually titled the booklet, "BJ's Accessory Shop-Hopping Day—September 3rd."

When we were ready to go, BJ offered to drive. "You're not driving, BJ," I stated in a matter-of-fact tone.

"Here you go, now you want to be the chauffeur on your birthday," was Sierra's response.

"No, seriously it's not a big deal. I want to," BJ continued.

"Listen, I still know the entire area better than any of you so it's final, I'm driving," said Neekoo.

Quite sweetly, BJ responded, "Well, that's your final word, sweetie, because I'm not going anywhere if I'm not the one driving."

"Hey, let's just go. Let her drive. We're not going to keep arguing about who's driving," said Sierra, whose patience for the back-and-forth was getting short.

Once outside Pink Bailey's, BJ walked us to the back. She was heading toward a parked BMW, and it didn't quite sink in until we were a couple of steps away from the car. I was the first to react. "You got your BMW!" I let out excitedly.

"No wonder she was fighting us to drive," said Sierra, shaking her head and smiling.

"This is beautiful," said Neekoo, walking around the car and caressing the body all the way.

BJ couldn't wipe the girly grin off her face as she announced coyly, "I didn't get my BMW; DeLuca did."

"What?" was the collective exclamation from Sierra, Neekoo, and myself.

"This chick!" started Sierra with feigned exasperation. "What do these guys not get for you?"

"Jealousy isn't a good color on you, Sierra," Neekoo chided harmlessly and called dibs for the front passenger seat. BJ, Sierra, and I were getting into the car when Sierra responded, "Trust me, I'm not jealous. It is simply unbelievable what kind of gifts this chica gets from guys, unbelievable." Our ride to the first stop on the shopping trip was treated to a soundtrack of details of exactly how DeLuca pulled it off.

It was a good birthday celebration for BJ, with all of us putting aside the fact that we really didn't care nearly as much for the shoes, bags, jewelry, and hats as much as we knew that BJ believed that shopping for them made her day almost more than they made her outfit. Some of the boutiques knew BJ by name. And when some of them found out that it was her birthday, she got a few freebie gifts as well.

We ended up back at Pink Bailey's, where the rest of us picked up our cars and all four of us headed back to BJ's for a nightcap.

"Why does any one person need this many handbags?" asked Sierra, grabbing three big bags out of BJ's car and heading toward the door of the condo.

"Or shoes," Neekoo chimed in.

"Keys?" Sierra called out. Tossing the keys her way, BJ called out, "Catch," in return.

"Sierra!" I called out, trying to get her attention before she was entirely out of my sight.

"I don't think she heard you," said Neekoo. BJ was laughing lightly. "Nah, she heard you, she just doesn't want to carry any more bags." I was by the trunk of the car, trying to grab the remaining bags, and I needed more hands.

Neeko, BJ, and I hauled the remaining bags up into the condo. We headed straight to BJ's bedroom, which led to her very-spacious walk-in closet—or to be more accurate, the adjoining master bedroom that she had turned into her closet. The smell of paint stopped us in time, and then we saw the note along the entrance of the closet. It was from DeLuca. BJ sank down to the floor to read the card. "Hey, I just wanted you to know that I was thinking about you on your special day and had your closet redone in our color. Let me know how your day went, even if it has to wait till tomorrow." He signed it, "Happy birthday, to the most beautiful girl. DeLuca."

While we were out shoe, bag, hat, sunglass, and jewelry shopping, sometime that afternoon, DeLuca had a closet remodeling team come to the house where, based on his approval, he had them totally reinvent her closet, paying closest attention to intertwining the color teal as well as creating easy-to-reach islands for her accessories. Before the makeover, BJ's closet was pretty much a huge room with wall-to-wall closet cubing and a large shoe-shaped chair together with an ottoman in the middle of the room. Both chair and ottoman were a plush velvet in black and gold, and those were the only items of color in the whole room. Happy tears trickled down BJ's face. She whispered, "I've got to call him." Then she dialed him through the speakerphone.

"Hey, babe," she called to him over the phone, the sex oozing from her tone.

"Hey, sexy," DeLuca responded with a slight baritone that really meant he was tired, but tonight it also turned BJ on.

"You know I would make love to you in this closet?" she asked him playfully. It was more of an invitation than a harmless tease.

"Looks like I did a good job then?" DeLuca asked. BJ was walking around her newly renovated closet as she was talking to her man and as she was taking in each detail. She couldn't stop smiling. Disregarding that we were in the room, BJ continued to express her gratitude in no uncertain terms. "A closet should not be making me horny, but when are you coming over?" she asked with a chuckle.

"You weren't kidding about that," DeLuca said, also through a slight chuckle.

"Of course not!" BJ exclaimed. "And don't worry, these girls will be leaving soon," she assured him. "BJ!" we exclaimed, feigning hurt. He didn't even know we were there.

"Your girls are there? They don't have to leave, babe. Why don't you come over here so that you don't have to be inhaling any of the paint fumes?" he said.

"That's cool. This chica needs her birthday sex," shouted Sierra for DeLuca's benefit.

"That's right!" BJ gushed. "That sounds like a great idea," she continued in response to DeLuca's suggestion. "Can't wait to see you, babe," and with that she got off the phone. Then we all tiptoed gingerly through her newly renovated closet, taking in all the details.

The whole room had been recarpeted with a beautifully textured, pale pink Berber. The chair and ottoman were entirely reupholstered with a suede-like fabric in teal with pale pink buttons, and they were no longer in the middle of the room because double-sided mirrors now hung from the ceiling in that spot. Inscribed faintly in the mirrors was the phrase, "simply, yes simply beautiful." Looking into the closet, on the right side, hung from wall to wall and covered in protective sheets were all BJ's dresses and gowns, color-coded from light to dark. Along the back of the closet was her business and business-casual wear (also color-coded), and on the left was all her casual wear. In front of the clothes were three light-brown wooden islands with drawers at the top and open shelves. The island to the right housed her closed-toe shoes, the middle island housed her pumps, and the island to the left had all the casuals—sandals and sneakers.

On the top of one of the islands, her jewelry was kept in customized jewelry drawers. On the left side of the closet was the new place for the chair and ottoman. As you walked out, in the very front of the closet were rounded pink hooks that held her bags and scarves. The crown molding was done in a nutmeg brown and all the walls in a shimmering gold with teal-and-pink sponge patterning all over. It was definitely BJ's dream closet.

It was almost eleven o'clock. She finally kicked us out of the house so that she could spend the last hour of her birthday with DeLuca, so we called it a night. She was out the door with us.

The morning after "the birthday to end all birthdays," I was alone at home when I heard the banging on my door. It was BJ.

"Hey babe," she said when I answered the door.

"What's going on?" She was still in her outfit from the night before.

"Before I divulge any details, I need to see what you have in your fridge for breakfast. I need a pot of coffee brewing, and I need to borrow some sweat pants."

"Are you crazy? You aren't going to fit anything I own," I said. I was five months pregnant and living in maternity clothes.

"Can you just get me some pants!" she insisted, heading to my guest restroom to take a shower. "You must have something from before the pregnancy," she scolded playfully. I went looking. The second I joined her in the guest room, she couldn't help but start talking about DeLuca and the night she had just had with him and how deeply she was feeling about him.

"And I promise I am not just saying that because of the gifts," she said.

"I know you mean it. If it was just the gifts, then you would have made that statement about many more guys before him."

We both laughed and went down memory lane over the many gifts—small, big, and mostly costly—that BJ had received over the years. She always managed to bag the rich ones. We were in the kitchen now, where BJ was doing some wonders with eggs, and I had poured both of us cups of black, decaffeinated coffee with organic honey.

"Remember that emerald and diamond ring that I got from that guy?"

"You mean the 'please date me because I really love you even if you don't even acknowledge that I exist' gift that you got from Steven … ummm, wasn't his last name Arden?" I recalled.

"Damn! You remember his full name! You're pretty good. I didn't remember his last name."

"I'm sure he would be happy to know that, after he dropped a pretty penny on that ring," I said.

"Hey, I didn't ask him to get it. But I will admit I was entirely surprised to find that he spent thousands—I wouldn't have bought something like that for someone I barely knew."

"He thought he was doing something nice, BJ."

"A diamond ring after three months of knowing me though? Come on, even though it wasn't an engagement ring or anything, even for me that was a bit much. Maybe diamond earrings or something, but a ring?" she said, shaking her head.

"Okay, okay, now speaking of diamond rings though, what's up with DeLuca, have you guys even talked about that?"

"I know he is trying to feel me out, and I also know that he will wait until he doesn't get any signs of hesitation from me before he even broaches the subject."

"Why the hesitation, BJ?"

"I can't even begin to explain it right now, because I do know he's a good guy and all of that, but I just don't know, I just don't know," and she ended that statement with a light, reflective look.

I didn't push for more; she had definitely thought seriously about a future with DeLuca, but still wasn't letting down her guard entirely with him, and there had to be a reason for that. I still had to add, however, "You know he's a great one, right? Not just a good one, a great one. He really knows how to handle you."

"I know," she said with a playful smirk on her face.

BJ was clearly on cloud nine after her birthday and practically lived over at DeLuca's. She would prepare him breakfast. He'd go into work an hour later than normal and didn't complain. BJ loved this new life even though she never said it. Sometimes she made stops at the dealership when DeLuca was there, and it pleased her to see the same salespersons who had once ignored her being overly nice to her. She reciprocated their greetings with a frosty cordiality.

I enjoyed listening to BJ's excursions with DeLuca because through them I saw a calmer, less frantic BJ who didn't feel the need to spend every waking hour at Pink Bailey's. They were both workaholics, but they managed their life together well. The closest park to DeLuca Inc. was along the George Washington Memorial Parkway, and oftentimes during the day, BJ would have them out at the park either for a picnic, bike ride, leisurely stroll, or even a silent lounge on the grass where they just enjoyed each other's company. Other times, in the evening, DeLuca would quietly come into Pink Bailey's where the hostess sat him at the same table each time and left him alone to await his lady till she was ready to leave. Then they would go and enjoy the rest of their day together. Life was good for BJ.

A few months passed, however, and it became a different story. I started noticing BJ place some distance between herself and DeLuca. I spent the night at BJ's when Michael traveled for a client meeting for a couple of days. Gourmet hors d'oeuvres, ice cream and cake, BJ's special recipe hot chocolate, and reruns of our favorite shows was just what my very pregnant body needed. Two hours into our slumber party, DeLuca called. BJ let the answering system pick up.

"BJ?" I said, wondering why she wasn't picking up.

"I don't want to talk about it, Rory," she said, and she turned the television volume up slightly. Her tone was sharp. It stopped me from making any further inquiries at that very second. I got up and walked to the restroom, even though I did not need to use it. As I turned on the faucet just to let the water run for a deceitful minute, I was fearful that there was something wrong with BJ and DeLuca, and it made me anxious. The side of me that knew my friend well enough told me not to push her, that she would come out with it when she wanted to, but I ignored it. I walked out of the restroom to rejoin her in the living room; I wanted to know if he had done something to her that she just didn't want to share. Had he cheated on her? All my rationalizations had me faulting him not her. The BJ that I had seen with DeLuca in the past few months had to be in love with this guy, so there was no way she could be at fault for any rift, I convinced myself. I needed to know something!

"BJ …" I paused. Then I added, "Can you just tell me if I should be concerned?"

"Concerned about what? No, you shouldn't." She was dismissive. She didn't offer any more than that.

Not being able to let it go, I kept pushing, but giving me that look that assured that she wasn't going to delve into it, BJ said, "We both just decided to take a break for a little while, but everything's okay. He was probably just reminding me of something that I forgot at his place or something."

I wasn't buying it, and before I let it go, I had to know. "BJ, you would tell me if he did anything, right?"

She looked at me and with sincerity that I believed, she promised me, "You wouldn't have to ask, because I wouldn't have been able to hold it in." Although reassuring to hear that, her statement then made me wonder what exactly she *was* holding in.

Five – *The Big ONE at Pink Bailey's*

I was responsible for the design of Pink Bailey's for its first anniversary, but BJ wouldn't let me into the café until Saturday morning; the event was that night. I had asked for at least part of Friday, but she wouldn't close it down on Friday evening. The Pink Bailey's Friday crowd was a dedicated one: mostly single women winding down their workweek (very often the same women each week), who just needed a feminine savvy place to relax and enjoy good friends, good food, and feel special. Earlier on when BJ noticed the group that would come in on Friday nights, she made it all about them, terming Friday night at Pink Bailey's, "Single Women's Escape and Treat" night—SWEAT—just corny! Needless to say, they were not going to be displaced.

The theme for the party was "Material Girl," which just meant lots of jewelry. Neekoo and I went to get the jewelry for the party. The deal was to get a few big jewelry designers into the restaurant to offer their items for sale at 50 percent off the retail price. I had suggested three-quarter mannequins wearing the jewelry and hung on the walls like art pieces, but Sierra had suggested instead that models from The Look should be hired as greeters for the entire night, and wear the jewelry with strategically placed price tags around each piece. I wasn't crazy about the latter, but I got the idea, so to appease Sierra, we used both ideas.

Starting really early Saturday morning, we redid all the hanging lights into crystal and pearl chandeliers, and continued with pearls as a consistent theme as the centerpiece for most of the tables. Half of the restaurant was cleared out into a dance floor, on which a temporary monogram of Pink Bailey's was glazed into the dance floor. The colors for the party were black and gold, and that included the dress code; BJ was going to be the only one in white.

The cake was a sight. BJ was annoyed at first when I told her that she would not be baking the cake. I had contacted Trisha, a baker from Virginia who catered some of the most sought-after events in DC, and before I finished the request, she said, "I know BJ. Don't worry; it will be just right." What that turned into was a delicious spectacle. I gave Trisha a few items of BJ's that she had asked for. The main cake or base of the cake was a replica of one of BJ's designer purses, but instead of where the designer logo was, she had placed the restaurant's name. Coming out of the bag was a replica of one of BJ's gold stiletto heels and a Pink Bailey's menu. The stiletto was chocolate, and the handbag was a yellow strawberry-swirl cake.

I wanted the cake to be a big reveal later in the evening, but BJ insisted on seeing it as soon as it came in. A smile slowly crept on her face, and she nodded her head as she walked around the cake. "So?" I asked. "Okay, okay," she said, still nodding. Phew! She loved it.

The guests started to arrive around seven that evening, and they looked glamorous. There were sparkling dresses, gold-sequined dresses, soft leather dresses, and they all were in gold. The shoes? I have never been a fan of stiletto heels—maybe because I could almost never wear them for over two hours—but these women rocked these heels with stylish ease; if it hurt, there was no telling. I don't think I looked good in the gold dress I had on; I should have gone with a pant number like Sierra did. That bulge in my lower abdomen wasn't supposed to be there, and it added an extra curve to the outfit; maybe that's what was making this all wrong. Granted, I had pushed out a baby not too long ago, but all I could see was that bulge that I wanted gone.

BJ, on the other hand, looked amazing. She didn't go for all-white as she had previously said she would, but instead it was a champagne-colored strapless gown that accentuated her entire delicate hourglass shape. There was something regal looking about BJ when she had her hair up, and that's how she wore it that night. It was in a simple bun with rounded rhinestone pins, holding her hair together and sparkling with each turn of her head. She matched the outfit with diamond stud earrings and adorning her neck was a barely visible diamond necklace with a canary diamond pendant that settled comfortably against her chest.

As I looked at my friend as she worked the room with her signature smile, appreciating everyone who had come out to celebrate with her, the only accessory that I could think of that was missing was DeLuca. He wasn't there yet. Entirely overstepping my bounds, I had personally sent him an invitation to her party. She needed him, at least that's what I felt, and I was sure I was right. I kept my eyes on the entrance, hoping against hope that he would show up.

There was food and drink everywhere. A section of the restaurant featured quartet seating, and each quartet had a different finger-friendly dish as its signature. So the setup was formed in the vein of a food tasting, but this food tasting was meant to eventually fill you up, as the especially efficient staff replenished each dish almost as soon as each menu item was removed from the table. I looked over at Sierra, who surprisingly was working the crowd in the most pleasant way. Small talk with strangers? Not her thing.

Neekoo was with yet another guy, and I was actually surprised that she came with him. Normally she didn't go anywhere with the men that she dated. None of us tried to keep up with them, as they never seemed to last. She also didn't bother introducing us to any of them for the same reason. So seeing this tall guy leading her through the room had me raising my eyebrows. From afar, I thought he was a prick—you know, the type who truly thought the world of themself and made sure you knew it too.

He was dressed nicely in a dark, well-tailored three-button suit and white shirt with no tie. For all my irritation at him, I had to admit that he did look good. He was dangling his keys, almost like he wanted everyone to know that he drove a Maserati; he was too obvious. As they walked my way, I was in a conversation with two politicians and one of the local radio personalities, and I was hoping Neekoo and her date wouldn't stop at our group. Unfortunately they did, and he lived up to almost every one of my preconceived notions about him.

While Neekoo hugged me, he was looking around impatiently. He seemed further irritated by our less-than-twenty-second catch-up, and Neekoo caught the cue and proceeded to make introductions. "This is one of my closest friends, Rory Carter," Neekoo said, and was about to introduce him when he took over.

"Hi, I'm Jason Masters," he said, shaking my hand. "Real estate guru Jason Masters, that is," he said with a side note. Yes, those really were his words, and I just looked at him with questioning eyes, wondering why that last bit was necessary. Thankfully, he did not further engage me in meaningless conversation and proceeded to introduce himself to each member of the group I was with. And with that last handshake with City Councilman Jackson, the Jason Masters life-bragging story began.

He told our group about several deals he had brokered for some of the prime real estate in the city and its surroundings, and although we may not have known his name, he assured us that we definitely knew his real estate. I was partially listening to still-talking Masters when my eyes gladly traveled toward what was the illumination of a friendly face near the entrance of the door.

DeLuca looked as dashing as ever, walking in his quietly confident stride, heading directly to the reason why he was there.

I wasn't the only one drawn to his presence. A few eyes were on him, wondering who he was. With a smile and a nod to each person who greeted him, he didn't break his stride until he was standing right next to BJ. She was being greeted by one of the guests and hadn't seen him walking toward her.

With his right hand traveling to rest on the small of her back in a motion to subtly move her in for a close hug, she was forced to face him, and in her eye was the glow that had followed her a little while back whenever she mentioned DeLuca's name. I smiled.

The smile on her face was equally as quiet as his, but hers was also lined with curiosity. After the kiss on the cheek, the hug they shared wasn't that of two friends but of two lovers after a moment of separation that they were happy was over. He had to share her, however, so their moment of ending-separation was a brief one as more guests came up to her to commend her on the success of Pink Bailey's. Then almost on cue, one of her songs came on. DeLuca led her to the dance floor, and the dance was theirs.

Sierra was standing next to me now, and we both had drinks in our hands. "Where did he come from?" Sierra asked. "I don't remember seeing his name on any of the lists." I had a telling smile on my face, and immediately she knew.

"No, you didn't. Does she know it was you?"

"Does it even matter?" I asked in a happy-guilty tone. "Look at her face, she deserved this, and it didn't look as if she was going to invite him, so I did. I wasn't really expecting him to show up."

"He was going to show up; he loves the chica. He was definitely going to show up," Sierra said. Switching gears, she asked, "You sent Vernon an invite, right?"

"Yeah," I said, noticing that he was a no-show. "Where is he?"

I reached for my mobile to send Vernon a text, and out of nowhere, a guy walked up to us. He came up to Sierra. At some moments like this, I would wonder like I thought every married woman did, *If it weren't for the ring on my finger, would I have been getting some curious suitors?* I would sometimes also think though that it wasn't the ring, but my size. I would have loved the opportunity to turn the suitors down; it would go a long way in stroking my image-ego. Sending a yelling text to Vernon about his absence, I made a mental note to check my schedule so that I could head up to New York to do lunch or dinner with him.

I excused myself from what had now become a conversation between the interested guy and Sierra, and made my way to the other side of the room to where BJ and DeLuca tasted some of the food items. I hadn't made it to them yet, when the emcee, who was one of the female local radio personalities, announced that it was time for the cutting of the cake. DeLuca was still holding on to BJ when she had to make her way to the table with the cake.

Within seconds of getting to her cake, as previously requested by BJ, our names were called over the mic to join her by the cake table. As we moved up to surround BJ, DeLuca eased away from her side before we could even stop him, and with the music keyed down and a pink spotlight on us, the whole room started singing happy birthday to Pink Bailey's. My eyes were on BJ; her eyes were searching into the audience. My guess is that she was looking to see if DeLuca was still there. I looked into the audience, but I didn't see him. At the end of the celebratory song, BJ quickly cut through the cake for a bite before they could whisk it away. She tasted a bit of the huge chunk she had cut, and with a mouthful she exclaimed, "It's really good!" The surprise in BJ's voice wasn't quite disguised. Leaning into Neekoo who was to the right of me, I said, "Thankfully the baker isn't in earshot." Neekoo nodded her head in agreement, while we were all smiles for the pictures being taken.

I saw BJ look out into the audience again, and the look was a slightly anxious and nervous one with a thinly veiled smile. I also looked out into the audience again to see if DeLuca was still there. I didn't see him, but by the time I looked back to the crowd that had come up after the cutting of the cake, BJ also was nowhere in sight.

I assumed she'd been engulfed by some guests or had hopefully found DeLuca. I began to wish we had hired a sitter and Michael was here with me. Neekoo and Sierra made sure they circled around enough times to wherever I was to make sure I wasn't lost in the audience. I didn't really know most of the people here, and I dreaded having to hear Neekoo's date speak about nothing again, so as I saw them seemingly making it my way again, I inconspicuously made my way to BJ's office behind the restaurant's kitchen. I was thankful for making my escape because I now felt the urge to relieve myself, and BJ's office had a private restroom. The light was on when I got back there, and there was someone using it.

Whoever it was hadn't heard me come in. It sounded like a continuous choking half-cough that didn't quite sound right. I didn't know what to make of the noise, and with anxious worry, I banged on the door. "Sierra is that you? Are you okay?" I called out. There was no answer. Instead, the noise now sounded muffled, as if there was an attempt to stop the coughing with a hand over the mouth or through a closed mouth. I had just seen Neekoo before I left the main lounge, so it couldn't be her, and access to this space was reserved for the four of us alone, so I called out again.

"Sierra, BJ? Are you okay?" I continued to inquire, this time tapping the door as well as trying to turn the doorknob. The door was locked. "Hey, whoever's in there, I'm going to call for help okay, just hang in there," I said getting my mobile out of my purse. At the same moment, the doorknob turned, and BJ opened the door.

Even though I had called out to her, I was still shocked to see BJ walk out of the restroom. "What the hell's going on, is everything okay?" All I was thinking was that something had to have gone terribly wrong in a record short time as this wasn't exactly the same BJ who had been shoving down chunks of delicious birthday cake less than ten minutes ago and blissful in DeLuca's sight.

"I think I had a slight anxiety attack," she responded as she moved over to her chair to sit for a few moments. She coughed a few more times to clear her throat and reached for her mouthwash and makeup kit that she kept in the desk. None of it sounded right to me, and without immediately processing what she had said, I reacted only out of concern when I asked, "Have you had these types of anxiety attacks before?"

"Yes. I just need to sit for a little while, and I should be okay." And with that, she poured some mouthwash into a cup and rinsed out her mouth in the restroom.

I began processing everything, and confusion started to take a stronghold of my feelings. *Gargling mouthwash after an anxiety attack?* I started to ask her out loud, but decided against it. I was convinced the timing was wrong. Instead, I rationalized. BJ was an all-around clean freak whom we all believed had some level of obsessive compulsive disorder, and it was common to find mouthwash, hand sanitizers, and wipes in different rooms in her house, office, glove compartment, and her purse.

As BJ walked back into her office, I teased her disapprovingly, "Only you would think of gargling mouthwash as the appropriate end to having an anxiety attack." She acted as if she hadn't heard me. She seemed a little nervous, and right after she cleaned off the sides of her mouth, sprayed air freshener through the office and the restroom, and reapplied her foundation, she flashed her beautiful smile asking, "Is anything out of place?"

"No, you look great," I said. It was the truth, but as sure as the feeling in the pit of my stomach assured me that something was amiss, it was also a lie. She looked great on the outside, but her eyes told me that things were not great on the inside.

"See you out there," she said, and before she whisked out of the office, I pulled her in for a tight hug. "You've done a great job here; everything's beautiful," I said, and she kissed me on the cheek and was gone.

It was about midway through our freshman year in college when it occurred to me that of all my housemates, I probably had the best family support system. Sierra and her brothers spoke sparingly. Although Neekoo was from the area, she preferred to spend little to no time at home, and that included the breaks we got from school. BJ tried to make it back to Arizona as much as she could, but that wasn't much. My mom had to be begged not to visit every weekend.

My dad never visited, or even called for that matter. But with him I've mostly felt like a live-in stranger anyway. When young, our conversations were sometimes like reporting to my principal. He listened to my periodic updates with a response of, "Good, good, sounds like things are coming along." The best years I had with my dad were in middle and high school. They were also my tough years when I joined one sports team after another with the hopes of losing considerable weight. We talked more then; our conversations went beyond updates on my weekly, monthly, or quarterly activities. We talked the sports; he played the sports with Vernon.

The tomboy in me comforted the overweight me. Since I was decent at many of the sports I played, each victory regardless of my size made me feel good. Tomboy Rory slowly but surely gave way to feminine Rory, and that widened the gap between my father and me, transforming our sports talks back into conversational updates. I began to get quieter around my dad. Actually, I was quieter with everyone as I was going through internal struggles with my weight. If being in this stage meant not having much to say to my mom because I knew exactly what she was going to say in the vein of being inspirational about my weight, it also meant then that I had nothing at all to say to my dad. I wished he had said something to me though, reached out in some way, but that never happened, and I must admit that a part of me has resented him for not recognizing my pain.

Before I left for college, living with my dad was like living with my mother's new husband who didn't quite know how to make a connection with his awkward stepdaughter. It probably wasn't the worst relationship to have with one's father, but then it wasn't even a relationship.

I have always thought that parents give kids too much credit when it comes to their state of mind. When I withdrew and acted as if I just didn't want to be bothered, those were the times that I needed my dad to pry, to ask me what was wrong even if he couldn't help, to want to really get to know me even if it had the potential to embarrass him. I never said anything, so that's where we've been, and as much as I know I love my dad without a shadow of a doubt and refuse to whine about the lack of a relationship, we definitely aren't close. This was the state of mind I was in generally when it came to my dad, and subconsciously it influenced the setup of my room in college, which BJ brought to my attention.

"Is your dad still living?" she had asked one day when it was just the two of us in the suite. I was lazing around while BJ was cooking. I was her taster for the evening, so I was pretty much on the cusp of the kitchen, yet still getting out of her way as she said I was "busying" her space. With a sudden jerk of my head and a quizzed look, partly at the question, partly at the random moment within which it was brought up, I responded in a slightly defiant tone. "Yes. What would make you ask that kind of a question?"

"You've got pictures of your mom and Vernon in your room, but not your father. I've never heard you talk to your father, and we've been living together now for a few months. Also, if your dad was in your life or alive, I assumed you would have spoken to him." As my answer, I noted that I had never heard her speak to her dad, but didn't give any thought to him being dead.

Perhaps it was psychological conditioning from not having a close relationship with my father, but what she noted as odd

I took as normal. Hence, I had never given any thought to the fact that BJ had never spoken to her dad on the phone, until the very moment that she brought it up about my dad. I wanted to retract what I had said as I now felt guilty for finger-pointing, when all she had really done was make an observation, but before I could, she said, "Mine might as well be dead." This being the last thing I expected to come out of her mouth, I was taken aback and silenced. She continued to cook without skipping a beat. She looked up and seeing the shock on my face, she chuckled slightly and added, "Don't worry, it's not like I really knew him or anything, so it would be like hearing of a stranger's death on the ten o'clock news." It was clear by the lack of a shift in my reaction that the added perspective didn't make a difference to me, so BJ gave me the whole story.

"My mother had me when she was seventeen going on eighteen, and they were high school sweet … well I'd say more so friends. My mother was extremely smart, book smart that is, but she wasn't as much when it came to guys. With them she was naive and really believed everything her closest male friend told her at the time.

"His name is Martin P. Holmes, and at that age I assume he couldn't keep his raging hormones in check. I think that because my mother never wanted me to feel as if I were a product of a rape, she puts it in such a way that deflects rape, but I have always taken it as that. On the night that she was "de-virgined," she was visiting him and they were doing their math homework in his room. It was sometime in the late evening. My mother, who was raised by her grandmother, was trusted to stay out as late as she pleased because she was responsible enough. Her grandmother also took in several foster kids, and the lack of a curfew could have come from her being too busy to keep an eye on a child who never gave her any problems. Hence, my mother being out on a school day at some guy's house, was the least of her problems.

"I don't know the whole story to my mother's parents, but they had two girls and gave them up to the state because they couldn't stay off drugs long enough to provide a constant supply of meals and clothing for their kids. So my mom ended up at her grandmother's, while her sister ended up being adopted by a nonfamily member. My great-grandmother never formally adopted my mother, and needless to say, my mother didn't grow up with a lot of guidance from any one direction and did a lot of 'raising herself' the best way she knew how. That meant becoming a remarkable student and staying out of trouble, which pleased my great-grandmother.

"But I don't think that's an excuse for her allowing my mom to be around boys at such a young age, you know? Anyway, about how I came about? My mother says that they had finished their math homework early and were watching a movie one day, and she didn't feel any different from any other time that she was hanging out at his place. He got up. 'I'm going to turn the lights off, okay?'

'That looks a little dark,' she responded after he started walking back to the edge of the bed where she was sitting leisurely on the floor.

'How about that?' he asked, leaning over his desk and turning on the single light from the desk lamp.

'That's better. I don't feel the light from the television drilling into my eyes anymore,' she said with a chuckle. He joined her on the floor and they went back to watching television. Then he started playing in her hair under the pretense of giving a head massage. He proceeded with his second move, which was to lean in for a kiss. She jerked, and he stopped.

"Now this is where I think she chose to describe things in a hazy manner to me when she was retelling the story. She says that with more persistence from him, she 'realized' that it was something cool to share with him that would probably make them closer, so she stopped resisting the kiss, and the kiss led to them having sex. I think that's bullshit. I have never believed this story, I know my mother, and when she was telling me what happened, I could tell in her eyes that she was holding something back.

"Two months after her first time having sex, she found out she was pregnant, but something had changed between her and Martin. Martin became more reserved. There was a mixture of frustration, confusion, shame, and disbelief going on with my mother as she contemplated what to do about her pregnancy.

"According to her, the frustration came from not being able to communicate with Martin and really feeling alone in figuring the whole thing out. She had attempted a conversation with him about it, and when he felt in her voice that she was leaning more toward keeping the baby, he first asked if she had told anyone yet. The answer was no. It was after that response that he then promised that he would be there for whatever she needed. Standing up for herself and communicating her own true feelings was not her strong suit. Instead, she bottled up all her feelings of confusion that stemmed from their conversation. How was he going to be there for whatever she needed, when he barely spoke to her, avoided most of her calls, and barely kept eye contact with her when they passed each other in public? She was alone in this, regardless of what he said.

"It was as if after that one act and the moments that followed, whatever naive film that had encased her for the last seventeen and a half years dissolved, and she couldn't stop beating herself up for not stopping this from happening, from not seeing the signs that led up to that moment. *How could she have been so blind?* she would ask herself during so many nights sitting on the California beach, not wanting to go home because a part of her wanted the wave to wash her problems away. At three months, she still wasn't quite showing and had successfully kept her morning sickness secret from her grandmother.

"She would leave really early in the morning for a workout routine at the community gym near the house and leave for school afterward. She went to the library after school where she would read up on everything she could find about pregnancies, and quiz herself to make sure that she was retaining all the information. She would do this several times through the week, retesting herself on the same information over and over again. On some days, she had to skip the library and head to her after-school job tutoring elementary and middle school kids, but on most days, after the library, she would leave for the beach and just sit there.

"When I hear people say they don't have friends, I wonder if they really know what that means. For my mother, it wasn't just a statement of assertion because she was taking a break from people who were bugging her or had let her down. No, it was her reality.

"School ended, and she had graduated from high school with honors, four months into her pregnancy. While many of her classmates, including Holmes, were going to use the summer to bid farewell to high school by taking steps toward transitioning into college, her after-graduation plan was to save enough money for a bus trip and a week's worth of a motel stay and leave for Scottsdale, Arizona. There was nothing special about Scottsdale. She read up on a number of cities in different states and looking at a map, she picked Scottsdale.

"She chose her day to leave strategically. On Tuesday mornings, her grandmother had about four infants that she watched. She almost never left their side until around one in the afternoon when their mothers came to pick them up, so she wouldn't notice my mom's absence. Although it's technically the definition of what was going on, my mom didn't see herself as running away, but as starting a new life.

"She agonized for hours about what type of note to leave for her grandmother. In her new maturity, she had analyzed everything about her life, and as much as this new reality wasn't what she had wished for herself, she really didn't think she owed anyone in her family any explanation.

"So what was supposed to start out as a letter requesting forgiveness and attempting an explanation of all that was going on, turned into a letter explaining that she was going on a school-organized road trip in celebration of graduation. She wrote that she had forgotten to tell her, and she wasn't sure when she would be back. She knew that because of her grandmother's preoccupation with the infants she watched, the lie would work for a little while.

"The trip took about seven hours on the bus, and although she was anxious, she wasn't nervous. Instead, everything she was doing at that moment was tempered by a matter-of-fact determination that left her with no choice but to put one foot in front of the other and not give too much thought to her situation. She arrived in Scottsdale somewhere between four thirty and five that Tuesday afternoon and went straight to a shopping plaza.

"Her plan even before finding where to stay for the night was to find a job, so arriving at a shopping plaza, she filled out several applications and was able to get two interviews—one at a fashion department store and another at a photography studio. The studio owner had also asked that she come back the next day. She had paid close attention on their ride up, and there were no motels, only hotels. She thought to try one of the small hotels. At the time, my mother had no strong religious or spiritual affiliations, but I have always thought that she had to have some angels keeping a watchful eye on her.

"Many wouldn't see being pregnant and living in a hotel maid's closet as a turn of good luck, but that's exactly the way my mother saw it. The concierge was a much-older gentleman who wore the most welcoming smile. She had approached him and asked him how much the rooms were; she was sure that if she walked up to the check-in desk, they wouldn't take her seriously. There would be too many questions and not enough answers at the desk, but something told her the concierge wouldn't have too many questions. She said that there was just something about him that seemed like he would help first and ask questions later if at all. He dressed the part, but like her, he didn't seem as if he belonged there. She got the feeling that he was on his second or third chance at life and would recognize it in someone else. She was right.

"He told her the rates, she sighed, and they started small talk;

none of it had him asking her questions that maybe he should have: Where are you from? What are you doing here by yourself? She chatted with him while thinking about what her next move should be. She decided that she would ask him about any nearby motels. As if reading her mind, he asked her to follow him. They went down to the bottom floor of the hotel, the floor that no guest really ever saw, with its own separate service elevator. Marie Manuelle, a robust middle-aged Spanish lady, was gathering some supplies in the maid's closet.

'Hey, Marie!' he greeted.

'What's going on, George?'

'My friend—'

'Sabine,' my mother quickly interjected, as they hadn't even done the routine introduction required of two strangers just meeting, '—needs a place to stay,' he continued without skipping a beat, 'and I thought maybe you could help.'

"My mother's birth name was Brenda Phillips, but on her bus trip up to Scottsdale, and in keeping with starting a new life, she had decided to take on the name Sabine Johnson. Sabine was French, and in her many readings, she had come upon the name and loved it from the moment she read it. Marie looked at my mother, and with a strong Spanish accent and a pleasant and musical voice, she said, 'Mmm, now where are we going to put you?' Continuing to George, she said, '*Ella es joven*' and back to my mother she said, 'But you are with child. This place may not be too comfortable.' She gestured around the maid's closet.

"From the moment George had played good Samaritan, even if only by gesture, my mother had decided she was going to be as honest as she could with him, and now with Marie, the two people who by no obligation whatsoever, were helping her. 'I speak Spanish,' she said.

"Marie smiled. My mom said in Spanish, '*Algo hará, y prometo que seré enteramente fuera de la manera, y ayudaré cualquier manera que usted me necesita,*' which roughly means, 'Anything will do, and I promise I will be out of the way and help any way you need me to.'

"With a smile of appreciation and approval, Marie followed with, '*Haremos este trabajo, y ninguna mujer embarazada hace trabajos forzados alrededor de mí,*' meaning, 'We will make this work, and no pregnant woman does hard labor around me.' What became her new home, one of the smaller-sized maid's closets, was actually the size of a single occupancy room in the hotel, but instead of a bed, tables, a sofa, and chair, there was a television, two cots, and an abundance of cleaning supplies and other supplies for the hotel guests.

"My mom got the job at the photography studio and at a department store and worked really hard at both places. Without management ever finding out, she stayed at the hotel, where Marie always had meals provided for her. Marie and George took her on as a surrogate daughter and guided her through living poor in the relatively rich Scottsdale area she found herself in. Although Marie didn't want her to, my mother would don a uniform at times and help with the cleaning chores on the first floor. Everyone who knew her fell in love with her. She carried her own weight and stayed out of everyone's way.

"She asked Marie if she could stay at the hotel just until I was born and then get her own apartment, so she could save as much as she could for my arrival. Her plan, however, was slightly interrupted. My mother was getting ready to head into the department store for work one early morning, a good two months from her due date. She started feeling some unbearable cramps, but there was no one around. Normally Marie came in about two hours after my mother left, but that morning, just after my mother's water broke, Marie walked in. Seeing the puddle near my mother who was profusely sweating and fighting tears, Marie knew exactly what was going on and swung into action. 'She's here, she's here,' Marie was saying with a smile as she helped deliver me in the bathtub in the form of a water birth. Marie had called for George to get a cab ready to head to the hospital.

"Maneuvering a new mom with screaming child through the first floor required a bit of creativity. My mother was in pure pain and barely keeping herself upright, yet she needed to get to the hospital to see a doctor. One of the cooks, who normally had a boom box near him to play music, brought it down to the room and pretty much blasted it so as to drown my screaming and deflect management from my mother. He was later written up because of the noise. My mom pushed one of the housekeeping carts as a support system to keep her up, and I was placed in a sterilized clear container from the kitchen that Marie draped with a blanket. That's how they made it through the short walk to the cab, which was parked in the service entrance.

"Understandably, a premature birth out of the hospital was frowned upon. Hence our reception by the hospital staff was a cold and disapproving one. A nurse grabbed me out of Marie's hands and saw to me first before they even addressed the fact that my mother had now soaked her seat in blood. She was admitted shortly after I was rushed into the neonatal intensive care unit. I weighed in at a little over two pounds. They informed my mother that they were going to release me only when I weighed at least five pounds. They asked her what name she was giving me, and with a confident, yet tired smile she said quietly, 'Bailey Irish Kennedy Johnson, yes, that's her name.'

'Four names for that little child. You are asking her to carry a lot.' Marie chuckled once it was just her and my mom in the hospital room.

"My mother explained the reasoning behind my name to her. 'I have never drank, but when I do, my first cup will be a Baileys Irish Cream. It's not that I'm naming my daughter after a drink, but what I imagine my experience to be when I taste it; I imagine it will be sweet yet strong, and that's what I desire her to be—sweet, but stronger than me. Kennedy? Well, from some of my readings, the only man I've wanted to meet is Robert F. Kennedy because of his resilience to follow his chosen path. When I read of John F. Kennedy's assassination, I thought it was crazy that Robert would follow the same path and meet a similar end, but I learned to appreciate that there had to be a conviction that led him down that path, and I would have wanted to know from them both, what kept that conviction alive in them. To that end, I hope nothing stands in the way of my daughter following her path. Not me. Not even her.'

"My mother had to leave me in the hospital when she was discharged two days later. Marie took her to her apartment complex where she lived, and although the conversation had never come up, it was clear why Marie hadn't offered up her place. It was occupied by Marie, her husband, and four granddaughters. All six of them were living in a one-bedroom apartment that was comprised of a living room and dining room space where all four girls slept, a bedroom that Marie and her husband shared, and a restroom that all six of them shared.

"Marie cosigned for my mother's efficiency apartment in the same complex. That first night was tough for her, and it wasn't because there was nothing in the place, not even a bed, it was because, as she had felt at the California beach, she was again alone. They had told her that she could come to see me in the hospital whenever she wanted, and at two in the morning, the first night in her very own apartment, that's what she did. She hailed a cab and headed straight to the hospital, where they let her sit and hold me once she was fully covered in sterile clothing for my benefit.

"I spent a month in the hospital gaining weight before I was good to go home. Although they told her I would be discharged around seven that evening, my mother had taken the day off and was by my side at eight in the morning, where she waited with me. While she was gone, Marie used her extra key to my mom's place and got the hotel staff to come into the apartment where they noted some of the household and baby stuff that she didn't have; then they went shopping to stock up on a few essentials. George picked us up from the hospital. When my mom walked through the door, her friends, not knowing if I was asleep, all whispered,

'Surprise.' For the first time in my mother's life, she felt like she had a family.

"I grew up knowing my origin, but seeing Marie as my grandmother, and the hotel staff as my real family. I learned Spanish from Marie and her family, and I learned how to cook from the hotel staff. Together they all helped raise me. Even when my mom could have afforded for us to move out to a nicer, bigger place, she didn't. We stayed in that efficiency two doors down from Marie and less than two miles from George. She stayed primarily for Marie.

"Whenever my mother had any extra money, she would pay for some of Marie and George's bills, and would make sure that once a month she bought their groceries as well as ours. She felt it was the least she could do, and although she had probably paid them back one way or another for what they had done for her before I even turned five, it wasn't the financial payback that my mother was responding to, but the goodwill that they had shown her those years back.

"My mother worked hard to send me to the best schools: first it was private school and then a public high school. Generally I loved my life—I really did. But knowing you are poor when everyone around you lives lavishly is tough. I have heard people say that when they were growing up, they really didn't know they were poor because their parents made it a nonissue. My mother made it a nonissue all right, but it didn't change the fact that outside of her world, I was mainly surrounded by people who had money, and tons of it. *I knew* we were poor.

"It was challenging enough to be ever so content with having less than everyone, but when I found out about my sperm donor's riches, I became bitter. In the month that my mother was waiting to take me home, she had called Holmes to inform him of my birth. In so many words, the same guy who had told her that he would be there for whatever she needed told her that it would probably be in her best interest to forget about him because he was in a serious relationship, doing well in college, and wouldn't be of much use to her.

"I remember it as clear as the sky is blue. In my junior year in high school, two of my rich friends wanted to visit California over the summer. My mom said I could go since my friend Lauren's aunt was coming with us and would be chaperoning our trip. Lauren's mom had a home in Malibu, and her aunt had rental property in Carmel. Malibu was the first stop where we were promised thirteen days at the beach before we headed to Carmel for eighteen days while Lauren's aunt handled some business matters. We drove up to a cul-de-sac of mini mansions that lined the beach. Like my mother, I love the water, and I was on the beach just about every day.

"One of the days that I was surfing, I ran into this girl that even I knew bore a striking resemblance to me, only she wasn't mixed. Lauren and I were together when I saw the girl, and Lauren was just as taken aback as I was. The girl couldn't have been older than ten and answered to the name Chloe. She was running back to the person she called father.

"My heart was racing because without any warning, preparation, or desire, I knew. I knew that man who called out for Chloe was the other half that made me. We locked eyes briefly, and an intense fear gripped me—fear that I would have to say something. I had never allowed my mind to entertain what any meeting with him would be like, and in that moment, I wasn't prepared for an impromptu happenstance. I quickly looked away.

"Lauren said it. 'Bailey, you look just like that man. I swear he has to be your father.' There was no mistaking it. Before he could have contemplated any move, I ushered Lauren in a different direction. 'Let's go, let's get out of here now. Please.' Following suit, Lauren was still exclaiming at how this was freaky that I would meet 'my father' this way, and we walked what became a longer route back to the house. The fear that had almost crippled me earlier, gave way to an intense feeling of rage. My chest was expanding at such a pace that I actually felt pain. I was walking so fast that Lauren had to skip a few steps to keep up with me. Eventually, the rage became anger, and I was no longer walking so fast. Lauren looked over to me a couple of times, but didn't say anything, allowing me to unapologetically experience all of my feelings. The anger remained.

"The days we spent in Malibu, I got to see the whole family—Chloe and Chad, their father, and a mother who was a nicely tanned white woman. I never spoke to any of them, not even to say hi. They had three cars. Why did they need three cars? A few times my eyes locked with his. I knew that mine were spewing hate, while his shot out a mixture of fear and defensiveness. At least that's what I saw in his eyes.

"Lauren wanted us to say something to him, arguing that no one would believe us that of all the places we found ourselves, we were neighbors with my biological father. It was a sign, she said. A sign of what? A confirmation that life wasn't fair? As awful as it sounded, I would have been a little more forgiving if maybe his wife was unattractive, or he had no kids and desperately desired some, or if he was barely making ends meet. No one had to tell me that my line of thinking was unhealthy; I knew this, but I felt that my thoughts were absolutely legitimate.

"I didn't see the point of confirming who I was to him. He seemed perfectly satisfied with his perfect family, so I was going to leave him to forget that I ever did exist. With each passing day, hard as I tried, I didn't resent his family. Chloe seemed sweet; she was energetic and strong-willed. A few times at the beach, she wouldn't stay with her mother. Instead, Chloe wanted to surf with us, and she was good—a natural with the water. Chad was a bit younger and never really left his mother's side. Mrs. Holmes was tall with dirty-blonde hair and bleached white teeth that gave her an illuminating smile. She was always in workout attire, so either she was a personal trainer somewhere or a workout freak. Either way, she had a perfect body.

"At that time, I hadn't been told the story of my sperm donor, only that of my premature birth. It was that trip that birthed my curiosity. I had never asked my mother; actually I had never even wanted to know about him, not until after that summer trip. My mother wanted to know the reason behind the sudden interest; I made up something, and that's when she told me about him. So when my mother was telling me the story, I had a face to put to the name, and I hated it.

"My classmates were lucky, entitled, and many of them didn't realize it. Their reality was so different from mine. I always had to act as if I was content in my bottom-dollar bargain items that my mother was so proud to find, while they had clothing allowances that surpassed what my mother and I spent each month to live on. I learned that rich people were treated very differently from poor people—and it wasn't always an issue of treating one better than the other.

"When rich people walked into almost anywhere, people deferred to them, became eager to talk to them, wanted to help them. With the poor, the look was often pity, sometimes disgust, and other times dismissal. How could I not appreciate what my mother had done for me and the life that she had provided me? It was the best that a young mother could have afforded at the time, and she gave up so much for me. With every part of me, I have always appreciated her. In the very same breath, however, my life in Scottsdale birthed within me the determination that as much as I could help it, I wouldn't be one of those looked at with pity, disgust, or dismissal."

Once a year since BJ had turned twenty-one, she gifted her mom with something unique. This year she chose Pink Bailey's anniversary as the occasion. It was about two in the morning, and the party was dying down. We were all going to head back to BJ's place for the night. Michael had given me the entire day and night off from having to do mommy duty. It was still three hours behind in Scottsdale, and BJ wanted her mother's gift delivered to her before the day was over.

BJ had tried having her mother move closer to her years ago, but Sabine wasn't going anywhere if Marie wasn't going to be there. Marie wasn't leaving Scottsdale, so that meant Sabine wasn't leaving either. She felt it was her duty to make sure Marie was taken care of as she was getting older—she was an active older lady, but years of cleaning up after everyone else had taken its toll on her in the form of osteoarthritis.

Sabine and Marie had since moved to a nicer apartment complex, but BJ wanted her mother to own her own house. That meant getting Marie a house. Within the past year, BJ did just that. Initially, she thought of getting both of them a townhouse each, but then thought that they would be better suited living together. Mr. Manuelle had long since died of a heart attack when BJ was still in high school, and even though Sabine had briefly moved in to help Marie out at the time of his passing, they hadn't discussed moving in together.

BJ had traveled up to Scottsdale a few times, unbeknownst to her mother, to pick out the townhouse and then to okay the work that she had requested to be done in developing a section of the house into a full suite for Marie. Her realtor had kindly agreed to drive Sabine and Marie to the house for their surprise. BJ got the call right when we were leaving Pink Bailey's, and the realtor was heading over to pick up Marie and Sabine. After the call from the realtor, BJ called her mom.

"Hey Mama, how's Marie?" BJ asked.

"She's good. What time is it? Where are you?" asked Sabine.

"You won't believe it if I told you, so I've asked a friend to pick you up," continued BJ.

"Believe what? What friend?" inquired Sabine.

"I'm in Arizona!" lied BJ. We were arriving at BJ's condo in DC at this time.

"By yourself?"

"No, Mom. Sierra, Neekoo, and Rory are here with me"

"Hey, Ms. Johnson," the three of us said loudly in the background.

"Bailey, get some sleep, we'll see you in the morning," pleaded BJ's mom.

"Joyce is going to be pulling up in about five minutes, Mom, so it's not like you're going to have a choice, and I don't care what you have on. I just want you to toast the restaurant's anniversary before the day is over, so hurry up."

"Okay, okay. I have to go and get Marie though."

"Okay, I'll call you in about five minutes; you should be with Joyce then."

We could hear the doorbell ring, then Mrs. Johnson said, "That must be your Joyce at the door now."

"Okay, call you back soon." And with that, BJ hung up.

Joyce told Sabine that before they could head to the hotel, she had to go home and change cars and leave the one she was in for her husband. She promised them that her house was on the way, and it wouldn't take long for them to do the switch out. The dutiful mother that she was, Sabine called BJ to inform her of these changes. It was a quarter to midnight, and Sabine was worried they wouldn't get to us on time. When Joyce got out of the car, out of earshot, Sabine grumbled to us, "Bailey, if we don't get there on time, you have to blame your friend, because it looks like we have to go through her house now to get to the other car in the garage."

She stayed on the phone, and the three of us had to muffle our laughter at the slight frustration in her voice.

"Mom, just go into the house. Is Marie out of the car yet?" asked BJ.

"I think we should just wait out here for her to bring the car out," said Sabine.

But Joyce was already by the door, holding it for them.

"Mom, please just go in the house, it's too late for you and Marie to be out there by yourselves. Go into the house, Mom. It will be quicker."

"Okay, okay. Come on, Marie."

Joyce led them into the house. On the kitchen table, Joyce had placed a big welcome basket and a very big and visible card attached to it with "Sabine Johnson & Marie Manuelle" inscribed on it. Without opening the card yet and immediately suspicious, Sabine asked BJ, "What is going on here, Bailey?"

"I don't know, Mom, what's going on?" responded BJ, feigning ignorance. Even though they were on speakerphone, the four of us were crowded around the phone on BJ's bed, waiting for the moment. We heard the tears before we heard the words. Sabine was reading the card.

> Hey Mama,
>
> This house is yours. It's my birthday gift to you this year because you are my best. Marie has her own wing, since I know this would have been a requirement to you accepting this gift. Joyce, my realtor, will be taking care of you and your move and anything you might need with regards to the house. I hope you like it.
>
> Love,
> Bailey

Sabine was in tears as she switched over to Spanish to talk to BJ. "My baby girl, I don't know what to say. I don't deserve you." BJ had tears of joy streaming down her face as she translated her mother's Spanish to us limited-Spanish speakers.

There was a series of, "She did this for me, for little me," from Sabine to no one in particular as Joyce was taking them through the townhouse. Marie's suite was on the first level with everything she would need. Marie, also through tears, kept saying, "May God bless that girl, may God bless that girl." Through emotion, excitement was taking over, as both Marie and Sabine started telling us everything about the house and how it was furnished. No one had the heart nor dared tell Sabine that BJ had flown up to Scottsdale a few times to orchestrate almost every single detail and knew what was in the house.

Not interrupting her mother's now full-blown excitement, BJ used my phone to call Joyce. It was now twelve thirty in the morning in Scottsdale, and Joyce had truly gone beyond the duties of a realtor. BJ wanted to assure Joyce that it was okay for her to leave, but Joyce told BJ that she was going to stay till they were ready to go back home if that's what they wanted.

After almost ninety minutes, Sabine finally remembered that they were supposed to be heading to meet us at the hotel for a toast and exclaimed, "Oh my gosh, Bailey, you know we totally forgot that we were supposed to be heading there. It's almost one thirty in the morning now. We'll come now, and we'll just act as if it's still the same day, okay?" To this statement, the four of us laughed, as Sabine hadn't figured it all out yet.

"Mom, I only told you that to get you out of the house. We are in Washington, DC."

"She tricked you." We could hear Marie laughing in the background.

"That means it's almost four thirty your time! You guys should go to sleep. Me, I won't be able to sleep tonight with all this excitement," said Sabine.

"I love you, Mom."

"Congratulations, Ms. Johnson," Neekoo, Sierra, and I chimed in. We hung up the phone.

Six—*Invitation Only*

BJ and I met up at my office to conceptualize her website, which she wanted changed to reflect a few more events and some of the charitable work that Pink Bailey's was getting involved with. Bella was with me that day and announced her godmother's arrival, although the distinct clicking of the stiletto heels against the hardwood floor did that for her.

"Have you seen today's *Washington Beat*?" asked BJ. She held the paper in one hand, as Bella held on to the right index finger of her other hand. I came around to join BJ who was going for the couch.

"No, haven't seen it."

"Why does Neekoo always do this?" complained BJ.

Since I didn't know what "this" was yet, I didn't respond, but flipped through the paper. I found it a few pages in: a quarter-page ad taken out by the paper, announcing their congratulations to the *Washington Beat*'s very own Neekoo Rahul for her recent award of the Elizabeth Bayo Journalism Prize. It was a prestigious prize, awarded by the Elizabeth Bayo Foundation every two years.

Elizabeth Bayo was a revered journalist who had broken so many rules and pushed open doors all in the name of getting the story. She entered a man's world when women weren't given the chance to get the big story. She was once quoted as saying that for her it wasn't a choice to cover such stories; she *had* to cover them to prove that her gender could do justice to any story. At the young age of forty-two, she had died of cancer.

After Elizabeth Bayo's death, an eponymous foundation was started. The foundation gave a single monetary award of $250,000 to a journalist who best emulated what Elizabeth Bayo had strived for professionally. The recipient could use the award as he or she saw fit. Coming to the decision of the awardee took two years; teams of media professionals all over the country sent in their nominees. Later, that list was pared down to ten. Several months of comparisons, justifications, and observations ensue until there is one person left on the list, all without any of the nominees' knowledge.

The story that had won Neekoo the award was that of the financial crisis erupting in the district and how it involved private health care. What had seemed like mistaken judgment calls were revealed to be deliberate schemes with a handful of powerful financial executives to blame. Neekoo not only broke the story, but the details of her three-part series resulted in the resignation of five financial house presidents and nine top-level hospital administrators. All of the key players were male.

There was a picture of Neekoo in the paper, a short bio on her, and several quotes from staff of the *Washington Beat* with their congratulatory wishes. Lastly, there was very limited information on an invitation-only reception to be held in two weeks on a Saturday.

Neekoo was that friend of yours who never said too much, but you felt had a lot to say. The one that you knew was upset, but would never admit it. BJ, who roomed with Neekoo in college, had always said if any of us were to go postal, no one should be surprised if it was Neekoo. I sat with BJ and dialed the phone, putting Neekoo on speaker.

"Hey, Neekoo, BJ's here with me," I said.

"Bella is here with me," said Bella in her little voice. We all laughed. "I am drawing a picture," Bella offered.

"Hey guys. Hey, baby Bella," Neekoo said unassumingly. She had no clue why we were calling.

"Aunty Neekoo, your picture in the paper," gushed Bella, giving away our reason.

I could tell that BJ wanted to get into it with Neekoo, but thankfully she decided against it. It wasn't worth it. Neekoo was so allergic to confrontation even in its most peaceful form that she almost always played ignorant by telling fibs. BJ and I would both feel it was a lie, but Neekoo would assure us that she hadn't been aware of it. Knowing that your friend told useless fibs was one thing, proving her a liar was another, and we had learned to pick which battles to explore when it came to Neekoo's unwillingness to share different things with us and then proceed to cover that up with little lies.

"Congratulations," I said.

"So should we wait to get our invitations in the newspaper, or are we not even invited?" muttered BJ sarcastically. I nudged her in the side.

"Oh BJ, stop being dramatic about it. I'll call you guys with the time and place soon," said Neekoo, sounding slightly distracted. "It's really not that big of a deal," she continued.

Turning to me and covering the mic on the phone, BJ asked in a mocking tone, "Not that big of a deal?" and then she added, "The sad thing is, she means that. She is delusional." Directing her comments back at Neekoo, BJ asked in the same mocking tone, "Dramatic? You really mean we're not going to have to call you and hound you for the information?" I dug into her side a little harder this time and whispered, "Stop it!"

Bella yelled, "Stop it!" to BJ in her child's voice. So much for me whispering.

"Well, forget their froufrou reception. We're going to have one for you tonight, just the four of us at Pink Bailey's," I cut in, volunteering BJ's services .

"What does froufrou mean?" asked Bella to our laughter. Her eyebrows were crossed into a little frown on her forehead, and she was so serious when she turned her eyes away from the picture she was supposedly drawing, and directed her question to BJ.

"Froufrou is when Aunty Neekoo's bosses have a party for her and they don't want us to come," BJ schooled Bella incorrectly. Shaking my head slowly, I corrected it with, "Froufrou means you won't want to be bothered with it, Bella." Ignoring me, Bella directed her follow-up question to Neekoo. "Aunty Neekoo, that mean I don't come to your boss's party?" Her little head was resting in her left hand with elbow on the table as she looked to the phone.

"No, baby, you don't get to go to Aunty Neekoo's boss's party," I told Bella. And in true three-year-old, short attention-span fashion, she was done with us, and out she ran to show one of The Look's artists the picture she had come up with so far.

"On a more serious note, Neekoo, we would love to be there for you on your big day, but—" "You don't have to say it, Rory. I want you guys there, and I will be there tonight with the information. What time?" asked Neekoo.

I looked at BJ for the answer.

"Is sevenish good for you?" A sigh escaped BJ's lips as she was shaking her head.

"That works for me," said Neekoo.

"Okay, it's set then," I responded.

"I have to go. I'll see you guys tonight. Love you."

"Love you," I responded and hung up the phone.

"I guess we should call Sierra now," BJ said with resignation in her voice.

"BJ, you have to stop it. I know how you feel, but—"

"But do you feel you can really trust Neekoo when she does things like this?" asked BJ.

"We are not going to have this conversation now." I tried deflecting the issue that as of now had no resolution.

"Think about it, if someone told me they got yelled at by

Sierra while standing in line at the bank, I would believe them. If they also said someone was gasping and she was the one that gave them mouth-to-mouth, and then quickly walked away, not wanting to be thanked, I'd believe that too. If I heard that you waited in line for five hours to get all of us tickets to a show that you knew we wanted to see and that you hated, it would sound just like you. Now what can you say with a measure of certainty about Neekoo?" asked BJ, sure that she had made her point.

She had, but again I deflected. "BJ, please don't start that conversation now, and definitely not tonight, either," I pleaded.

"As long as you know I'm right and agree that it's pretty screwed up." Knowing within her that she was right, thankfully BJ let it go.

College wasn't much different when it came to Neekoo. That very first day when BJ and I moved this little, unassuming girl into the room, we were sure she was only shy initially and would eventually open up. But that day never entirely came. She had moments of being seemingly outgoing and social, but they were few and far between. She didn't enjoy small talk, and instead would listen to you as you engaged in it. We pretty much made up her group of friends because she wasn't great at making new friends. She just didn't seem very socialized, and we all just chalked it up to her different mix of cultures.

Neekoo was a bookworm who liked her own space, and we did the best we could to respect that. In that first year, BJ and I really just wanted all four of us to get along, and we did, but we also found that concept meant different things to all of us.

With Sierra it meant that we indulged her through late-night partying with some of her teammates, which often lasted through the wee hours of the morning. It wasn't just the noise, but the disregard of time, space, and resources. For Neekoo it meant that we let her have her space—inordinate amounts of it. Often no explanation of what was going on came with Neekoo's solitary escapes, which wasn't always cool. All four of us felt some form of responsibility for each other at varying degrees, and it was sometimes hard to be responsible for someone whose whereabouts were likened to CIA secrets.

For BJ and me, it all meant going with the flow. This equation was pretty much the case through college, with moments of Sierra being a little more considerate, moments of Neekoo choosing to spend more time with us, and BJ and I pretty much being the most dependable and consistent through our college tenure and beyond.

Because of Neekoo's writing skills and work ethic, she was referred to the school paper by most of our professors and landed the position initially as staff writer and later editor in chief. She was an involved writer: the same girl that some had never really heard in conversation, shined at interviews. She always had the details that no one else seemed to be able to get their hands on. Either she had a secret weapon that the rest of us didn't know about, or people just found it easy to talk to her.

In our junior year, BJ and I decided that Neekoo just wasn't really good with girls. With guys however, the girl was a magnet! And inexplicably so. All her visitors at the suite were male. Sometimes they would be in her room, other times they stayed in the living room, and since the guys were normally more outgoing, they would engage in conversation with all of us. She did stories on some of the guys but that explained only a handful; she didn't do stories on the other guys who couldn't keep away.

BJ and I often wondered what the draw was. This isn't to say her sheer beauty wasn't reason alone, but we're talking about a girl who wasn't quite social, having a revolving door of men. None of it made sense—Sierra swore that the girl that we believed was so innocent was probably a closet nymphomaniac—but then Sierra thought the worst of everyone, even jokingly.

I never shared it with anyone, but on two instances I felt that there could have been some weight to Sierra's preconception of

Neekoo. The incidents were identical: I had to come back to the suite for something I had forgotten before making it to my next class. I literally walked into a guy as I opened the door to the suite; he was tucking in his shirt and smoothing out his pants. He seemed nervous, but Neekoo, who was fully dressed and was not disheveled, didn't miss a beat as she turned to me and asked if we could walk to our next class together. I didn't think anything of it until two days later when the same thing happened. It was a different guy, and again Neekoo acted as if he was nonexistent and proceeded to ask me about a book assignment that was due that day. What would I ask her? What *could* I ask her? I brushed it all off, refusing to even imagine Neekoo in that light. She didn't have a boyfriend, and I couldn't see her randomly having sex with all the guys who visited our suite.

Generally, we just couldn't place Neekoo, but we accepted her exactly as is; she hadn't stolen any of our things or maligned our names anywhere on campus, so mysterious as she was, Neekoo was our girl.

With a hug for Neekoo and a slightly raspy, "Hey, chica," Sierra was the first to greet her as she approached our table. Sierra, BJ, and I were already seated at Pink Bailey's.

"Hey, babe," responded Neekoo in her signature sweet and low voice. She wrapped Sierra up in a warm reciprocating hug. The "BJ" that came out of Neekoo's mouth next was one of cautious resignation. I had tried talking BJ out of not bringing anything up, but there was no telling exactly how she was going to handle this whole situation. It was clear that BJ was especially unhappy that Neekoo hadn't told us about the news before reading it in the paper. For BJ, the lack of communication spoke volumes about our friendship. Her feelings were probably valid; I just didn't think this was the time to bring it up. Regardless of how we found out, this was still a big moment for Neekoo, and I wanted her to have that moment.

"Neekoo, Neekoo, Neekoo," greeted BJ with a kiss on Neekoo's right cheek. "You look good," she continued. We saw each other several times a week, and Neekoo didn't look any different than the last time we saw her. Also, Neekoo was probably just getting off work. Perhaps it was BJ's way of communicating *something*; I didn't get what she was trying to say. I left it alone.

"Where's Bella? After our froufrou conversation from earlier, I was so sure she was joining us for the rest," said Neekoo.

"Congratulations, Neekoo. This is such a big deal." I jumped right into giving Neekoo the floor so she could tell us about the whole ordeal.

"I forgot. Actually, I just pushed it aside. The announcements came out a week ago, so yes, I had an opportunity to let it sink in before the rest of the world found out today." She paused, looking at BJ, the main person she was trying to convince that this, in fact, wasn't intentional.

"You're whack. That means we've seen you since you found out, and you just held it all in?" said BJ initially. She then added, "Anyway, let's hear it. How did you find out?" giving Neekoo some assurance that this wasn't going to be an attack. She just needed Neekoo to know that she was supportive, but still had to express how she felt about how we found out.

"Well, I walked into the building that Wednesday morning, and as I normally do, I had my headphones in my ears, playing no music. I felt something was odd. I don't know why, because nothing was out of the ordinary, but I just felt something was going on. I got to my floor and from the minute I stepped onto the floor, I heard people whispering. The advantage of course was that they didn't think I could hear them.

'I don't think she knows yet,' someone said.

'She doesn't seem the type who would even care about it,' another said.

"As they whispered, they smiled in an attempt to cover that

they were talking about me. I smiled back and just before I walked into my office space, my copy editor patted me on the back with a 'Congratulations.' I took the headphones off and greeted her. Then Susan, the copy editor, said, 'You're the toast of the paper!'

"What are you talking about?" I asked her.

'You won the Elizabeth Bayo award! Can you believe it?' Susan said with excitement."

Neekoo paused. "I don't know how to explain how I felt. It's different if you knew you were being considered, but the process of the Elizabeth Bayo award is so guarded that the only time you find out is if you are the selected recipient. So although I am sure I was excited somewhere deep down inside, it really didn't sink in immediately. Five minutes after I got the news, I had to revisit an assignment that I was working on, and that was it. I didn't really have the time to celebrate the news, so I conveniently put it aside and delved right back into work. My parents don't even read the *Washington Beat*, so I wouldn't be surprised if they don't even know yet."

There was a slight smirk on BJ's face; she took that last statement to mean that we shouldn't be up in arms about not knowing since Neekoo's parents didn't even know yet. Nonetheless, the fact that BJ had to hear it from *someone else* didn't sit well with her.

"You're not already engaged as well are you?" asked Sierra with a mocking tone.

"What?" I asked, confused.

"Hey, I guess we shouldn't be surprised if we found that out in the paper too," added BJ chuckling.

"Anyway, what big story are you working on now?" asked Sierra. "Are you doing an exposé on the bullshit of psychotherapy?"

That came out of nowhere, and we all couldn't help laughing. Sierra successfully changed the subject from having Neekoo defend herself and lightened the mood. BJ wasn't as upset anymore. She picked up the diversion with a toast, "Here's to the future Pulitzer or Nobel laureate!"

"And here's to women who rule the world," toasted Neekoo.

"And to the men who try to tolerate us," I toasted.

"Talking about men who try to tolerate us," started Sierra, "remember that guy from BJ's party?" She directed the question mostly to Neekoo. "Yes?" Neekoo asked.

"I think he needs to give you a lead or something, Neekoo. He's been trying to reach you and bugs me about you not returning his calls."

"I have his number; I'll give him a call," said Neekoo.

"He said he didn't have yours, and I wasn't going to be the one giving it to him," said Sierra.

"Thanks. No he doesn't have it." And Neekoo didn't offer any more than that. We continued with our dinner.

The day of the reception for Neekoo's award ceremony, there was something in the air. The reception was to start that evening around seven o'clock, and I just couldn't seem to get it together. I woke up that morning with a head cold or allergies that put me in a somewhat irritable mood all morning. I got into the office much later than I had planned and shut my door—I never had my door shut. I was a dud and shouldn't have gone in that day as I got very little done.

I didn't leave the office till five o'clock that evening. It wasn't from lack of trying or that I couldn't tear myself away from the design that I was working on at the moment. No, it was pure lethargy. Starting at three o'clock, I looked at the clock and told myself I would get up from my desk in a half hour. That happened every half hour until five. I called BJ during my search for an impetus to leave and asked her what she was wearing to the reception. A dressy dark grey pantsuit, she answered, with some brown stilettos. Then I called again; I asked the same question. She asked if I had been drinking. That was my cue to go home and take some medication before I truly embarrassed myself at the reception.

Later on, after searching my closet, I settled on a red sleeveless cocktail dress with a cardigan, gold shoes, and accessories. Drugged up on cold medicine, I headed out to the Mandarin Hotel where the reception was being hosted. Sierra and BJ were already there; they were standing outside of the reception hall, waiting on me. Their countenance gave it away—it was going to be a bitchy night.

As soon as I walked up to them, Sierra started. "If she didn't even tell us about winning the award, do we have to be here?"

"What?" I wore a clearly confused look on my face and shook my head. "I'm not going through this again. We've been through it too many times. She had her reasons."

"Have you checked your phone all day?" interjected BJ. I pulled out my phone.

"Oh, sorry, I've been out of it most of the day, I didn't even hear you calling," I said, noticing missed calls and a text from Sierra, asking to carpool.

"Thanks to you, I got lost," snapped Sierra. Now I knew that Sierra's mood had nothing to do with not being told. She had gotten lost and needed a venting source.

"I don't even think she would care if we weren't here," grumbled Sierra.

Two seconds from total frustration, my tone was full of exasperation when I said, "We're here! We are going to make sure that she knows we are here for her, and then you can leave."

"What's gotten into you?" said BJ, not expecting me to respond in kind to the grumblings.

"I'm fine. Right now I don't really want to be here anymore than the two of you, even if for different reasons. I feel sick and just want to be in bed, so let's just put on happy faces and pretend as if we all really want to be here."

To this, BJ laughed and said, "Nice to know that even cheerleader Rory doesn't want to be here. Okay, now we can all have a really nice time." I smiled.

Neekoo was standing nervously by the coat check. BJ leaned

in to give Neekoo a kiss on the cheek and rubbed her right arm. "You actually look a bit nervous."

"I am," Neekoo admitted. "I don't really talk to more than half of the people here."

"You don't really talk to more than half of the people *anywhere*, Neekoo. Come on, let's go in," said Sierra. As we were getting closer to the table marked "Reserved—Guest of Honor," I noticed Neekoo's mom already seated at the table. She looked beautiful in her champagne pantsuit and silver brooch. Giving her a hug, I went and sat by Mrs. Rahul.

Neekoo's coworkers, local bigwigs, and members of the Elizabeth Bayo Foundation filled the room. The reception was held in one of the hotel's smaller ballrooms, with a capacity of three hundred people. We were about two hundred at the reception, seated eight to each round table.

The room was set up as it would be for a simple wedding reception. The furniture was black and all the linen, including tablecloths and chair dressings, was gold and white. Gardenia floral arrangements served as centerpieces. We were seated in the middle of the room with Neekoo's mom and a few of her coworkers. The reception, although sponsored by the *Washington Beat*, was organized by the foundation, so coupled with placards of the *Beat* on the walls were also placards of the foundation. It was there that we heard about the details of the co-nominees who were in attendance. Neekoo, who was the youngest of the lot, was in amazing company.

There was a guy at our table who made it a point to mention that little detail a few times, and there was something about the way he said it that indicated he wasn't being congratulatory. "I don't think it's possible to do all of that without either making a double of yourself *or* adding a little fiction to your work every now and then," he mentioned with a bit of a smirk. Everyone ignored his comment, but I shot him a dirty, disapproving look. Again he mentioned, "Is she even thirty yet? She must be the luckiest hardworking person ever to have gathered that much under her belt already." Again we ignored him, but he was definitely getting at something. His name was Matt, he also worked at the *Beat*, and from the accounts of his coworkers at the table (when he left for the restroom), he was disgruntled about just about everything.

This wasn't our crowd. Our crowd was fun and welcoming. It wasn't that the people there were altogether pretentious or anything, but they were definitely bland and stiff. Half of the room had to be five years from retirement, and the rest, who were our age group, took themselves too seriously. The best part of the evening? Realizing that the host had probably had one too many drinks. She made a few mistakes, including mispronouncing Neekoo's name during the announcement of the video reel highlighting some of Neekoo's award-winning work.

Neekoo seemed to be going through the motions with each occurrence and not taking any of it to heart. It was even worse when she got up to thank everyone. Her award was officially presented to her, and she must have given the shortest acceptance speech I'd ever heard. It was like receiving the best actress award at the Oscars, except she simply got up there and said, "I couldn't have done this without the help of so many. Thank you." That was it, and she came off the stage. I would have liked to hear her talk about what inspired some of her work or maybe thank the one person or people who inspired her. Instead, quite shyly, Neekoo was seated within three minutes of her rising to accept the award.

In response to her acceptance remarks, probably meaning to say this just in his own head, Matt said, "What kind of fucking selfish acceptance was that? She didn't do all that stuff by herself, and who exactly is 'so many'?" He had a point. In some way or another, others were probably thinking the same thing, but to hear him say it, it sounded really bad.

Sierra had had enough of him. He was seated about three seats to the left of her. Sierra turned directly toward him, leaned in to the table, and said "Excuse me" to the two persons whose space she was temporarily invading.

"It's Matt, right?" asked Sierra. He lifted his head in a slight nod of acknowledgment. "I don't really know who the hell you are, but what's your problem?" she practically barked. And without waiting to hear a response from him, she continued, "Did you ask her out and get turned down or something? Or is it that you think this award should be going to you? Well, do something award-worthy and stop giving us your play-by-play criticism, okay?"

Sierra didn't wait for a response as she flashed a smile of apology to the two seated to her left and adjusted her body back to the center of the table. He didn't respond, not verbally and not to Sierra. His head tilted back in astonishment as members of the table were looking at him for his reaction. He opened his mouth, shut it, shook his head, and then got up. He straightened his sports coat, and as he walked away he said, "I've had enough of this bullshit anyway." Everyone was pretty much engaged in their own conversations, or pretense at having a conversation, that the one-way exchange between Sierra and Matt hadn't even caused a ripple.

It wasn't a great event, it wasn't even a good event—something was wrong here. Matt's obvious disdain of Neekoo's recognition had Sierra and me wondering whether any of the people from her paper who were supposed to be there to celebrate her, were even in her corner—it seemed too much of an act for some. Many of them there were there out of respect to the Elizabeth Bayo Foundation, and few murmurings went around about Neekoo not really deserving it. I immediately felt bad that the four of us were quibbling earlier on about not wanting to be there.

The handshakes were weak, the hugs were air-filled, and the smiles were penciled on—and quickly erased within two feet of departing Neekoo's presence. I couldn't help but feel that Neekoo had to notice this was going on. I whispered to BJ, "Do you feel dirty?"

"I don't know what's going on here, but they really should have checked off an enemy list before sending out the invitations," was BJ's reply. By the looks on my friends' faces, all three of us felt it, and we couldn't wait to leave the room.

The day after the reception, I had to call Neekoo because it was all I could think of when I left the reception. "Neekoo?" I said when she answered.

"Hey, Rory, what's going on?"

"Okay, I'm just going to come out and say it. What was that about yesterday?"

"What do you mean?"

"Neekoo," I warned in a tone that begged her not to go down that road of oblivious innocence. The air the night before had been thick with negative energy. "You can't tell me you didn't feel all those people not really being happy for you?"

"I don't even take that stuff seriously. That's just the business. Everyone wants to get ahead. My colleagues want to be the ones receiving that award themselves."

"But Neekoo, yesterday was something else. These people acted as if they knew you didn't deserve the award. I know you work hard, so I believe you deserve every writing award there is, but that energy yesterday was bad," I insisted. Everything I knew about Neekoo and the friend I had come to love was innocent, so in my heart she deserved everything good. In my heart, I couldn't accept anyone not seeing the purity that I saw in Neekoo. No matter how cutthroat her profession was, I was finding it hard to accept that her coworkers couldn't see what I saw.

"Really, it's nothing, Rory. Are we still meeting this weekend for your clean-up-the-city thing?" That's how she dismissed the whole issue. If there was something going on with her, I couldn't get her to tell me.

"Yeah, we're still on," I answered, trying to keep the resignation out of my voice. "I love you, Neekoo."

"Love you too, Rory."

SEVEN – *A little sex with your morning paper?*

I had been approached by an organization for women that brought together all levels of working women from different professions in the metro area to literally clean up the city once a month. The activity had two parts. Early in the morning, a large team of women would pick up garbage along different high-traffic streets, and afterward, smaller teams would go to preselected homes of the elderly and help them around the house. I had signed up all four of us, and we had to report for duty bright and early at seven thirty on Saturday morning at a community center in DC. Sierra was the only vocal one with her resistance. "You already signed us all up without asking?" she said when I rang to fill her in on the event.

"Yup, we'll love it," I said.

"We're going to love picking up trash on the side of the street on an early Saturday morning instead of sleeping in. Sure. Have you run this by Ms. Obsessive-Compulsive yet?" Sierra asked.

"I am sure I caught BJ while she was occupied with something else because she didn't even raise the fuss you're raising. She just said 'sure,'" I said.

"Cool, but expect her to freak out when it dawns on her what she just got signed up for," Sierra said, laughing.

"Not even Neekoo gave me any fuss. I've already signed you up, Sierra."

"Not even? Are you kidding me, like you expected Neekoo to say no. As long as she wasn't out working a story, you don't even need to ask her," Sierra said in mocking laugh.

"Whatever, Sierra." I couldn't help but smile. Sierra was right. Neekoo never said no to whatever we asked her to do. Sierra on the other hand also supported, but I wished she didn't always have to say how she felt about it, especially knowing that she was still going to say yes. "So you'll be ready when I come by?" I asked her, as I now needed to get off the phone.

"Sure. If you remember, give me a wake-up call just in case," Sierra said, and we hung up.

I forgot to give Sierra that promised wake-up call, but thankfully she didn't need it.

"Sorry," I said, squirming as I rang her from right outside her door.

"Don't worry, I wasn't relying on your wake-up call," she said as she opened up the door and hung up the phone. We walked back to my car. As was I, Sierra was wearing black exercise pants and the When Women Clean shirts that she had sworn she wouldn't wear because she didn't want to look like we were wearing a uniform. She saw me look at the shirt with a faint smirk on my face when we got into the car. "I'm just being a sport, so remember this," she said. I started laughing, and Sierra just shook her head. Earlier that week, I had taken the shirts, gotten each of the girls' names monogrammed on the back, and cut off the sleeves.

BJ was second on my route, and she had ditched the sneakers that we were all asked to wear, instead donning a pair of expensive-looking name brand monogrammed sling-backs. She'd gone with a stiff-necked black polo underneath the When Women Clean shirt and adorned herself in coral jewelry. Announcing her agenda for the morning, she said, "You didn't say I had to like being there, just that I had to go," making it clear she was primarily there for the company and not the task. Neekoo also was ready when we got there. Water bottle in hand and ankle weights on, she looked ready for a brisk morning run.

There were about twelve volunteers at the community center that morning. We would be split into groups of four together with two team leaders for the second half of the task. We gathered our tools of sanitary gloves, garbage cans and bags, garden pin forks, and we piled into the white van waiting to transport us to southeast Washington, DC. Like the four of us, everyone came with a friend, but we all made the effort to get to know each other.

In addition to the four of us, there was a high school principal, a college basketball coach, a vice president of a local car insurance agency, a retail buyer, a security guard from the Library of Congress, a professional dancer, an interior designer, and a veterinarian making up the group of female professionals joining the When Women Clean team that weekend. Six WWC team leaders joined us, including the founder. She was a former health-care worker who left the business and opened up one of the best adult day cares in the metropolitan area. Her name was Susan Francis.

When Francis was making her career transition, she planned on being an independent activities director for senior living companies—every company she contacted liked the idea. She went to work, starting the nonprofit organization Three Score and Ten, and vigorously pursuing grants, many of which she attained through private foundations. In the first two years of the business, she and her team of adult activities facilitators went to the centers, but as the demand grew, she got enough money to get a large and new building, a few vans, and a bus. So starting in year three, the adults were transported to the center, which was good as they got to meet mates from different centers, through which romantic relationships were cultivated and much more. Participation wasn't limited to elders from the centers alone, but was open to anyone sixty and over who lived alone. It was through her interactions with this group that she found that a number of them—fiercely independent—couldn't always get a few things done by themselves and would appreciate the help, but didn't want to reside in senior housing. WWC came calling.

If anyone had told us that we would have fun picking up street trash, I would have scoffed. The security guard from the Library of Congress started it all off; she was a pure comedian. Her name was Stacey. She kept most of us laughing so much that picking up some of the nastiest things off the ground wasn't so nasty after all. Stacey was especially fond of the prima donnas in our group. BJ was one of them. "This one knew she wasn't picking up anyone's trash today," Stacey said, tilting her head in BJ's direction.

BJ smiled. "And I am not ashamed of it. I am here for moral support," she said as she gave a cute one-shoulder shrug.

"We should all look to see if we find some stilettos out here, so that we too can be stylish trash pickers," continued Stacey. We laughed lightly.

The jab taken at BJ for not wearing practical shoes did not bother her one bit. In fact, she said, "Hey, truth be told, we'd probably get a lot of publicity if all of us were doing this in heels. Now that's a story."

"All right, all right, Ms. Fashion's got a point there. But this girl over here in a skirt?" and with that, Stacey moved on to the next target of her friendly chiding. Stacey was right on the money on most things she joked about with all of us. No one got upset. Before we knew it, two hours had passed, and we were back in the van, heading back to the center where we would get cleaned up before dispersing to our predetermined elder's home.

Our elder was Denise Black. "DeeDee, that's what everyone calls me, so that's what you have to call me now, okay?" was the introduction we got when we arrived for our second task for the day. From the looks of it, her house wasn't in bad shape, but our two team leaders, Beth and Kathy, had a long sheet of tasks that we had to work on in the house. Thankfully, the two of them, like all the AAF who went out on the home tasks, were certified home contractors. Between them they had certifications in carpentry, electric work, masonry, and more.

Ms. DeeDee was in her early seventies, and she had lived in her home for the past forty-five years. It was the first and only home she and her husband had purchased when they started their family. He'd died of natural causes five years prior, a day before his seventieth birthday, and Ms. DeeDee wasn't leaving her home. In her words, "I'm leaving just as Kenny did, right from my bedroom." We smiled. She had two children; the older child had passed away at twenty-seven from complications of a heart condition he'd been born with.

Their daughter now had a family of her own, and they lived clear across the country in California. They barely made it to visit Ms. DeeDee, with the last time being two years earlier. She sent her mother money that Ms. DeeDee didn't spend. She kept it in a savings account that she planned on giving to her daughter's children. She didn't make a lot of money she boasted, but "I have enough … enough to get by with no complaints."

Per instruction from Ms. DeeDee, we started in the kitchen. Why? "Because ladies don't work on an empty stomach." Nodding her head, she led us to the kitchen where she had prepared a brunch for "my workers coming to help a little old lady today."

"You young ladies of today starving yourselves to death. It's just not good, all of you, looking so skinny," she admonished us, and then looking at me she added, "You, you look nice, don't go looking like them now, okay?" I smiled. It wasn't quite stated as a compliment, but it was her form of it. "Thank you, I couldn't even look like them if I tried, and trust me I've tried," I said.

"No, no. Keep that meat on your bones," Ms. DeeDee said, shaking her head.

We let her say whatever she wanted. The company was good for her, and knowing that no matter what, she enjoyed the fact that her house was alive with more than just one warm body, we didn't mind stomaching the words she had for us, even the potentially insensitive ones. Her words to Beth for example, while we were all forced to chow down on brunch that we weren't hungry for, were, "All those muscles, they scare me on a woman. You're not one of those that's taking those injections to become a man are you?"

We actually burst out laughing. "No ma'am, no hormone injections here, just a lot of hard labor, that's all," Beth said.

"Now remember, men like 'em a little feminine now, not a woman that could probably beat him up."

It was clear to us that Ms. DeeDee didn't mean any harm; she was old-school and said things as they came to her, and generally felt she was right. It was also clear that although she wouldn't be able to help us out much, she wasn't going to simply let us do the work either. With the television remote in her front apron pocket, she circulated between the kitchen, the living room, and the rooms we were working on.

Our main rooms were the utility room and her attic, which had since been remodeled into a bedroom. With the utility room, we—or more accurately Beth and Kathy—needed to install a new HVAC unit to help kick more air into the attic bedroom. The four of us were working on her sewing room. It was formerly her daughter's bedroom.

Our task for that room was stripping all the wallpaper off, painting the walls, reupholstering the few pieces of furniture in the room, and altogether updating the room. A team had met with Ms. DeeDee about a week ago and asked her what she wanted done. For her it wasn't chores, it was updating a few things, so they had picked out colors, themes, and accessories for the spaces that we were working on. All the items were donated. When we got the list for the room we were working on, BJ whispered with exasperation, "I want to go back to cleaning up the street." BJ was the best person in there to jazz the place up, but as anyone who met her would realize, hers was the vision; it was for someone else to put that together.

So we started. With masks and scrappers, we got rid of the antiquated wallpaper. We were happy to see it go, and even more so after we heard Ms. DeeDee's commentary. "Can you believe it? Debbi picked that out when she was fifteen. No, I won't miss it." And she breezed back out. The wall beneath it was perfect, and we got right on our task of priming before applying the two coats of maroon paint. We were moving fast, making fun of each other, but mostly at BJ whose pace was the slowest of the four of us with no apologies. Her biggest challenge was going through all of this and not getting paint on her.

Louder than we had heard her voice since the moment we met her, Ms. DeeDee said, "I know I've seen her before. The little girl is on the news!" We had no clue what she was talking about. Sierra and I were already in the living room, and Neekoo, BJ, Kathy, and Beth (who had all been working in the utility room) came to join us in the living room where the only television in the house was. "Sit, sit, sit, it's coming back on," said Ms. DeeDee. "The little one is on the news," she said as she touched Neekoo's shoulder.

Ms. DeeDee was excited. "I have my own local celebrity in my house working for me; I feel special!" she said. "I don't have TiVo or any of those high tech things that you young ones are into, so let me know when Jason comes back on." She headed into the kitchen to get all of us some lemonade. Jason Warner was the anchorman; she called his name as she would a good friend. Simultaneously, we poked fun at Neekoo, knowing that the news we were about to hear could be anything.

"You eloped and got married and didn't tell anyone—that's it right, Neekoo?" asked Sierra.

"You didn't!" I shot a reprimanding glance at Neekoo.

"I swear, whatever this is, will be news to me too. I have no clue what this is," responded Neekoo. The look on her face was genuinely one of confusion. She was now standing behind one of the sofas, looking intently at the television.

"I've got it, I've got it," BJ let out excitedly. "She's dating a seasoned oil tycoon who's buying out the *Beat*."

"What?!" I exclaimed at the outlandish justification that BJ gave. Neekoo shot a quizzical look at BJ, "Really?" The segment introduction music came on, and Beth called out to Ms. DeeDee, "Jason's coming back on." I went to get the glasses of lemonade for Ms. DeeDee, and with everyone but Neekoo and myself seated; we listened to Jason's newscast.

He opened by saying, "The Elizabeth Bayo Foundation has released a statement addressing inquiries that the foundation has received about its latest recipient, Neekoo Rahul. The statement released by Jennifer Roman, a spokesperson for the foundation, reads, 'We stand by our selection of Ms. Rahul as this year's recipient of the Elizabeth Bayo Journalism Award. However, in response to the number of queries we have received, the foundation will launch its own investigation into the nature of the relationship Ms. Rahul had with some of her sources.'"

Warner continued with the conclusion of the story, "It has been reported that since the presentation of the award, the foundation has received numerous queries for an investigation to be held on the nature of the relationship Ms. Rahul had with sources of some of her well-known stories. Accusations have ranged from unethical conduct to false promises. Stay tuned to WSWA for the latest on the Rahul investigation."

Throughout the newscast, the room was silent. The minute the story was over, Ms. DeeDee blurted, "Vultures, vultures, vultures. Little one, I don't know what you did or didn't do, but men do worse. As long as you didn't make up any of your stuff, forget them all I say." She continued in her defense of Neekoo as if she had been there when the stories were researched and knew all the tactics. "She didn't do anything a guy wouldn't do. The men are never persecuted like the women. But what does an old lady know. It's like my Kenny used to say, 'Women are the stronger sex; brave enough to do the crime, time, and sing about it when need be.'" I looked over to Neekoo as Ms. DeeDee was talking, and her face looked ashen.

Ms. DeeDee ignited a short one-way conversation about gender inequality, with the focus on her sharing some stories mostly from her youth and her experiences being passed over for promotions as well as losing a job because of what she believed was gender inequality. It had been less than two minutes since the broadcast, and standing there listening to Ms. DeeDee, it was awkward not knowing what to say to Neekoo who had only managed to say "wow" quietly through a very deep breath. Thankfully, Beth got up and said, "Now that that unwelcome break is over, let's try to get back to work." "Here, here," said Sierra.

Sierra and I went back to the room we were working in. BJ had gone over to Neekoo and without saying anything, gave a rub on her right shoulder, and both of them came in to join Sierra and me. I wanted to say something, but I didn't know how to start and really, what exactly to say. Sierra looked as if she was about to say something, but it was Neekoo who spoke first. "I almost wish I didn't get this award. I heard about the queries to the foundation yesterday, but there was nothing specific."

"I'm sure a complaint came from that guy who sat at our table," said Sierra. Remembering the disgruntled colleague of Neekoo's at the award ceremony, BJ and I agreed, joining Sierra in reminiscing about that evening and suggesting different ways in which he could use his time. Eventually Neekoo lightened up ever so slightly.

We finished at Ms. DeeDee's house around seven that evening. Two to three hours could have been shaved off if she hadn't interrupted us several times for any reason she saw fit. It was clear she loved the company, and when we were leaving, we promised to drop in on her every now and then, take her to the movies, or spend an afternoon doing lunch and the spa or something.

Her response was, "An old lady hangs on to such promises,

so don't get me all excited if you're not going to come through now."

Barely out of Ms. DeeDee's house, Sierra called us all out. "You all know we just lied to that old lady," she said with a slight laugh. BJ began to motion in protest, to which Sierra said, "I know you aren't trying to claim you will be here. Really, to scrape off more fifty-year-old wallpaper?" We all laughed.

"I might take her to a movie or shopping," BJ said meekly.

"I know that right about now, I need a bath," said Neekoo.

"That is a great thought," I said.

"Yes, we stink!" said BJ, and we started piling back into the van.

"How's my garbage lady?" asked Michael as I walked through the door.

"You know we did more than pick up trash, right?" I rebutted jokingly as he gave me a kiss on my cheek.

"Mamee!" Bella screamed through the house. All my little girl had on was her underwear.

"She was just about to take a bath when we heard the door," explained Michael. She ran and jumped into my arms, bubbly with kisses.

"Smells like you had meatballs for dinner," I said, planting a kiss on her forehead.

"Tell her, Daddy, tell her," she burbled out.

"I promised I would tell you that she helped with the dinner. She portioned out the exact amount of spaghetti to be cooked."

"Good girl! Now we really need to get you that bath since you need to be in bed soon."

I got the recap of her day; her favorite part was being able to boss her father around. We ended with Bella attempting to read one of her favorite Dr. Seuss books. She was nowhere near sleepy! At the tender age of three, she had taken after both her parents, being more of a night owl. Like most nights that I put Bella to sleep, I had to pretend that I was so exhausted, yawning through some of the passages that I was reading, until Bella in her sympathy voice said, "Mamee, you're sleepy! You can go to sleep now, I'll fall asleep soon."

I watched her once, and right after I left the room she continued to read aloud, making up quite a few brand-new words that she definitely couldn't read. She was pointing at the pictures and laughing to herself as if Dr. Seuss had told her a personal joke. This continued for a few minutes until the yawning started, the scratching of the eyes, and slowly but surely, she would fall asleep. She was a good child.

I joined Michael in the basement, where he had some spaghetti and meatballs, garlic bread, and red wine waiting for the two of us on a side table. "Come on, babe." He motioned for me to join him on the sofa, where I sank in to receive a soothing foot rub. He mostly drank wine because he had already eaten dinner since he didn't know when I was going to be home. We filled each other in about our day as I ate, and he started with, "Did BJ pick up a single thing?" I chuckled while filling my mouth with a forkful of my dinner.

Before I could bring it up, Michael, assuming that we hadn't gotten a chance to see the newscast because of our street cleanup, cautioned me, "You should know that Neekoo's in the news, and it doesn't look great."

"I know, we saw it," I responded.

"Is she okay?" he asked, sounding like the concerned surrogate brother he had become to my friends.

"She will be," I answered. My sigh came out deeply, starting from my diaphragm, and induced a yawn. I was tired, and unconsciously I repeated it again, "She will be." I was partially trying to convince myself of the desired truth in that response.

"Do you think you could take about three weeks off of work?" Michael asked out of the blue.

"Mmmh, I would have to work remotely, but I can trust my

team well enough to run things while I'm gone," I answered. "Why? Are we going on a very long overdue romantic getaway?"

"For three weeks! There isn't that much romance in the world!" Michael teased.

I got the couch pillow that was closest to me and hit him with it as we both laughed. He reached over to give me a kiss. I fought him—for less than five seconds. I knew where this was going, and making love with my husband was an activity that I would never fight.

The next week was a nightmare for Neekoo. One source after another came forth, making ridiculous claims about how Neekoo got her stories. There was one story, however, that was gaining credibility because of the consistency and frequency amongst different sources. Sierra had called early that morning to tell me about the story. "Get the hell out of bed and go pick up your paper. Neekoo's in it again," she ordered.

"She's been in the paper a lot—" I started to say and wanted to ask what was so different about this one.

She cut me off with, "Yes, but this one's really bad."

"I'll call you back," I said as I had now picked up the paper and slowly walked back into the house. I sat at the kitchen table to read the story. It was featured in a competing paper's weekend edition. It was now almost two weeks after the news first broke, and they had what they called an "exclusive exposé" on Neekoo's "indecent proposals." The headline read, "A little sex with your morning paper: indecent proposals from star journalist of the *Washington Beat*." My heart sank as I read the story. Not having passed the very first long paragraph, I called BJ.

"Do you think Neekoo's read this yet?" I asked, my heart sinking deeper with each word I read. "Why are they trying to ruin her career? What the hell is going on here?" I exclaimed in frustration just as Michael walked in to start the coffeemaker.

"What are you talking about?" he asked as he gave me a morning kiss on the forehead.

"It's this article," I responded.

"Neekoo's award again?" asked Michael. I nodded. BJ was still on the phone, but I started recapping parts of the article out loud for Michael's benefit. I started reading a particular line in the middle of the article: "Suffice it to say, Neekoo Rahul has taken the journalist-informant relationship to another level. Welcome the sexformant to the—"

Michael interrupted. "Sexformant? Really? Wow, your girl is in for the worst publicity nightmare."

I started summarizing. "It says that coincidentally, none of her sources were female; most of her information was gained through sex exploits, dating some of the men, and having one-night stands with others."

"They are going to reduce all Neekoo's journalism experience to these claims," said BJ through the phone. The resignation in her voice was heartfelt.

"You must be near the last of it," I noted to BJ. I read the line BJ was referring to: "Rahul got the inside scoop on her articles. It is how she got to be the first to break most of the hard-to-get behind-the-scenes facts on even some of the most controversial incidents in the metro area."

"Did they name any sources?" asked Michael.

I was still reading. "I don't think so," I said. I hadn't come across any in the article.

There were details, like hotel rooms and flights that coincided with stories that Neekoo had written. The paper claimed that their sources were men who had slept with Neekoo and not secondary sources. The writer assumed the Elizabeth Bayo Foundation was probably going to hasten their investigation to come to a decision, writing, "It is yet to be seen whether results of the investigation will lead to the foundation stripping Neekoo Rahul of the prestigious award."

"Ever since this thing started, Neekoo hasn't really said how it has affected her, and I think she is just hoping it's going to go away, but I don't think they are going to be satisfied until they see her lose this award. Winning an award shouldn't give anyone the right to crucify you like this. What they are talking about is personal," I ranted. Even though I still had the phone to my ear, I had forgotten that BJ was still on the other end. "BJ, BJ?" I called into the phone. There was no response, so I hung up. I did not call back immediately.

In a deliberately calm voice, Michael responded, "It's not that personal if she got the stories that way, Rory."

"You know Neekoo!" I stated, clearly upset. "This shit isn't her! I just know it isn't her."

"Do you?" Michael asked. He saw the disapproving look on my face as I shook my head. "Babe," he said in a soothing voice, "I'm not trying to aggravate you; that's your girl. But you need to get her to talk to you, and not just about how she feels, but if any of this stuff is true."

"What do I sound like by asking her if this stuff is true, Michael? What kind of friend would I be?" I asked.

"You'd be a real friend, giving her some relief," he said in a matter-of-fact tone that led me to believe that he knew something more. So I asked, "Giving her some relief? What do you mean? What do you know?"

"Nothing," he said.

"Michael," I started in a cautious tone, but he cut me off as he picked up his cup of coffee and planted a kiss on my forehead. With a strong tone said, "I'm not keeping anything from you. I'm heading to my office," and he left the kitchen. I wasn't satisfied, but I wasn't going to nag him either. As much as I still didn't know how I would ask any question regarding all these allegations of Neekoo, Michael did not need to point out what I've known since I heard the news. Neekoo needed to tell us, her girls, that none of this stuff was true. I called BJ.

"I'm already on it," BJ said as her greeting when she picked up the phone. She was going over to Neekoo's, where she was going to stay for the weekend just to make sure she was okay.

"That sounds like a good idea. I think we should all go together," I said.

"That's cool," BJ agreed. "Can you get Sierra?"

"Okay, we'll meet you there, since I still have to shower," I said.

"Sounds good, see you soon," and we hung up the phone.

By the time I was out of the shower and was getting dressed, Bella had roused from her sleep and was in my room. I decided to take her with me to Neekoo's. When Sierra, Bella, and I got over to Neekoo's, we were greeted by a Great Dane at the door that scared Bella half to tears. Holding on to me tightly and backing into me for protection, she let out a yelp-scream. Sierra moved in to stand between Bella and the dog and to maneuver the dog back into the house. Now clearly shielded, Bella peered around Sierra to scold the dog with, "Bad, bad, bad." I chuckled at Bella's determination to *show* the dog that she wasn't entirely afraid.

"When the hell did you get a dog?" exclaimed Sierra. Signature Neekoo move: we had seen her within the past week, but no one had heard about a dog.

"This thing looks like a horse. What possessed you to get something bigger than you?" continued Sierra. There was a little smile, maybe even a hint of laughter through what was clearly a tear-stained face as Neekoo hugged Bella.

"What's your dog's name?" asked Bella, thankful to be in Neekoo's arms and looking down at the dog instead of at eye level with it.

"How about you name the dog?" responded Neekoo. She hadn't given the dog a name yet.

"Alice," blurted Bella, excited that she was naming the dog.

"I think it's a boy, Bella," I responded, seeing the unmistakable package that defined his gender still hanging out between his hind legs. "How about giving it a boy's name like David or Jack?" I suggested.

"No, he looks like a tiger. His name is Tiger," said Bella, so sure of herself.

BJ was in the kitchen making some soup. The aroma filled the apartment quite nicely. We all headed into the kitchen, and I started helping BJ set out the bowls. Sierra took a seat, and Bella, who was now on the ground, kept staring at Tiger. The two were probably sizing each other up, not knowing what to make of the other. Any dogs she had been around were no comparison to Tiger in size. We soon ignored the two as Tiger was gentle enough and made no moves toward hurting Bella. She especially liked it that the dog followed her anywhere she went as she moved around the apartment, smiling behind her when she noticed she had a one-dog entourage.

When we sat down to eat the soup, the television was off, the newspapers were on top of the kitchen buffet, and music played in the background. Sierra launched into it, "Are you waiting for one of us to ask you if any of the stuff we are reading or hearing is true?"

"Yes," was Neekoo's very simple response. Her tone was desperate.

Instead of asking the question she wanted, I started to say, "I just can't believe any—"

At the same time, Sierra was saying, "Hey, it doesn't matter to us either way I'm sure, but is it true?"

"Yes, most of it is true," Neekoo said as tears welled up in her eyes; she forced a weak smile on her face. My eyes widened and then receded into a questioning crease. I was not prepared for that. In fact, I was shocked.

"Wow, and I thought I was the slut among us," joked Sierra.

"Sorry, babe, you do not have a nice enough attitude for guys to stay around long enough for you to be a slut," provided BJ in a dry tone.

"No, chica, it doesn't take being nice to a guy to get him in bed, so if that's the role you're playing, you and DeLuca might never make it to the altar," Sierra jabbed at BJ.

"What the hell?" I asked, looking at Sierra, taken aback by her statement, even if it was a joke.

"Oh, please, I don't take Sierra seriously. If she knew what she was talking about, she'd have someone by now, right?" They continued back and forth just like in college. BJ had to stop first because Sierra didn't know how to, and her bark was always the meanest.

As they ended their thankfully short jabbering, I turned back to Neekoo. "When you say 'most of it is true,' what exactly do you mean?"

She sighed. "I don't know how to explain it, I really don't. It just happens each time. I seek out the story, not the guy. It doesn't happen the way the paper makes it sound. With each story, there's always a guy who knows the details that those I'm supposed to be interviewing don't really want me to know. They pursue me. One thing leads to another, and I get my story. It might be questionable to those making the inquiries, but I stand by my stories. Nothing I wrote was embellished, vindictive, or unethical. Should it matter exactly how I got the story? Guys use women all the time. I haven't done anything different, so I don't think it's fair or even right to have me persecuted because I have done my job." The tears streamed slowly down Neekoo's cheeks, and a voice that slightly wavered at the beginning of her statement, cracked and became a little angry by the end.

There was so much sincere emotion in Neekoo's argument. I was concerned about the fact that she was sleeping with all these men, because if that part of the story was true, she had bedded quite a large number of men. I hoped that she had been careful and hadn't contracted anything yet. I was rationalizing. As she continued speaking, I struggled to support my friend. I didn't want to judge her, but I couldn't understand how any of this could be happening. I looked at Sierra and BJ, but they didn't seem to be taking it the way I was. They looked on and listened, letting Neekoo get it all out.

"This is unreal," I said under my breadth. Either no one heard me, or they just didn't react.

Neekoo continued getting the quasi-confession off her back. "Generally I don't think about it as good or bad. I'm getting my job done, and that was just part of it. I did feel bad when I would find out that a number of them were married …" She couldn't look at me when she said this, and as the only married one of the four of us, I did feel a pinch of betrayal.

I rolled my eyes and slightly shook my head when I asked, "Them? There was more than one married man you slept with?"

"Yeah, there were at least two that I became aware of, and one of them had kids. It was unfair to them," she said and paused.

How altruistic, I thought, now *she reflects on her actions being unfair to the kids?*

Neekoo finished with, "But … but that was the responsibility of the men not to hurt their families that way."

"Wow," I breathed out, not being able to effectively process all this information.

BJ and Sierra looked at me and then back at Neekoo. We were all silent for a moment. The weight peeling off of her, Neekoo asked, "So what do you think? I really want to know what you guys think."

I wasn't in her shoes and didn't want to judge her, but how could I not? I disagreed with everything she had admitted to doing. I was torn, but I kept telling myself that I needed to support my friend through this ordeal and that had to be my focus. Thankfully, BJ responded first. "I'm more concerned about *you*. I don't agree with the witch hunt to make it seem as if you are a terrible journalist because of how you got your stories. If you went through a war-torn area to get your story each time, everyone would be applauding you instead of persecuting you. It's no different than an actress sleeping with executive producers and directors to get a more noticeable role; no one rallies around to get her stripped of her acting nods."

"It's not the same thing as an actress, BJ," I said. "I also am concerned about you, but especially because you see this as part of your job, Neekoo. I am glad you've made great strides in your career, but you've also probably left some unhappy people along the way. And yes, I am referring to the families of the men you slept with. You seem to feel no real remorse for some of the lives that might get destroyed if their names are revealed through this." I had launched into a somewhat spirited reprimand, even though in my head I kept telling myself to focus on supporting Neekoo.

"You are both focusing on two totally different things here," Sierra noted. "Rory, your issue falls more along moral codes, and if that's all we are to focus on here, as much as it is an issue, it's personal and Neekoo has to deal with that internally. On that point, I don't think she should be persecuted for it. Everyone's moral codes and limits are different. Now with BJ, your stance is an issue of work ethic, good or bad, and until the names of these men are revealed, the witch hunt will be initially focused on her work ethic."

Almost clinically, Sierra had done what only she was emotionally and professionally equipped to do. I felt Sierra steering us through some form of group therapy. "When you asked about what we thought, you must have guessed that you would get a mixed batch of emotions, right?" Sierra asked Neekoo.

"Of course. And honestly, I expected something like this," Neekoo said.

I felt the need to frame my earlier comments, as I was kicking myself for not listening to my inner dialogue. "I am going to be here for you, Neekoo, you know that. And I hope you don't think I was judging you. I just have a problem with some of what you did, but that's my problem." Neekoo just smiled.

"Hey, even sluts have supporters, so you've got us," said Sierra.

"And this one being crude about it all, just doesn't help," I said, shooting Sierra a disapproving look. I seemed to be the only one who had a real issue with what Neekoo had done, as Sierra and BJ were vocal in lending their support to Neekoo no matter what. Did this mean I wasn't a true friend? I didn't have a problem with Neekoo getting her stories, but sleeping with men for them?

BJ and Sierra's ability to seemingly compartmentalize Neekoo's act of sleeping with these men from the act of gaining her story was something I was going to have to learn to do. That was not going to be easy for me. Neekoo was going to have enough detractors, and I didn't need to be one of them. I needed to remain strong in my support of her through what was definitely going to become a full-blown public scandal before it died down.

"Do you know what the process of the investigation is going to be?" asked BJ.

"No, not yet," answered Neekoo.

"The paper's conducting one as well?" BJ asked again.

"I'm not sure, but I don't think so. I guess I'll find out very soon," said Neekoo.

"Hey, I don't know how it works in the news world, but are there some specific rules that you guys have to follow to get your stories?" said BJ.

"There aren't any actual rules. The purview of what you go through to get a story changes with each story, as I'm sure you can guess," Neekoo explained. She got up from the table and headed to her living room.

Leaning toward me, under her breath, Sierra muttered, "The rules don't apply to nymphos." With a very light chuckle, I shook my head slowly. Trust Sierra to voice that right now. I hoped I was the only one who heard her.

Standing up to head into the kitchen, BJ effortlessly changed the subject with, "I think we should go and get massages." No one responded.

I had followed her with my mug to get a coffee refill, and in a low tone I said to her, "Neekoo knows I'll be here for her no matter what, right?"

First BJ nodded, then she said, "No matter how bad it is, and no matter how little she tells us right now, we need to see her through it." She paused for a bit and then added, "Sierra's right. No matter what one's crime, everyone needs a support system, and between the four of us, you are typically the most selflessly supportive person. You have a right to feel whatever you are feeling, just try not to let it take over, okay?"

As she was talking, I was nursing the rim of my mug and reflecting on all she had said. BJ came around to give me a kiss on the cheek, then walked out to join Sierra and Neekoo in the living room area. She said, "You guys are not jumping on my massage idea, but we need to do something. What games do you have in this place?" She found Neekoo's *Michael Jackson: The Experience* and challenged each of us to a level. We took her up on the challenge, with either Neekoo or Sierra winning each time. It successfully lightened my mood.

The rest of the day went well; we weren't avoiding the issue, but we didn't beat it to death either. Also, Bella and Tiger gave us barrels of laughs as they became good friends by the end of the day. Tiger had taken to Bella so much so that when he lay down to take a nap, he allowed Bella to curl up against him, serving as her pillow. I decided late to spend the night at Neekoo's, so I called Michael and asked if he could get Bella and me some clothes for the next day. BJ had already brought her clothes as she had planned on spending a few days with Neekoo. Sierra was going to have to use some of our things.

That evening, DeLuca called to speak to BJ and check on Neekoo. He offered her use of his legal counsel if it came to that. It was kind of him. And this of course sparked a conversation along the vein of where DeLuca and BJ were in their relationship. They were so of and on that I had given up on keeping tabs on their status. My only hope was that they would end up 'on' for good at some point. BJ revealed that they were currently back on, and were moving slowly, more so because of her. We already knew the latter half. DeLuca was crazy about her and patiently waiting for her to make up her mind. By her account, they were in a pseudo-relationship, doing away with the formal commitment, therefore dissipating any expectation either had of the other. Whatever.

Late on Monday, I found out from BJ that Monday morning had been eventful for Neekoo. She got calls from every major network asking for "her side" of the story, to which she gave no comment, not even to clear herself. I thought she should have said something, even if to simply say that she was deferring all comments until the Elizabeth Bayo Foundation was finished with their investigation, with which she was cooperating. The other set of calls came from the *Washington Beat*; some were calling to check on her, but the most important came from her editor in chief, who wanted Neekoo to come in to tell him the truth, just so he knew why he was supporting her. He promised that the *Beat* was behind her; he just wanted to know the truth. They agreed that she would come in that day around two for a meeting.

Victor Augustine was in his office and dismissed everyone when Neekoo got there. He was old enough to be her father plus a few years. Today he didn't entirely play the role of her boss, but a concerned father figure. He asked, "So what statement do you want the *Beat* to make, you know we've got your back, right?"

She said pretty much the same thing to him that she said to us, leaving out a couple of things here and there.

"Is there any fabrication in any of the stories in question?" Victor asked.

"No," Neekoo answered.

"Did you write all of the stories?"

"Yes."

"Did you cross ethical boundaries that we would disapprove of?"

"Haven't we all?" said Neekoo in the same tepid voice with which she had answered all his questions. Victor smiled, left eyebrow raised. Neekoo then added, "Yes. Yes, I did."

Mr. Augustine got up and came around to the edge of his table, closer to where Neekoo was sitting. "I don't want to know the details; it's safer that way. If this thing gets any messier or gets legal, I may not be able to avoid the details, but at that time, I would want it to come from you, understand?"

"Yes," Neekoo answered.

"Also understand that you will always have a job here, but—" Neekoo cut him off with, "I know." What Neekoo knew was that when there was no avoiding it, regardless of the 'lifetime job' sentiment, he would terminate her.

"You need some time off?" Victor asked, but it was more of a statement. Neekoo shook her head. She got up to leave his office, and he reinforced his statement. "Whenever you need to, take a few days off, okay?" Neekoo nodded and went to her desk. There were some reporters who kept circulating the front steps of the *Beat*, attempting to get the "latest developments" for their newscasts. Neekoo didn't leave the building until very late, after the reporters were gone.

After a week went by of Neekoo dodging reporters to make it to work and back home, the Elizabeth Bayo Foundation requested a meeting with her. Sierra couldn't make it, but BJ and I were there. Local reporters were camped out in front of the foundation's DC office, awaiting their decision. The foundation had announced that they were nearing a final decision, so reporters were poised, each hopeful to be the one revealing the decision early for their station. To deflect a heightened circus act, a representative for the foundation had advised Neekoo to enter the building using a service entrance. We were able to entirely escape the prying mics of the persistent reporters.

Neekoo was dressed as if she were heading out for an assignment: an old pair of sneakers, a pair of faded blue jeans, a light pink tank top, and brown leather fitted jacket, and her brown leather satchel. Her hands went from going in and out of her jacket pockets to smoothing the strap of her satchel many times. Noticing Neekoo's unease, BJ asked, "You okay?"

"Yes," escaped from Neekoo's lips in a deep whisper. It was all Neekoo could do not to walk right back out the very long hallway we had just ventured into, headed toward the foundation's reception desk. Up until this very moment, I had not observed any physical unease coming from Neekoo regarding the situation. It confirmed within me what I had already suspected: Neekoo was internalizing everything, and she was taking all of this a lot harder than she allowed herself to let on.

We finally got there, and they were waiting for her. The receptionist was kind. She looked at us and through her questioning gaze, you could almost see her making the mental decision against asking BJ and me to wait in the reception room for Neekoo. She told us to follow her to the conference room where the meeting would be held.

We entered the empty conference room. I reached for the water, while BJ reached for the coffee, both of which were on a serving table on the right side of the room. Neekoo first sat at the table, placed her hands on it, then slowly ran one hand through her hair. She got up from the table, pushed the chair in, and then came back to join us. Neekoo didn't reach for anything; she just stood there next to BJ with her hands in her pockets. Drinks in hand, we made our way to the chairs at the end of the large conference table. We waited for Neekoo to join us, then we all sat down.

"You know they are not going to take your award from you, right?" asked BJ. "I mean, what could they legitimately accuse you of to take the award from you, you know?"

"I'm not really worried about them doing that, I just hate that I have to go through this. It's as if I am being scolded by my parents for something they thought I wasn't old enough to do yet. You know that feeling?" Neekoo sighed and sank down into her chair.

Again, my internal dialogue cautioned me against saying anything critical right now. *Not the right time,* I cautioned myself, but my tongue started a different dialogue all its own. I loved my friends, and whenever I was critical of their actions, I usually chose nonthreatening words to express myself; not this time. "Neekoo, this is probably not what you want to hear, but each time I hear you talk about this, I wonder if you realize that you are selling yourself like a prostitute, only the pay is the information you get." I hated that I just likened her to a prostitute. BJ's eyes were large as she swung her head in my direction, lost for words. There was deafeningly uncomfortable silence that settled in the room for about ten endless seconds.

Neekoo took in a deep breath and breathed it out in an open-lipped sigh. A pursed smile settled on her face when she turned to me and started to say in her typical low tone, "I am—" But she didn't get to finish her thought, as just at that moment, the panel from the foundation walked into the conference room. My heart was racing and I felt like crap, and not because we were moments from finding out the foundation's plan for Neekoo.

There were five of them in total. They looked relaxed, and a couple of them had smiles on their faces: three men and two women. They introduced themselves as the finalizing board that made the decision on the recipients of the award, and when the queries had surfaced as to whether or not the foundation should replace the awardee for the current year, that final decision was also theirs to make.

One person primarily spoke, a Ms. Stanton, the chairwoman of the board, and she kept it short. "Ms. Rahul, it's no secret that we have received numerous requests for you to be stripped of the award, but the criteria of the award states that we must base our decision on the accuracy of your stories and the information gathered. As much as we are concerned about how you got your information, it strikes us that it is hard to determine or judge whether or not sexual indiscretions were the sole method by which you gained and developed your stories. Our decision is to have you retain your award. We wanted you to hear it first from us in person before our news conference tomorrow. Okay?"

"Thank you," responded Neekoo. There were no unnecessary

formalities afterward. As they wished her the best with handshakes, they invited us to stay as long as we needed to in the room before leaving, and they walked out. Neekoo sat back deeply into her chair and looking up at the ceiling, all she could muster was, "Wow." Her eyes glistened a bit, but no tears fell.

BJ immediately reached over and squeezed Neekoo's hand. "I told you they weren't going to take it!" said BJ proudly. Still not knowing what her response was going to be to my earlier comment, I simply squeezed her hand.

"Now I only wish the reporters will stop hounding me," she responded with a heavy tone. She was audibly sad. We got into the car, and it was a mostly silent ride. She hadn't resumed her response to my statement, and I was mulling the statement over in my head, thinking about how else I could have said it and still meant the same thing. I was also thinking about what I could say to her to clean it up; for crying out loud, I had called one of my best friends a prostitute!

There were no reporters at Pink Bailey's when we got there, and we headed to the back, in BJ's office, entirely out of sight. Sierra couldn't join us for the victory brunch. BJ ate enough for all three of us, and I teased her by asking where she put it all, since she never gained a pound. She excused herself shortly after we ate, giving Neekoo and me a chance to talk.

"You know I wasn't calling you a prostitute," I started, trying to get it out as soon as I could.

"I know," she said.

"I just wanted you to see that you are too beautiful and too smart to use your body in that way."

"I know what you meant, Rory, and seriously, it's okay. I'm not proud of it, but as hard as I know it is for you to accept, it became a means to an end."

"But that means you get no real pleasure from the sex, and you don't feel attached to any of these guys."

"You wouldn't understand, Rory," she said as she got up and

started walking the office, but not quite pacing. "You wouldn't understand," she said again.

"And I guess I never will," I said under my breath, in resignation, as my hands raked through my hair. I got up, went to give her a hug, and said, "I'm here, Neekoo, whenever you need me. I need you to know that I'm here. I want to share the burden with you, and I just don't know how. I'm sorry that it came with such harsh words, but I love you so much."

Neekoo wore a sad smile on her face and without any noise to accompany them, the tears trickled down her cheeks. I wiped her tears away with my bare hands and pulled her in for another tight hug. Without warning, I was spent. Now, I was in tears.

EIGHT—*Seriously, where is my spa treatment?*

The foundation called a news conference the day after we met with them. Their statement was:

> We are a foundation that takes our nominations seriously, and we investigate the integrity of our nominees. In the past few weeks, we have reviewed the inquiries into some of Ms. Rahul's sources and are upholding our decision about the award bestowed upon Ms. Rahul. If all journalists had to reveal their processes and sources for all stories, we might not all be proud, and although some of the actions journalists take blur ethical lines, we find that the issue here is of personal boundaries. We wish Ms. Rahul the best in her career and look forward to more hard-hitting stories from her.

I was in my office when I listened to the initial newscast. They made a good point that even I hadn't thought about. Yes, Neekoo's stories typically covered getting facts and information from what would be whistleblowers on some of our top executives, be they political, financial, or corporate, and she got the truth about all of those stories out there. For stories whose subjects never really wanted their dirty laundry aired, as the foundation rightly insinuated, getting those facts couldn't be a simple task. Society, which happened to include myself, just wasn't comfortable with the methods that Neekoo had chosen.

I called BJ. "Yeah I saw it," she responded before I could ask. I knew she was going over there, as BJ had been spending a few nights at Neekoo's through the whole ordeal.

"You should come over too, you know," BJ said.

"I don't know. Michael's been very understanding, but I think I should stay around there tonight."

"You know Michael doesn't mind. I feel like all of us should celebrate the foundation's public announcement together."

"You're really trying to use us as guinea pigs for a new recipe of yours aren't you?" I asked.

"You'll have to be here to find that out. And don't act as if you don't love being my guinea pigs as you call it," BJ playfully snapped back.

"I do love your tastings. I'll see what I can do," I replied.

Shortly after I got off the phone with BJ, DeLuca called me. He asked about BJ. "How's your girl doing?"

"She's good. Are you guys in your no-talking phase again?" I asked.

He gave a dismissive half laugh then said, "I've never been in a no-talking phase with Bailey." I noticed that he called her Bailey. I hadn't heard him call her that before, perhaps it's what he called her when they were alone together, or when he was thinking about her in a certain way, I didn't know.

"She's been spending a lot of her free time checking in on Neekoo," I offered.

"I know she's been there for Neekoo, but I just needed to know how she's doing beyond her frequent responses of 'oh, I'm fine.'"

I heard the concern, but there was something else there; it was slight, almost unnoticeable, but it was there in his voice. I pressed him a little, feeling that I may not get another chance to ask him my burning question. "What went wrong with the two of you? When you guys are on, you are so good together."

"I'll leave that to your girl to fill you in with the details," was his frank response. For whatever reason, I was expecting him to be entirely dismissive. And not that he shared anything specific, but all the same, he didn't beat about the bush. Instead, he inferred that he should not be the one giving me that information, but BJ, and he was right. Nonetheless, I pushed him for more.

"That's true, but I want to hear your side of things," I told him.

He laughed a little. "I know what you're doing," he said, but added, "You're going to have to get it from her."

"Okay," I breathed out.

"I'll be in touch, say hi to Michael." I said good-bye and hung up the phone.

I was now more curious than ever. I called Sierra to get her take on things and to find out if she was going over to Neekoo's later on that day. I got her voice mail. I tried refocusing on work but failed. I asked Cynthia to take over. Neekoo's issues were swimming through my head. I felt useless and helpless, as I couldn't do a thing for Neekoo but criticize her actions. I wasn't just internalizing her issues, but I was also struggling with keeping a real friendship going on without judging, and at the same time still holding true to myself. I was in a state of anxiety.

And then there was Sierra, who I suspected could be back on her drugs if she ever did stop. Since she had shared her drug dependency issue with me, I found myself always reading different things into her behavior. I probably needed to better educate myself on what actions would be exhibited by someone addicted to prescription drugs. I didn't even remember the names of the drugs she told me she had taken. And now DeLuca was reaching out to me to check on BJ? I took that to mean there was probably something wrong that had nothing to do with their relationship. I had been on the scale countless times a day over the past week and seeing the number induced a headache instead of reducing any anxiety. I started feeling the need to escape everyone and everything for a little while. My mind was on an uncharacteristically selfish path, and with Cynthia in charge, I rushed out of the office by noon.

I knew the plan was for us to go over to Neekoo's, and I was going to make it there eventually, but at that very moment I just wanted to be alone. Well, almost alone. I called my brother, who I hadn't spoken to in a couple of weeks because he had been traveling. He had moved to New York since leaving college—just close enough to my parents that he still went home on the weekends for home-cooked meals and for Mom to occasionally do his laundry. It was refreshingly pitiful. My mother loved having him home of course, so even though she complained about his laundry for example, she wouldn't have had it any other way.

I got Vernon on the first ring. "Hey, kiddo, what's going on with you?" he said.

I wanted to know what he was doing, and if he was busy. He claimed he always had time for me, so it didn't matter what he was doing. "Well, can you pick me up from the train station in about three hours? I want to come up there to do lunch."

"Is everything okay, Rory?" he asked.

"Sure, everything's fine."

"Okay, I'll be there." I didn't call anyone else at that moment. I didn't even feel the need to call Michael and tell him I was going to New York for a couple of hours. It was his day with Bella, so I didn't have to make plans for her, either. I turned my phone off, drove down to Union Station, and caught the next Acela train to New York City.

Vernon wasn't running late as was his norm, but was right there as I got off at Penn Station. He greeted me with a kiss on each cheek, and then a third, and to that I said, "Which country were you just in?" He tousled my hair as his response to my teasing. I laughed when I added, "And I bet it's not going to last."

"Hey, at least I can use it to impress the ladies."

"When are you going to grow up?"

"With you as my twin, I don't have to," he responded in a warm voice that toned down our teasing. We walked in the direction of Broadway and Madison Square Garden, getting immediately engulfed by an array of street vendors. I leaned closer to Vernon to avoid being constantly hit in the shoulder by passersby. He wrapped an arm around my right shoulder and gave it a tight squeeze. I felt that he knew something was wrong and that was his way of communicating it, almost as if to say, "It's going to be all right."

"So what are you in the mood for?" he asked.

"Anything, really," I responded. We both loved different types of cuisine, so there wasn't really ever a miss at any restaurant we went to. We lunched at a beautiful Zagat rated Vietnamese restaurant about a thirty-minute walk from Penn Station. We sat upstairs at a table overlooking their outdoor seating and were one of only five groups seated upstairs. "So how are Mom and Dad?" I asked.

"Yeah, Mom said you've been avoiding her calls."

"No, that's not it. I've just been all caught up with Neekoo's whole situation." He wanted to know how she was doing, so I filled him in.

"You are having a problem with the fact that she probably slept with a few married men along the way, and she didn't think to take you into consideration before she did it," Vernon stated. I knew he really wanted to say, "I don't want to offend you, but I need you to hear how self-serving you might be taking this, when it isn't really about you."

"I know it's not about me, Vernon."

"It's not just that, Rory. You have to try to understand that if Neekoo were taking this as a moral issue, she wouldn't have slept with them, but she's not, and you can't impose whatever your moral standards are on her. She's single. Chances are, she doesn't or wouldn't have the same inhibitions that you would, and you should be okay with that." I knew he was right, I did. I was making this about how it affected me. Everyone had pretty much pointed this out, so I knew the problem was me.

"Have you said any of this stuff to Neekoo?" Vernon asked.

"Well, somewhat."

"Somewhat?" he asked. I told him about calling Neekoo a prostitute.

"What?" He leaned back into his chair and cocked his head to the side. "You called her a prostitute?" Although he wore a slight smile on his face, his tone was one of disbelief.

"I know, I know," I said, the dejection oozing out of my voice as I shook my head slowly. With elbows on the table and my head cradled in my hands, I said, "I don't want to talk about this anymore."

"Yeah that's a tough one, but you and Neekoo need to figure out how you feel about all of this, otherwise your friendship will be strained. And if you can't see things the same way, at least agree to disagree and really be there for her, without your issue with her actions having to flare up later." I was silent.

My heart was really heavy, and I really didn't want to focus on this anymore so I switched the subject to him. I wanted to know if he was seeing anyone and how things were going with him. He turned the rest of our lunch into a lighthearted affair— exactly why I had come to see him. It was now five o'clock, and I wanted to beat traffic when I got back to DC, so instead of rushing out, I stayed on in New York for another hour. We used that hour to window shop, after which I headed out to Penn Station and was in Union Station just before nine.

Once in DC, the phone rang. It was the third call from BJ. Again, I pressed the ignore button. I am sure she expected a response from me about being at Neekoo's hours ago, but instead I headed straight home. For that small moment, the only role that made me feel important and whole was that of mother, so I went home to my girl. I needed a hug from my Bella.

When I got home, she was writing a book entitled, *Me and My Best Friend Tiger*, and when she was done, she was going to read it to him. So far, so good. It was pure scribble, but she knew what the scribble meant, so I promised her that when she was done, we were going to have a special reading party at Aunty Neekoo's so that she could read the book to Tiger.

Michael asked no questions, which was strange. He wasn't the pestering type, but I was gone for hours and hadn't checked in with him. It was my habit to do that, so I expected him to inquire about my whereabouts. Not a single question. Although I was thankful for his desire not to know, because I didn't feel like being interrogated or shrinked by him, it also made me feel that he was hiding something. I ignored my normal curiosity.

"BJ wanted you to call her when you got in," he said.

"I was supposed to join her at Neekoo's, but I wanted to come home and see you guys first."

Michael came over and stood behind me with his arms wrapped around me, then he gave me a kiss on the neck and the cheek. "It's going to be okay. You guys are going to get through this." He said "you guys"; he didn't make it about Neekoo, but all of us. I thought that was strange, but I dismissed it.

Holding on to his strong arms with my head nestled against his chest, I whispered mostly to myself, trying hard to believe my words. "I know, I know," came out of me in a soft, almost inaudible voice. "I guess I should make it down there before BJ believes I forgot," I said.

"Are you spending the night there?"

"No, I'll be home."

"I don't want you driving if it gets too late. I think you'd be better off staying over."

"If I didn't know any better, I'd think you were trying to get rid of me." I gave him a kiss and went looking for Bella. I played our game, which always tickled her pink. It was our version of hide-and-go-seek.

"I hear little footsteps in the hallway," I called out, going into each room, calling Bella's name even though I knew exactly where she was. When I finally found her and feigned surprise, she was so excited, she jumped up and down repeatedly on her bed, proud that she had "won." Although she wasn't ready to go to bed, I got her to settle down, read her a book, and turned off her lights, knowing that once I left she was probably going to climb into my bed to fall asleep until Michael would pick her up and tuck her in for the second time.

I went back to the kitchen where Michael was having a cold beer. He got up when I entered and gave me a long, tight hug. A cloud came over me, and I just cried as I stood within his arms as he rubbed my back. He still said nothing, but simply wiped the tears from my face and then gave me a kiss on the forehead. I smiled when I looked into his eyes. He wanted to say something, but now wasn't the time to get into it. I had to be a caring girlfriend and head over to Neekoo's house to see how she was doing. I gave my husband a long kiss and headed out to my friend's house.

I didn't call before getting there; I just showed up. Sierra and BJ were already there. Shortly after my arrival, BJ quietly led me to Neekoo's bedroom. "Where have you been? I called you all day. Did you get any of my calls? Seriously, where have you been?"

I told her where I had gone, but didn't get into the details.

"You know we have to spend the night, right?"

"Why? That's what Michael said, but I didn't think we were going to," I said.

"We're spending the night, Rory. It's a good night for a slumber party—"

"Slumber party? Really?" I said with cynicism.

"Tonight's a good night to get Neekoo dealing with how she really feels about the whole ordeal she has been through so that she can start leaving it all behind, at least now that it's all officially over."

"And here I was hoping that you were putting us through a tasting," I said.

"Don't worry, I cooked." With that, BJ and I headed back to the living room where Sierra was trying to find out what alcohol Neekoo had in her house—not much, since Neekoo wasn't a big drinker.

Sierra didn't drink at all, so I asked, "Why are you looking for alcohol? You don't drink."

"I don't need it, but that chica needs to get drunk, because she is acting as if her life is over when she should be overjoyed."

It was the truth. Neekoo was literally sitting there and staring into thin air. She seemed to have become emotionless, but I didn't think alcohol was the answer.

"I need you guys to eat some of this food that I cooked, because Neekoo pretty much ate nothing and I have stuffed my face," BJ said. I helped myself to a little bit of the dessert. I was so tempted to have some of the shepherd's pie that she always made with kidneys, but I didn't dig into it. I brought out the one bottle of red wine that I found after rummaging through Neekoo's kitchen, and I also got some lemonade and ginger ale for Sierra and myself.

It was now almost eleven, and although I had stubbornly not packed a bag, it looked like I was staying. With wine, lemonade, ginger ale, and lemon tarts as our game pieces, we started playing "I have never" which Sierra had suggested. Normally the game was set in motion with one person stating that they had never done a particular thing, and anyone else in the room who had actually engaged in the act, had to take a swig of their drink. The game could be played with any theme in mind, and that night we played it with sexual content, because Sierra and BJ thought that would be most interesting.

"I'm going first," started BJ. "I have never kissed a guy's ears," she said.

"What?" the three of us said as we each took a sip of our drink.

"That was weak," Sierra scolded, and then she gave her challenge: "I have never had sexual intercourse with a guy without him first going down on me." Only Sierra sipped on that one, and at the same time I playfully screamed out, feigning innocence, "Oh my ears!"

"Hold up, is that right?" BJ asked. "Aren't we supposed to be saying the things we have not done? Sierra, you mentioned what you have done," she said, confused.

"I think Sierra just feels like us knowing her sexcapades," said Neekoo with a dry smile.

Neekoo was a good sport; she was indulging us and couldn't care less about the game. She was in her tank top and pajama shorts with her blanket around her. She was just about to mention her second escapade when her doorbell rang. BJ went to the door, but no one was there. She picked up the brown box that was left at the doorstep.

"Did you order anything?" BJ called out as she brought the box in.

"No," said Neekoo.

"You sure? Looks like you may have ordered a bag or something," I said.

"Nope, it looks more like a Mercedes Benz key box," said BJ, placing it on a table and turning the box around.

"Not to sound pessimistic, but it could very well be a fucking bomb," Sierra noted.

"It can't be a bomb," I said, really doubting that anyone would go to that much trouble to cause Neekoo harm, but I still took out my mobile phone, predialed 911, and left my finger on the "talk" button just in case.

We were still contemplating the possibility that it could be a bomb when Sierra, who had introduced the idea of the potential danger, started opening the box. There were four identical blue-and-brown pouches, and each had one of our names embroidered on it. Even lethargic Neekoo was genuinely curious and reached out to take hers when Sierra handed it to her. We opened the pouches, with a mixture of surprise and excitement.

"This is beautiful," I said. Each of us now held a white gold-link clasp bracelet with our name inscribed on a round charm. On the other side of my name was inscribed "sexy." On the other side of Neekoo's appeared "loving." BJ's was inscribed "selfless." And on the other side of Sierra's, she read "warm."

"Did you order these?" BJ asked. She looked at me with the same look of curiosity I was sure I had on my face.

"I was just about to ask you the same thing," I said.

Sierra looked down into the box, took the tissue lining out, and saw the card. The card had the picture of hot stones in sand on the outside, and on the inside it read, "Because you deserve it. You have reservations starting today to join us for some of our signature services at Willow's Spa and Sanctuary." The card was signed *Vernon, Michael, and DeLuca*.

"Damn, they're good!" said Sierra.

It now made sense why Michael had wanted me to pack a bag. The card said the reservations started that day, so we needed to leave. I immediately called Vernon. "You could have said something, you know!"

"And spoil the surprise?" he asked in a light tone.

"It was better for all of you to find out together. Are you guys there yet?" he inquired.

"No, we just got the card," I said.

"The resort has been waiting on you for a few hours, so you might want to give them a call to let them know you guys are on your way."

"Thanks," I said, and we hung up. The next call was to Michael. "Now I know why you were trying to get rid of me for the night."

Before I could say more, Sierra took the phone out of my hand and pressing the speakerphone button, she asked him, "Who came up with 'warm'?" They both laughed, and so did we. Neekoo called the resort, and they said they would expect us anytime that night.

"Oh my gosh, we're really going to the spa!" exclaimed BJ. "I had asked for us all to get massages a week ago, and the gods heard me."

"Sure, the massage gods heard you," Sierra teased with a smile on her face.

"Mmm, I can't wait to get a nice mud bath and a hot stone massage," I said.

"I want to try something that I haven't tried before, so we'll see," Neekoo chimed in.

"Who's going to keep Tiger?" asked BJ. It was too late to knock on any neighbors' doors, so I called Michael and asked if we could drop the dog off when I came to pack a bag. I knew Bella would love having him over.

I was the first one out the door, and I didn't see my car. My exclamation didn't come immediately as I kept telling myself that maybe I had parked in front of another one of the townhouses and had forgotten, but as I surveyed the sea of cars and didn't see mine, I panicked.

"Where is my car?!" The panic was short-lived.

BJ had recognized a car in the lot and said in a slightly unsure tone, "That looks like one of DeLuca's cars." The guy drove up to us and said that our cars had been delivered to our houses and that he was supposed to drive us to the resort. He had already picked up a bag for me from my place, so we asked if he could drop Tiger off, afterward. The driver called DeLuca when we got in, as DeLuca had requested.

Over the car's speakerphone DeLuca called out, "Hey babe," referring to BJ.

"Hey," she greeted in response.

"Your car is with me. Michael has Rory's," he said, filling us in.

"Thanks, DeLuca," we called out through the car.

"You are quite welcome, ladies, you are quite welcome." It was

Friday, and they booked us a stay for the weekend. We needed this. This was definitely better than staying over at Neekoo's and cheering her up; now we could all get pampered.

None of us had been to this spa or even heard of it. Neekoo said it sounded a little familiar, but as we drove off the highway down what seemed like a deserted road, even she was sure this was new to her. About a quarter of a mile off, we saw what we hoped was the spa. We drove up to a mini mansion surrounded by beautiful flowers and woods, with cabin-like bungalows. We headed into the foyer of what looked like a very well-decorated main living room. A lady named Ivory welcomed us.

Ivory led us out of the main house through a garden path that was serenely lit. We got to our cabin—number four. It was a mini apartment with a log-and-rattan theme. There was no television, and no doors on the restroom and kitchen. This was an unusual spa.

Before Ivory left us, all she told us was that because we had come in really late, we would have our briefing at six the next morning before our first session at seven. We didn't bother asking her any questions. We were tired and really wanted to go to bed. Everything in our rooms was simple and mainly brown and white. Like we did in college, Sierra and I shared a room and BJ shared with Neekoo.

When I got up at five thirty to prepare for our six o'clock briefing, my body hated me. I just wanted to roll onto my other side. Neekoo poked her head into our room to ask if we were up.

"Something like that," Sierra responded.

Neekoo, BJ, and I were showered by the time there was a loud knock on the door, our signal that we were needed in the main house. We waited on Sierra before leaving and finally got to the main house by six fifteen.

Ivory escorted us to one of their receiving rooms, where we were greeted by a middle-aged woman named Mercedes who introduced herself as a therapist. We were seated on big ottoman-type structures and before doing anything else, she directed us to do some deep-breathing exercises. We looked at each other. "Does this all seem a little weird?" I whispered to Neekoo, who was the closest to me.

"A little," Neekoo whispered back.

The spas I was used to visiting didn't normally have me doing any exercises, and had already taken down my desired services by now. There was no way Vernon, Michael, and DeLuca knew what services we wanted, so I was expecting someone from the spa to ask.

We finished the breathing exercises, and then she started. She had profile sheets on all of us so she knew our names and tried to match up the name to the person. She was a pleasant lady, but we were getting a little impatient and started fidgeting in our seats. In a huffy attitude, Sierra got up and asked, "Is there any real reason why we had to get up this early to do nothing? Can someone give us a list of our massage options, and why are we meeting with a therapist first?"

With a sweet smile, Mercedes answered, "And you must be Sierra." Sierra didn't like that. "Normally this first session we actually do individually, but we can also treat the four of you together. So after reading this letter from your friends who sent you here, you can let me know which setting you prefer for this first session, okay?" It was all so mysterious that ten more minutes of the continuous closet talk would have had me packing my bags. Mercedes handed us the letter.

My heart was pounding. Everything about this felt like an intervention without everyone there to express their views to you. Sierra, who was the most impatient and annoyed of us, tore open the envelope. "What the hell is this? I'm getting tired of this. Are we getting massages or not?" But she stopped ranting as she started reading.

> Ladies,
>
> Sierra, you are going to have a few words

> for us when you find out what's going on, but we can take it. BJ will probably start pacing the room once she finds out, and Rory, try not to hyperventilate, everything will be okay. Now Neekoo's probably the only one who's going to take all of this in stride, so in absentia we say thank you for understanding. And to all of you, if you think this is intrusive, we are sorry you think so. But we aren't sorry for doing this. You really are at a spa. It was the only way to do this for you, of course, but more importantly, you are at a spa treatment center with professionals to help you realize fully what we see when we see you.
>
> BJ, this is Anthony writing right now: You are the most beautiful, caring, selfless, and driven woman I know, yet to know that you have to purge almost everything you eat and entirely deny it, concerns me. I have felt the pain of this because I know you want to believe that I don't I know, yet I do, and I think it is the main thing keeping you away from me. I am yours now and forever and will see you through this, even if you hate me for orchestrating you getting this help.

BJ was in tears. I had my eyes closed tight. I couldn't believe what was going on, but Sierra continued reading,

> Neekoo, this is Vernon. You are good at what you do, and I refuse to judge you, but this might be a good time to look into a few things. Rory teases me about being always good for a fun time, but your time with these men doesn't seem like it was fun for you. For that I am hurt for you, and I feel there's something else there that you aren't

> sharing with anyone. I need you to have the last word, but you have to find out what that will be.
>
> My wife, my love, the mother of my perfect child—and the one who doesn't always see how beautiful she is. Who doesn't fully realize that not every man is searching for the skinniest woman but the woman she is inside, the woman we fall in love with because of how she makes us feel even when she is not in the room. To me, you are the sexiest woman alive, but I'm afraid that unless you see it on that scale, you'll never really allow yourself to believe how physically attractive you are. You are and have always been the one I want to wake up to every morning, but I want you to stop waking up to the scale.

Everyone but Sierra was in tears by now. "Sierra," she read out her name and then came the knot in her voice. She tried, but couldn't read it out loud and read the rest in silence. Her hands trembled and the letter fell out of her hands. I walked over to Sierra, and before I could reach out to her, she turned away from me. I was breathing heavily, my stomach was turning and my eyeballs were burning from the free-flowing tears trickling down my face. Neekoo had been standing closest to Sierra. She continued where Sierra had stopped, as Sierra walked out of the room muttering, "This is fucking stupid."

> Sierra, it's your boy, Vernon. First I need to say, don't be mad at Rory. She loves you and it's not her fault that I know this. And come on "chica" as you would say, I've spent time with you, and baby girl, you have a drug problem.
>
> I know you've admitted it to Rory, but that's not enough. You need help to get through this,

> and I know the longer you stay like this, the more damage you are doing to yourself.
>
> We hope you aren't too mad at us, but we will risk that for you dealing with your individual issues. We thought the only way you guys would really do it, is if you were to do it together, even though you haven't shared all your issues with each other. We want you to know that as the men in your lives, we are going to stand by you no matter what and for us, that means making you realize that you aren't weak for admitting your demons and addressing them. We believe it will make you stronger.
>
> We love you,
> Vernon, Michael, Anthony

My heart was pounding so hard that all I could do to calm it down was to take in very deep breaths through tears, trying hard *not* to hyperventilate. Head buried in her knees, Neekoo was curled up in a ball on the floor. Her head must have been spinning. None of us could look each other in the face. Sierra walked back into the room. Her eyes were bloodshot red. I didn't know what to expect from her. The whole room was tense.

In an unusually quiet voice, Sierra said, "Rory, I told you that in confidence. I didn't even know how I wanted to deal with it yet, and I told you—and you told them? Who else did you tell, Rory, who else did you tell?" By the end of her statement, her anger came back into her hurt voice. The accusation of betrayal cut deep, but it was warranted.

I didn't say anything. What could I say? I know it wasn't easy for her to tell me about her prescription drug dependency, and I made that clear to Michael when I told him. It was never supposed to leave our living room, and he had obviously shared it with Vernon and DeLuca.

"Who else knows, Rory?" She was screaming at me now.

I reached to touch her hand, which she brushed aside, and with tears in my eyes, I apologized. "I am so sorry. Maybe I shouldn't have shared this with Michael."

"Maybe? I'm a therapist, Rory. I know that it was getting out of hand, and that's why I confided in someone. I—not Michael, not Vernon, not even you—should make the decision for me as to when I get that help. That's a decision I make." There was a gentle knock on the door, but none of us answered. Sierra reached for my purse and got my phone out of it.

"Call him. Call Vernon and ask him if he told my brothers, because if he did, I want nothing to do with you ever again." I knew Vernon and her brothers kept in touch every now and then, but he wouldn't have shared anything like this with them without running it by me first. At least this was what I was banking on when I took the phone to dial his number.

There were no pleasantries, and from the tone of my voice, I was sure he knew that we had found out why we were really here. I asked him, "Did you tell Sierra's brothers about the pills?"

"No, I didn't," he responded. Sierra asked me to ask him again to make sure, but I really didn't need to. He heard her through the phone and asked to speak to her.

"Tell him to go fuck himself," she responded. "I'm not staying here," Sierra said. "I know how to deal with my issues, and I'm not doing it here, and definitely not after being betrayed."

Neekoo was the one who responded, "Obviously none of us are dealing with our problems well, Sierra, and we are the only ones in denial about it. We might not like the way that they've done it, but think about it. How else would you want them to go about this? We are finding out stuff about each other that for as long as we have been friends, we should have shared with each other by now. And I am probably the biggest one at fault with that. We are living these double lives as super put-together women, but we're internally crumbling, and we didn't expect anyone to eventually take notice? I mean look at me …" Her tears flowed easily, but she didn't stop talking.

"I've slept with so many men, I don't even remember names anymore, and I've justified it as being okay, even though I don't feel good during any of the sexual exploits. I need to stay. I can't speak for you, Sierra, but I think we *all* need to stay."

BJ, who had been pacing the room as predicted, hadn't said a word since the letter was read. She had gone over to Neekoo's side when she was making her case for all of us staying. The gentle knock on the door was back again, and this time Mercedes came back in. In a soft, very caring voice she asked, "So how are we all doing?" No one answered; we were all engulfed in our very own thoughts. Sierra, with back turned, was looking out the window. Neekoo and BJ were seated on the floor, and I stood against the wall.

"It's important to us that you aren't here against your will, so after finding out why you are actually here, I need to know if you are deciding to stay." All but Sierra slowly nodded. She handed each of us a profile sheet. There were numerous characteristics on the sheet that we were supposed to fill out, giving the spa a better perspective on our issues.

"You will be staying with us initially for a one-week period, after which you go home for one day on the weekend. You will return to spend a two-week period with us and then have another one day away, followed by a final seven days with us."

I looked up, contemplating a protest, but she quickly continued, "Also, since you came to us as a group, many of your sessions will be together, but you will also have individual sessions with therapists specific to your needs, on a daily basis. Your friends, bosses, and coworkers have assured us that it will be okay for you to spend this time with us, so there should be no problem."

We all felt so defeated, and it wasn't just the intrusion into our lives by our loved ones anymore; we had supported each other, yet secluded each other at the same time. Maybe being here was good. It had to be, but as we sat there, it was hard not to think that it was easier being angry at the guys and at each other.

How did they do it? We found out later on that their plan had been in the works for a long while. During one of their on-again periods, BJ was spending the weekend at DeLuca's, and he found out about her habit. She had arrived at his place on a Friday evening and let herself in. When he walked into his house, he called out for her because he had seen her car outside. There was no response. She wasn't in the kitchen or in his library. He headed toward his bedroom, and as he walked in, she walked out of the bathroom. "Hey, babe, I didn't hear you come in," she greeted. He motioned to kiss her, but she deflected it and flopped onto the bed.

They spent a quiet evening together, during which he noticed she brushed her teeth at least three times in a four-hour period. He joked, "Oh so that's how you keep those pearly whites." On that Saturday, they skipped breakfast for a scrumptious lunch that BJ put together. After they both sat down to healthy servings of her dishes, DeLuca wanted to go for a quick run so he went into his bedroom to get into his running gear.

Very shortly after she was sure he was gone, BJ had gone into the restroom to purge the meal she had just eaten. DeLuca had forgotten his headphones and was back in the house and up to the bedroom too soon for BJ to be done in the bathroom. He heard what sounded like a choking cough and tried to open the bathroom door, which was locked. He banged on the door, wondering first why it was locked and secondly what could have happened to BJ in such a short period of time to have her choking in the bathroom.

He heard the toilet flush, and BJ spraying air freshener before she opened the door. He was concerned and asked her if everything was okay. She told him that she thought she had a stomach virus or something and that she would be okay. He remembered that he had smelled the same mixture the day before and asked if she was going to see a doctor since it had been a couple of days.

"A couple of days?" she asked, wondering what would make him think that. She thought she had covered her tracks too well the day before.

"Looks like the same thing happened yesterday when I walked in, so you must be dealing with something that's staying with you a little while," he responded with concern.

She said she would see the doctor the following week if it persisted.

He left the subject alone and went to the kitchen to make her some tea and gave up his afternoon run. By the end of the weekend, BJ made herself purge a couple more times, but didn't have to explain too much of anything since she had now established with him (for that weekend at least) that her trips to the bathroom were necessitated by her "stomach virus."

A couple of months after the case of the mysterious stomach virus, BJ was back at DeLuca's, and it was almost a repeat of the stomach virus attack, but DeLuca wasn't buying it.

"Babe, we need to talk," he started.

"What's wrong?" BJ asked.

"Don't you think you're getting too many stomach viruses?" he asked.

"What do you mean?" she said dismissively.

"Maybe because you don't want me to know that sometimes you make yourself throw up after you eat?" DeLuca proceeded with caution, searching BJ's face for a reaction.

"You don't know what you're talking about."

"Maybe you're right, but it's not a stomach virus, babe," he asserted.

BJ was getting angry. "When have you seen me throw up?"

"I don't have to see you perform the act to now know that something is wrong, and I just want you to get some help."

"I don't make myself throw up. I've never done that here, and I need you to drop this subject." BJ was getting loud.

DeLuca stepped closer to BJ and smoothed her hair as he said, "You said you've never done it here, but that means … Anyway, babe, if you're bulimic, we—"

BJ waved his hand away from her head. "Bulimic?" She started shaking her head. "You're not dropping this. I've got to get out of here." She chuckled nervously as she walked to the closet and started gathering her items to leave.

DeLuca sat on the bed and quietly said, "I don't want you to leave. Tell me what you want me to do, to keep you healthy," he continued. He was now standing in front of her, holding on to her arms in a motion to halt her from packing.

"You don't need you to do anything. I just want to leave," she said, knowing that she was about to break down. He let go of her, and she left.

DeLuca didn't let it go. He didn't press her, but spoke to Michael. His assumption when speaking to Michael was that I knew and had shared it with Michael. The guys assumed that the four of us told each other everything; they also further assumed that I shared a lot with my husband. This was mostly true, and I trusted my husband not to divulge that trust. So when Michael was approached, he acted as if he was aware of BJ's purging and suggested that DeLuca find some form of intervention and treatment for BJ that would work.

DeLuca insisted that *I* should be the one to set it up, as he felt that it would be easier for BJ to take from one of her girlfriends. Michael knew that I hadn't told him anything about it, and he put the ball back in DeLuca's hands, making the argument that this was DeLuca's moment to let BJ know he was going to see her through anything. They planned to get back together with a plan of action.

Neekoo's public scandal came at an opportune time. Michael, who now knew about all our issues, started the conversation with Vernon, that it might be a good idea to get all of us help at the same time and get through our demons together, as opposed to singling any one person out as the focus of an intervention.

Vernon thought it was a great idea, and he set the ball in motion, researching various places. He stumbled upon the women-only center in Virginia that handled an array of addictions and dependencies in a spa resort-like setting. DeLuca and Michael agreed that this was the right place, and the arrangements were made with the facility.

The next step was to reach out to our jobs and make arrangements for our absence without divulging any details. Michael handled that aspect. Neekoo's was easy, as her boss had already suggested she take a paid leave of absence for a little while because he knew the toll the public scrutiny had taken on her. Mine was a simple call to Cynthia, asking her if she could take over for a month. She always did this whenever we went on our vacations. This was why Michael had been asking me about taking a vacation.

BJ's also went smoothly. She had since taken a step back as the head chef, so that area was already taken care of. DeLuca paid a management team to take over BJ's daily tasks at Pink Bailey's for the period that BJ would be gone. Sierra's was a little tougher, but they ended up convincing her cotherapists to take on her patient load. Everything was done without a single one of us suspecting a single thing. They were good.

As Mercedes was reading to us the schedule for the rest of our week, I looked around at the four of us. We were beaten. Sierra's look was distant, and although she had mentioned her need to leave, she stayed in the room with us as we all barely took in what Mercedes was saying. Thankfully, Mercedes also handed us a booklet that detailed our schedule and promised that things weren't going to be as bad as they seemed at this moment. We still weren't saying anything to each other.

NINE – *Mirror, Mirror …*

"I'm going to have you meet with your individual therapists for about a half hour because they need some specific information from you, and then why don't we take a break for about an hour to get ourselves together before meeting in the Meditation Room?" And with that, Mercedes led us each to different rooms.

"Hey, Mrs. Carter!" greeted a bubbly five feet three, petite lady who had the body of a twenty-one-year-old and a face that was ageless. I was hoping she was at least somewhere in her late twenties. *She has to be a size zero,* I thought. "I'm Toni," she said in greeting as she reached out for a hug. *Why does everyone always think the big girl needs a hug?* was my first thought. My second thought was, *How could such a big voice come out of such a little thing?* I didn't bother introducing myself since she started with calling out my name, but I did interject after the second "Mrs. Carter."

"Umm, yeah, I'd rather be called Rory," I said.

"Oh, sorry," she said sweetly, "Rory."

"Yes, each time I hear it, I think my mother-in-law is around."

"Sorry about that."

I listened to her talk—or, point of correction, she talked and I heard the words coming out of her mouth. And then I couldn't help myself. I said, "I hate to ask you this, but how old are you?" I wasn't going to be too happy if the only person they could get me was an image of skinny perfection who had just graduated and looked every bit of it. How was that supposed to help me? She brought back feelings of indignation from high school that I would have sworn were gone.

Stop it, Rory! I told myself.

"Absolutely no offense taken," she assured me. "I get asked that all the time." She whipped out her driver's license from her wallet for proof and said, "I'm turning forty later on this year. I am so excited about it!"

Forty! See, that's the thing with skinny women; they freaking don't age either! None of this was starting off well. I didn't like it. I wanted to be back living my life, regardless of what Michael thought about me benefiting from this. I thought I was doing just fine before someone stuck a skinny, effervescent forty-year-old who could pass for twenty-five, in my damn face.

She continued with her questions. "So someone who thinks the world of you thought you could benefit a little by spending a month with us and solidifying a good self-image. How do you feel about it?"

"Well, the truth is, I really don't know yet. I don't know if I appreciate any of this. I've had a lot of issues with my weight when I was younger, but not as much now."

"Do you still revert back to those days when you didn't like your weight as much?"

"Not quite," I said, and I suppressed a self-directed chuckle as I had taken one of those journeys within the last few minutes.

"And when you say not quite, what exactly do you mean?"

"Well it's no longer an issue of not liking my weight, as I—"

"When did you last get on a scale?" she quietly interrupted. I gave a reflective smile and rubbed my right earlobe. Perhaps Michael had mentioned something to her, I thought.

I didn't answer her question directly; instead I said, "I do have moments where I wonder about different situations and what the turnouts would be if I were a little smaller."

"Now, you don't have an ideal weight that you carry around in your head do you?"

"Of course I do," I said, looking at her as if she was crazy. *Who doesn't?* I thought.

"It should be based on how you feel though—" Mercedes started to say.

"Sure," I said with sarcasm. "You can tell yourself that it's not about the number, but how you feel. But you feel better when you aren't so heavy, so we're back full circle to the number."

Mercedes smiled, followed with a gentle laugh. She asked, "So what's that ideal number?"

"Wow." I breathed out. "Let's see, I would say about 155, 160 would be a nice number."

"And how much do you weigh now?"

"Ahh, the last time I checked, I think I'm around 180ish." I was giving out the numbers as if I had to think hard about them. These were numbers I carried around in my head like the pin numbers to my bank account. I had been on the scale that day!

"You are just making my day! Normally I have a few women come in telling me that their goal is to lose anywhere from forty to sixty pounds in a month, and it's not always the healthiest choice. We just need to get you into a healthy, beautiful "you" mode, without focusing all on your weight."

As I became more tolerant of her style, I began to like her. The smile I wore betrayed my thoughts.

She smiled back and then reached out her hand to touch mine. "Your weight is only the beginning. I am okay with us starting there because I gather that it is always lurking in your mind, and seeing you at your healthiest weight is important to me. However, we will work on you seeing that it in no way defines you." She paused and gave me a demure smile. "We're going to work on this together, right?"

"Sure," I responded.

Sierra's therapist was Lola. She was older and looked statuesque. She wasn't going to indulge too much of Sierra's nuances. That's what Sierra needed. Lola knew what she was dealing with in Sierra, so initially she handled everything with the same flippant attitude with which Sierra treated her. Only she wasn't as rude or obvious as Sierra was.

There was a couch in the room as well as a high bar stool that looked as if it were there just to complete the décor. Lola didn't sit until Sierra did. Sierra took the stool, placing her at higher eye level than Lola. All of this was necessary for Sierra to feel in control. It worked. With the simple nonverbal assurances that Lola had given, Sierra was more open and less combative than she would have been if she were being "handled" as opposed to being treated as an equal.

Once seated, Lola shifted her glasses and looked at her notepad while she spoke to Sierra. "You've had an impressive fast track in pediatric therapy. I read one of your articles last year actually, when you gave your analysis on the high-profile case assigned to you of the boy who killed his mother." This invited Sierra to engage with Lola as a fellow therapist, which she did. During her commentary on the article that Lola was referring to, Sierra had now gotten up and was comfortably walking the room.

"Am I correct in saying you've recognized your own dependency and were looking for the right time to start dealing with it head on?"

"Yes, no one would have even known about this unless I said anything," replied Sierra with a trace of an indignant tone.

"And what was that timetable looking like?" asked Lola.

Sierra was quiet.

"I'm sure with the type of patients you deal with, you don't necessarily leave the timetable and decision to go into therapy to them. You trust them to rely on guardians to create that timetable for them." It was a statement that rang deep within Sierra because it was true. She knew all of this, but she had willfully ignored it; her timetable for dealing with it just wasn't coming any sooner.

"Yeah, I really don't know when I would have gotten around to it, because I truly never have time," Sierra said offhandedly, giving herself an excuse.

"Yet you use the pills to function?"

"Well, not on a daily basis. I can go several weeks or months without the pills, but then again, when I'm on them, I can be on them every single day for three straight weeks."

"Do you have any on you now?"

"Of course," Sierra responded matter-of-factly. "I didn't know I was coming to a treatment center!"

"You know we have to search your belongings—"

Sierra cut her off. "I know, I know the drill. In fact, shouldn't you have done that when I came into your 'spa'?" she said in a mocking tone.

"Not if you weren't staying," said Lola, exuding the perfect picture of calm.

Sierra took out the little satchel from her pocket that was holding a mixture of her pills, and she handed it to Lola. "Thank you," she said, acknowledging that Sierra could have made this a lot harder. They walked out of Lola's office and headed to the cabin to unload Sierra's bags of more pills.

Dallas wasn't present when Neekoo walked into the office, so Neekoo took the liberty of finding out about her therapist in advance. She had only one degree on the wall—her bachelor's—but the name tag on the desk read Dr. Dallas Greene, so Neekoo surmised that her therapist wasn't showy; Neekoo liked that. Dallas loved dogs. Mounted on the wall was a picture of her and a black and a golden retriever in a chaise lounge. She had a mixture of books in her office library. There was a Koran, a Bible, and several other spiritual books on one shelf. On another shelf there were hardback copies of J. R. R. Tolkien's *The Hobbit* and *The Lord of the Rings*, an anthology of Shakespeare's works, Machiavelli's *The Prince*, and Octavia Butler's *Kindred*. Neekoo picked up Dallas's hardback copy of Paul Coelho's *The Alchemist*, made herself comfortable on the couch and started reading

Dallas introduced herself into the office with a rush through the door and a breathless monologue, "I'm so sorry to keep you waiting. I had to take my dog Betsy to the vet quite unexpectedly this morning; she woke up with a weird … I'm sorry, there I go, giving you a rundown of my dog's hospital adventure, not even knowing if you like dogs."

Neekoo had stood up and turned round. Book clutched against her chest, her statement was simple: "I got a Great Dane not too long ago. I am becoming a dog person."

"Who's keeping your dog while you are here?"

"My girlfriend's husband, but their three-year-old daughter, Bella, is probably trying to take care of the dog," to which Dallas smiled warmly. Dallas walked over to the couch area and sat down.

"Please, please sit," she said, motioning to Neekoo to resume her earlier spot on the couch.

"So you just got a dog, what's the story? Gift from a boyfriend?" Dallas sounded like a giddy girlfriend. Neekoo, who had been splitting her visual focus between the book and Dallas, raised just her eyes to look at Dallas. The look was disapproving.

"No, not a gift. I got the dog after a recent investigation related to my work," Neekoo said.

"So the dog is serving as a bodyguard?"

"No. I became paranoid about being in my house alone, so I got a dog, that's all."

"Do you mind telling me about the investigation and what led to it?"

Neekoo gave a journalistic rundown of events, as had been

reported in media. Dallas never interrupted her, not even once. When Neekoo was done, all Dallas asked was, "Would you do it all again?"

"Do I have to talk about that right now?" Neekoo looked down as she was about to tear up.

"No, you sure don't," answered Dallas. "All I would like us to do with this meeting is both agree on why you are here, even though you don't have to get into the details today."

"I first thought maybe I was promiscuous, but then I thought that's not the case since I don't go looking for it. Then I thought maybe I was a sex addict, but the same reasoning applies. They have been acts of convenience more than anything else. I know why—at least I think I do. I guess I'm here to be honest with myself? I don't know."

"Do you think your sexual encounters were excessive?" Dallas asked.

Neekoo was quiet, then answered, "I guess so."

It was clear Neekoo wasn't going to delve into it just then.

BJ was pacing in her therapist's room, more nervous than scared. She hadn't had a chance to talk to us about the secret that she had kept, and now she might have to talk about it to a stranger. As she was pacing, she kept having internal conversations convincing herself that she wouldn't have to get into it today. It was too early. They wouldn't make her get into it right now, would they?

Willow walked in barely two minutes after BJ was let into the room. She was soft spoken. She was one of the more fashionable and stylish therapists. Willow had on a pair of dark jeans rolled up right above the ankles and a white, loose three-quarter-length artist's shirt with a silk scarf adorning her neck. Her open-toed pumps were a mild fuchsia, showing off perfectly pedicured toenails with black nail polish; her manicured fingernails matched.

Willow pulled off the look effortlessly, and BJ took note of every single detail. They were perfectly matched for each other. BJ liked what she saw, and from the moment that Willow walked into the room and unknowingly allayed BJ's fears, BJ knew she could do this.

They talked fashion first, and afterward in true BJ style, *she* started asking the questions.

"I could be wrong, but you don't seem as if this was your first profession, was it?"

Willow chuckled. "I began as a massage therapist, and actually started listening to a lot of women's problems then. When I offered them advice, to my surprise, they took it. They always came back to me—some of them weekly, others biweekly, but they all came back and gave me updates on how their situations were going, through each of our massage sessions. Then I got into a car accident and found that I couldn't always stand for the long periods of time that I was used to, so I went to school and studied psychology, became certified, and here we are."

It wasn't the story BJ expected to hear, but a "eureka" moment went off in her head. "You are the owner."

"Yes, I am the owner," she said.

"Any reason why the center only takes women?"

"Regardless of how crazy women are with each other, get the right set of women together and they heal better with each other. That's the premise on which we rendered our services when it was just a spa, and it's the same premise we use now since combining it with a treatment center."

"Interesting," commented BJ, more so perfunctorily.

"Our staff does include men, and you will meet them once you get into your treatment routine. Some of our fitness trainers, nutritionists, therapist assistants, and physicians are male, but for your one-on-one sessions as well as your group sessions, you will be meeting with only female technicians."

Willow wanted to know about BJ's family. BJ told her about

her mother and Marie. "Was your father in the picture?" Willow asked.

"No, not really."

"*Not really* allows for a window where he might have been there sometimes, would that be true?" Willow pressed.

"I don't consider myself as having a father. He was never there for my mother or me. My mother would say differently; she would explain that he wanted to be and couldn't. But that's a lie. I've had no relationship with him."

"Have you sought him out?"

"Boy, you start in heavy on the first day, don't you?" said BJ, wanting her to stop with the "father" line of questioning. "I thought that, according to DeLuca, I was here for some other reason."

Denoting the underlined feeling of betrayal in BJ's statement, Willow offered, "I believe you are here to learn healthier ways to trust yourself, and I was curious to find out how far back there might have been issues of trust."

"All you had to do was ask me who I trusted, and I would have told you."

"But I couldn't ask you that question when you don't even trust yourself."

There was silence. Not indignant silence from BJ, but contemplative. Willow didn't interrupt her silence. BJ settled into her chair and got a little more comfortable, and with eyes closed as if trying to remember every single detail and not leave anything out, BJ told Willow the story her mother had told her about how she entered the world. BJ left out crossing paths with the person she blamed all her habits on, as she still felt Willow was getting into heavy subjects with her a little too soon.

Back in the cabin after her luggage had been searched for any other prescription drugs, Sierra had started reading through the schedule booklet. Neekoo and I happened to walk in together. Sierra greeted Neekoo with, "You'll be happy to know they are going to make us do yoga and Pilates."

"I'm sure we are going to have a few mandatory things to do here, but honestly, I'm beginning to feel like, if there's anywhere I am being made to do anything, this place isn't half bad," responded Neekoo.

We were seated in the living room area of our designated cabin. As soon as BJ joined us in the living room, Sierra immediately stopped reading. "I'm sorry for being a bitch to you earlier, Rory. I know you care and I don't think you're a blabbermouth. If you didn't even tell these two, it had to be out of concern for me that you told Michael," reasoned Sierra.

It came out of nowhere, and I was shocked. "Change of heart?" asked BJ.

"I don't know, man," said Sierra with her head down. "I just feel bad that I came at you that way." I went over and tousled the top of Sierra's hair. "You're good. I couldn't have predicted any of this." She looked up and said, "And I guess Neekoo's right; seems like a good place to explore all our crap." I hadn't seen her look this vulnerable since college.

"For two seconds there, when you walked up to take Rory's phone, I was afraid you were going to hit her, and I had no clue what I would have done," said Neekoo.

Sierra laughed lightly at Neekoo's statement. "Nah, I wouldn't have done that, although I was incensed. Boy, I'm nuts!"

"Yes, you are!" said BJ, shaking her head.

"I think we all are," I said, and Neekoo corrected me. "It's not just what *you* think, Rory, but obviously your guys think we are some kind of nuts, so we're here." In her unassuming style, she had lightened the mood, and we all laughed while shaking our heads.

Our first day there was marked by anxiety, intrusion, revelation, and homesickness, but also some fun. That day was a little slow. After our initial one-on-one sessions with our therapists, our next task was meeting a group of other spa residents who were either working in groups like we were or as individuals. Most of the interactions we had with the other residents included outdoor fitness, outdoor meditation, once-a-week group therapy sessions, and meals.

After the meet-and-greet, we had to see the in-house physician for quick physicals. Then we went to the outdoor meditation session, which was weird. All the guide said was, "Meditate on anything."

What the hell?! Meditation is not easy. In fact, it's downright impossible the first time. Your mind wanders to everything, even the things that you are trying so hard to block out. We were sitting next to each other, cross-legged on the grass. BJ was on a mat.

Our meditation guide was sitting in the middle of the circle of about twelve of us. She asked us to close our eyes and take in deep breaths, then she said, "Meditate on anything, and let your mind take you to where you need to go and then stay there. Feel your soul, feel your spirit."

Again, what the hell?! As someone who hadn't done this before, two things were going on in my mind: first you ask me to meditate on anything (and right now, all I can meditate on is your voice telling me to feel my soul and my spirit), and secondly, this can't be useful since it sounds like hocus pocus.

I tried, I really did, but that session for me, at least for that day, was a joke. Here's what I meditated: *I wonder what Bella is doing right now? Boy I miss my husband's body! This is what I get for trusting that guy with everything! No access to his amazing body and staying here to fully relearn mine—how ironic! Is my underwear matching? I was wearing a pink-and-black bra and my black boy-shorts. That was a close enough match. We haven't eaten yet; I wonder if BJ will approve of the meals they serve us. BJ critiquing their meals would be funny. She said her personal therapist was the owner; knowing BJ, she would tell her directly about the meals. Okay stop—really, what am I supposed to be meditating on? How do I feel my soul or my spirit? Am I supposed to know what that feels like? Do I really want to know what that feels like—it sounds as if it would actually feel a little spooky. Maybe I'm supposed to have an out-of-body experience to know what it feels like.*

I had a full hour of those kinds of thoughts and found out later that I wasn't the only one who had a stream of random, unconnected thoughts. So if that's what meditating was, which I was sure it couldn't be, then I guess we meditated on "anything" as the guide had directed. I was thankful when at the end of the hour, she said, "If you had a stream of random thoughts, that's normal, especially if this is the first time you are doing this. But the more you dedicate time to trying to control your thoughts on one specific thing, or even on nothing at all, you will gain better peace from your practice of mediation."

Now why didn't she start with that?

We broke for a general session of a light lunch of salads and fruit-infused water, and then there was yoga. You had to be there to appreciate what happened in that room. There were teams of us doing yoga in different rooms, and thankfully for us that afternoon; it was just the four of us in our room with Laila, one of our fitness guides who was a certified yoga instructor. She asked if any of us had practiced before and to our regret, only Neekoo had her hand up. Neekoo had asked us to join her a few times for yoga, Pilates, and spinning classes, and we could never make it. It would have been nice to be able to say we at least knew what we were doing.

"Not to worry," promised Laila in a soft voice.

We hadn't gone with her on any other fitness exercises yet, and I was hoping that this wasn't the way she was going to be giving us instructions toward any other fitness exercises, because I couldn't see that soft voice inspiring me. She started us off with diaphragm deep-breathing exercises, and between Sierra and me, we didn't know we could push our breath down to our abdomen until then. Laila held my stomach against her right palm for me to really feel the breath. I started to yawn.

Then we went into what she called the sun salutation routine, which initially was a piece of cake as it simply had us standing up with our hands together in the form of a prayer. But then we went into this thing called the downward dog. I'd never seen a dog do that. Now doing the pose wasn't as difficult for Sierra, but still the three of us had to stop the noises coming out of our bodies. Neekoo was just fine.

It came from Sierra first, and all of us acted as if we hadn't heard it. And then Laila came over to me and separated my legs a little more and tilted my pelvis to better align my back, and although I was now probably doing the pose correctly, there was no mistaking the noise that came out of me. We couldn't ignore it. At first I thought pure and utter embarrassment was going to engulf me right after the moment it happened, but it didn't.

We started with slight chuckles while we were still trying to keep the pose, and then BJ let one out, as well, and we all burst into laughter. Laila had to let us have that moment. Our bursts of laughter were gut-wrenching and cathartic. Laila assured us that it was very natural to have those "body acoustics" during our first few yoga sessions, depending on the stretches. And she wasn't lying, because through that session all three of us—Sierra, BJ, and myself—created more "body acoustics." It was memorable.

That first week went by without much incident; if there was camp for adult females, this is what it would feel like. They had us talking about our issues and engaging in exercises that didn't make us feel as if we were at a treatment center. The massages that we received every other day didn't hurt either. We didn't terribly mind being there anymore, and counting down the days to Friday when we would be allowed one full day away from the center, was a bonus.

We started the mirror exercise on day three of week one. It was scheduled after dinner and our evening walk on the grounds. The four of us were back in our meditation room with two other residents on that particular day, and initially it felt a little strange. The choice was ours to sit or stand in front of the wall-to-wall mirror, and we had to look into the mirror and express whatever it was we saw.

So you are sitting there with the inability to escape your own eyes, and with fear of what you could possibly see. It was intimidating because the exercise required that when you got comfortable enough, you had to verbally express what you saw aloud, in the small room where everyone was going to hear every word you uttered.

That first day, the whole room was silent, even though I am sure that like myself, we were actually engaging in the exercise within ourselves. It was hard not to do the exercise. Staring into your own eyes, you started seeing things about yourself that you liked, loved, hated, and tolerated.

Day two of the mirror exercise wasn't much different from day one. The six of us were back in again, and you could smell the detachment in the air as we strolled in. Sitting there in front of the mirrors that day, there were smiles and tears. Laila, who was our guide for this exercise as well, just sat behind all of us, smiling serenely.

Day three of the mirror exercise was a breakthrough. It was a Friday, and we were leaving the treatment center the next morning to return by Sunday afternoon or evening at the latest as we were instructed. It started with Dorothy, a twenty-seven-year-old, who was described as a fully functioning drunk.

She worked as a bartender in one of the upscale bars in Georgetown and never drank on the job. She barely slurred or lost her balance when under the influence, and the only giveaway that she had drank herself to her limit was the uncanny reaction of passing out even though there had been no other symptoms leading to it. One day after work, she had gone to another bar to drink, after which she proceeded to drive herself home. No one stopped her, because she wasn't slurring and didn't miss a step as she walked out of the bar to her car. She was halfway home when, with the immediacy that only three of her friends had witnessed, she passed out and drove straight into a tree. It was three o'clock in the morning, and there were very few cars on the road.

An older gentleman driving about thirty-five miles per hour at most, to his part-time job as a security guard saw the car and stopped. He walked over to the driver's side where this young lady was slumped over. Initially he thought she was dead, because when he opened the car door, touched her, and called out, "Miss, miss," she slumped out of the car into his catch. He dragged her out of the car and laid her on her back. He patted his pockets, looking for his mobile phone. He didn't have it on him and looked toward her purse in the passenger seat, removed her phone, and dialed 911.

Awaiting the arrival of paramedics, he knelt by her side and was about to perform CPR when he realized that she was breathing. He stayed with her until the paramedics arrived. He had made several attempts to talk to her, but there was no response. It was remarkable first that she was alive, but to his naked eye, she had no mark on her from the accident. Once at the hospital, tests confirmed that the accident was alcohol related. She was lucky. She hadn't endured any major injuries, internally or externally.

When they looked through her phone for a parent's number, they found none with that designation, or no last name matching hers, but they found a number with the designation "Emergency Contact." It was to her best friend Mike, who got to the hospital in less than fifteen minutes after the call. They explained what they thought had happened, and Mike inquired about an emergency detox program. The best they could do was keep her there for forty-eight hours to make sure that nothing was wrong with her, after which they had to let her go.

Mike was hit with the implication of what had just happened. Dorothy could have died; she could have killed someone and wouldn't have been aware of any of it. He went into overdrive; he called two other friends, told them what happened, and asked them to start seeking a treatment center and an interventionist.

He asked the nurses the same thing, and they gave him a list of places, one of which was Willow's Spa and Sanctuary. The call to Willow's was the third, and final.

When Dorothy woke up and saw Mike sitting next to her in a hospital room, she knew what had happened. They had joked about it before, that one day she would have one of her "pass out" moments behind the wheel. Mike had mentioned then that he almost wished she was a belligerent drunk, because then people would know that she was drunk and possibly try to stop her from driving. No luck there. Dorothy started crying deeply, and it took her a moment to get the question out: "Did I hit anyone?"

Mike shook his head slowly. "No." He didn't beat up on her; he just stroked her hand, telling her that she was the luckiest person alive. She had totaled her car and left more bruises on the tree.

Dorothy couldn't stop crying. They didn't get much of a fight from her when they conducted the intervention the next day. In fact, before they gave her any details, she said she was ready to go.

"I should be dead," said Dorothy through tears, looking directly at herself through the mirror. "I have been so selfish and irresponsible. How could I not see what I was doing? I don't even like the taste of alcohol." By this time Dorothy wasn't just in tears, she was on her knees, shouting out while crying. She was lashing out at the person in the mirror. She continually repeated, "I can't be selfish anymore, I can't be selfish anymore," over and over and over. It was powerful, even though we all heard her, the tears I was crying weren't just for her, but for me, and I think that's what all the rest of us in the room felt.

Like a domino effect, since Dorothy started, everyone else went too. Neekoo went after Dorothy, and she started by shaking her head so hard. It was almost as if the harder she shook, she would physically get the thoughts out of her head. BJ, who was sitting closest to Neekoo and wanted Neekoo's pain to stop, motioned as if to stand, but Laila quickly went to BJ and had her sit back down. Neekoo didn't say much through her tears, but her words were piercing: "Nobody loves me. How can anyone love me? I don't even love myself. Why would anyone love me?"

The force of this exercise that I detested continued. I found myself spilling out my communication with myself, revealing my insecurity and my desires. "I am more than my body! I am not defined by being fat. I am beautiful. I don't have to be skinny. I am not my mother. My father needs to accept me the way I am. He needs to love me for being so different from everyone else in the family. I am still his daughter."

Laila pressed the intercom once without saying anything, and within a minute, four more guides came in. They brought blankets, pillows, and warm drinks for those who had exerted so much energy in the mirror, they were now spent. Sierra was already expressing herself, but I heard her better when I stopped. "How could she love you and not stay? She said she loved you, but how could she leave you? She shouldn't have been able to leave you like this. She didn't even love you enough to stay. Why wasn't it him? Why didn't he just leave? You aren't as bad as everyone thinks you are. You actually care; they just don't know it. But …" She stopped and couldn't look at herself in the mirror anymore, but instead, like the rest of us, she curled into the fetal position and just lay there on the floor.

What the guides knew that we didn't was that we would feel like this—wrecked with headaches and no desire to leave the room—but stay in the position that we were in, eyes closed, feeling the innermost of our pain, praying that with each moment we lay still, things would change.

The last day before leaving for our first off-center break, we were breaking into ourselves. The mirror exercise was practiced as a group the first week and the last week only; other times, it was your decision to come in and consult yourself through the mirror. There was something about expressing your inner thoughts aloud in the midst of others that requires you to be brave enough to think *fuck it!* and it validates those emotions as real.

BJ wanted to scream, I could tell. She wasn't going to say anything; she kept wiping her tears away and tried to look away from herself in the mirror. She looked a little angry. One of the guides went to sit by her and another went to sit by the sixth woman in the room, who had started talking. Then BJ stared longingly into the mirror. "How could you not want to meet a child you helped create? What makes it easy for you not to have anything to do with a life you helped create? And it's not as if you never wanted kids, just not me. What was wrong with me? Why weren't you there? Why weren't you there?"

All six of us spent the night right there in the mirror room. I was beaten and didn't care to move. We felt better in the morning, and leaving that day couldn't have come any sooner. I know that I needed a break from the emotional outpouring that we'd been through. We looked a mess when we walked to our cabin to get ready for breakfast. And as much as that was probably the toughest emotional thing we had done, strangely I felt better than I had about myself in a very long time. After breakfast, we headed back to our cabin to put things in order before leaving, and then headed out to the garden.

DeLuca's driver came to pick us up around two in the afternoon after we had done our group yoga meditation session. DeLuca had wanted BJ to spend that day with him, but she wasn't ready to see him, so she asked if she could stay over at my place. Neekoo asked Sierra to stay with her. Sierra's body language looked as if she was about to turn down the offer, but she decided against it. The center trusted that because Sierra wasn't currently dependent on her pills, she would be responsible enough not to take a step backward by taking them. It was a trust exercise, and she knew her bags would be checked upon re-entry together with her getting tested. Neekoo suggested the sleepover to take away the temptation entirely, and she said, "I know Willow told us that they are trusting all of us to be around our vices and not dabble in them, but I'd like us to stay together and clean out your place of any more of your pills."

Sierra smiled and nodded her head slowly. "Touché."

The first thing Sierra did when she got to her house with Neekoo was have a de-drugging party. She first discarded the bottles that still had prescription drugs, and next went all those empty bottles that she had kept for years. She treated Neekoo with a few stories along the way, many of them sad and indicative of the pain that Sierra had been suppressing for so long; there were also moments of laughter.

"Mameeeeee!" yelled Bella as I walked through the door. Bella ran to the door with Tiger close behind.

She had heard Michael announce, "It sounds like Mommy's home," as he himself headed down the stairs. She flew into my arms, and I hugged her so tightly, even I forgot that I had only been gone for a week. It felt as if I had been gone for much longer.

"Why are you crying?" she asked, wiping the tears from my face.

"I'm just so happy to see you, that's all," I said as I tried to hold her head down on my shoulder.

But the ever exuberant child of mine kicked her head back and said, "But I'm really, really, really happy to see you, but I'm not crying." This made me laugh.

BJ had walked past me to greet Michael. "Hey, Mr. Carter," she said with a bit of cynicism and shaking her head. She never called him Mr. Carter, but Michael. She didn't have to say more than that. He smiled.

"Hey, hey," he greeted her back and gave her a hug.

I couldn't quite look into Michael's eyes when he walked into the room. After giving BJ a hug, he came to me and placed a warm kiss on my right cheek. "I'm going to take your stuff upstairs," he said.

"I forgot to tell you when we just came in. BJ is going to stay with us through tomorrow afternoon," I called after him.

"The guest suite's all yours," Michael told BJ, when he walked back in, taking my hand to lead me upstairs to our room. Bella was coming after us, but BJ called her back, telling her that they both needed to take Tiger for a walk.

"So do you want us to talk about this?" asked Michael.

"No, we don't need to."

"But I know you are upset with me."

"No, not anymore."

"But initially you were."

"Of course, but I'm not ready to talk about it yet." And then I stopped with the attitude and had to let him off the hook. "I'm not mad that you did it. Well, I wasn't really mad at first, I was just taken aback because I knew absolutely nothing about it. But I understand why you did it, and I understand why you had to do it for all four of us, but I still don't know how I feel about you not saying anything to me, about how you think I saw my image. I understand, but I just don't know how I feel about it right now."

"You know I love you, right?"

"Always," I said, and I gave him a hug and a kiss.

"So how are the other girls taking it?" Michael asked.

"Sierra's probably going to have more than a few words for you the first time she sees you, but if I were to take a guess, I would say they are on the same page as me right now." And before he made any suggestions, I cautioned him, "I wouldn't say anything to them yet. You guys have us in this thing for another three weeks. Give us time; we'll let you know how we feel along the way."

"Okay, but they can't go hating us or anything, especially BJ with DeLuca," said Michael.

Tiger, BJ, and Bella were back from their emergency walk by the time we were done upstairs, and Bella wanted to go to the mall. I thought that was a great idea—anything to spend some time with my little lady.

But BJ came up with a better idea. "How about we head over to my place for a second so that I can pack what I will need for the next two weeks, and then we can head to Tyson's Corner for some shopping for Bella, and then manicures and pedicures?"

"Yay," screamed Bella as she ran into her room to get her stuff for shopping. Her desire to go shopping? Now that was purely BJ's influence on her.

We rang Sierra and Neekoo to find out if they wanted to come along, but there was no pick up. By the time we got to the salon to get our nails done, we desperately needed the foot massages that they started with, thanks to all the walking that we had done in five hours. We were the last ones to get there just before the doors were locked, and we didn't get out of there for another two and a half hours. I normally only allowed clear nail polish on Bella's nails, but today we let her get whatever color she wanted, and she wanted a different color for each nail. Bless her heart! Michael called to find out where we were as it was already ten o'clock and no dinner. I asked him to order some pizza for all of us, so that it would be there by the time we got home.

When we walked into the house, there was sweet-smelling sauce in the air. He had made some seafood over angel hair pasta for Bella, and rotini for the rest of us.

"So you just let me talk on and on about ordering pizza?" I said.

"I just needed to get an idea of when you guys were coming home, without me having to cook and then save it to be heated in the microwave, that's all."

"Well, thanks for the nice surprise."

"It looks as if you guys bought up the entire store," he commented, looking at the bags we had brought in. Bella had already gone into her room with a bag and put on one of the outfits. She tugged at Michael's pant leg. "Look, Daddy," she said and twirled for him to admire her outfit.

"You look gorgeous," he said, sweeping her off the floor and placing her in a chair in front of her plate with a dinner napkin over her dress. It was late and she wasn't really hungry, but she didn't want to go to bed.

"You look sleepy, Bella," said BJ when she tried to feed her.

"Noooo," said Bella shaking her head and ending with a yawn, which she quickly covered up with her little hands.

"Oh, oh, I saw that," BJ teased her. Bella laughed, trying to stifle another yawn.

"Come on, babes," I said, reaching out to Bella. "I think we should go to bed," and I carried her out of her chair to take her up to her room.

"Mwah." BJ blew her a kiss. "Sweet dreams, Bella."

"Mwah." Bella tried reciprocating. I was planning on staying with Bella for as long as she would stay awake, and that was short-lived. She was quite sleepy and drifted off within ten minutes of us reading one of her stories.

I was leaving Bella's room from tucking her in, when I heard my mobile phone ring. It was a little after eleven. It was Sierra and Neekoo on the other line, wanting to know what we were doing. I headed into BJ's room and put them on speaker. "We're probably going to be sleeping in less than an hour. We called you guys earlier so that you could go shopping with us."

"We must have been asleep for about three hours," responded Sierra.

"And that's why you guys can't sleep now," teased BJ.

"Hey, BJ," started Neekoo in a begging voice. "Do you think you could whip us up some dessert at Pink Bailey's?"

BJ said, "Yes!"

"Oh, one more thing," said Neekoo. "Could you bring Tiger?"

We had a blast! BJ did this sparingly—opening Pink Bailey's in the wee hours of the morning just for the four of us. We started in the kitchen, keeping BJ company as she whipped something up. Afterward, we all ended up in her office, where Tiger was waiting.

We reminisced over the first yoga session we had with Laila and had a good time making fun of ourselves. We left Pink Bailey's about four in the morning.

Ten – *Unbeautiful Revelations*

After that moment of outburst from Sierra shortly after our arrival at the center, none of us had confronted each other about how we had been able to keep so much from each other. Everyone knew that at some point, I had problems with my image; they knew my biggest struggle.

What did it mean that BJ couldn't let me know that she was bulimic? But then she hadn't even admitted it to herself. And even if she had told me, what could I have done?

Sierra had told me something about her vice, and I hadn't done anything. My husband, brother, and DeLuca were the ones to finally make the move for all of us. What did that say about me? I made a mental note to discuss these issues with Toni when I got back to the spa.

My thoughts were interrupted when my mobile phone rang. Sierra gave me no opportunity to let out a greeting. "Where the hell are you guys? We were sure you guys would beat us here."

"What time is it?" I asked, lying in bed with Bella who was watching cartoons.

"It's three thirty in the afternoon, Rory."

"Oh my gosh, are you serious?!" I exclaimed, knowing that

they had asked that we were back at the center between two and four, Sunday afternoon. I had been comfortable just lying in bed after breakfast, telling myself we had time.

There was no way we were going to be there by four, and I hadn't showered or packed. I hung up the phone with Sierra and popped into the guest room to check on BJ. Not only was she not ready, she wasn't even up.

"BJ, BJ," I called out as I shook her. "We're running late. You wanna start getting ready?" She turned over for a second and then got up. I went back to my room with Bella trailing me. I hurriedly got ready.

When we finally reached the spa, we drove up the driveway and saw Sierra and Neekoo waiting outside the receiving hall.

"Were you afraid we were going to skip out on you or something?" said BJ to Neekoo and Sierra as we got out of the car.

Ignoring her comment, Neekoo asked, "Did you speak to DeLuca at all?"

"No, I didn't. He called, but I'm not ready," responded BJ.

"You're not mad at him are you?" continued Neekoo.

"Nah, I'm not mad at him. Truthfully, right now, I'm just scared to talk to him, and I wouldn't know what to say."

"You didn't see her barfing either, did you, Rory?" This was Sierra's way of being concerned.

"Sierra! You are in rare form! You didn't pop any pills in the last twenty-four hours, did you?!" I rebutted.

"I flushed all my pills down the toilet. Now what?" responded Sierra proudly with a smile on her face. I looked at Neekoo, and she nodded in agreement.

"Well good for you, I'm glad to hear it"

"Well, did you?" Sierra pressed BJ. "Your guys got us into each other's business, so now we better stay in each other's business."

"No Sierra, no barfing yesterday, satisfied?" answered BJ.

Sierra's tone changed almost immediately into one of concern. "You know I mean well." With a smirk on her face, BJ nodded.

We had the option of going to yoga mediation for an hour with Laila or the fitness gym for two hours with Mercedes, and the four of us opted to head to the fitness gym. They interchanged depending on their schedule, and we preferred Mercedes for the gym. Laila's voice just didn't motivate me to pick up that extra ten pounds on the weight bench, but Mercedes's sometimes screaming voice did it. I did sixty minutes on the treadmill and then interchanging different weight machines for forty-five minutes and fifteen minutes of interval stretching. Neekoo and Sierra headed to the swimming pool afterward, and BJ and I headed to a hot tub.

I called Michael to wish Bella goodnight, but she was already fast asleep. Michael said DeLuca came by the house that evening. I couldn't be on the phone for long periods of time per the spa rules, but I wanted to quickly find out more. "Is he okay?"

"Yeah. Yeah, he's okay. But he wanted to see his girl. He feels like she's really mad at him," said Michael.

"He should just give her a little bit of time," I said with compassion. "I'm sure she's going to talk to him soon, but I don't think she's mad at him. She'll come around."

"I hope she does soon. He really loves that girl."

"I know," I sighed. "Babe, I do have to go now, okay?"

"All right, I love you," Michael said. I hung up the phone.

Week two started light for us, with routines of yoga, Pilates, gym workouts, trust exercises, long walks, individualized mirror exercises, and more. During one of our one-on-one daily sessions, I had spoken to Toni about the issues of betrayal that I was feeling with regards to my girlfriends and not knowing how to approach the situation. She said she would like the four of us to get together near the end of the week to have a group session. It was Thursday evening, and we met in one of the common rooms with Willow and Toni.

They had us seated in an honesty circle; we had to be honest in answering any of the questions asked of us, no matter how painful. I was hoping we weren't going to have a séance or anything, because once seated, they placed votive candles and holders in the middle of the circle.

Willow did most of the talking. "First I want you ladies to know that you are strong for being here, and your individual progress should be commended. Many of us women believe that at this age, we should have everything sorted, but very rarely is that the case, especially if we have never dealt with any of the ghosts in our past. You are each dealing with those ghosts, but sometimes it is necessary to share the burden. So I need each of you to pick up a candle. You will ask each other a question or address each other with an issue. The person responding will have their candle lit, and once she begins talking, no one is allowed to interrupt her until she is done or the candle burns out."

We all looked at each other, and Laila chimed in with a smile, "Oh come on, the candles aren't long," and we all laughed, revealing that most if not all of us were thinking the same thing: *How long will I have to keep talking, for the candle to burn out?*

Since I had given this some thought, I dove right in. First I asked if I could address more than one person at a time, to which the response was yes, but they both had to respond individually. I was going to address BJ and Neekoo together, but then decided against that.

"BJ, I feel hurt and betrayed by you, but I also know this isn't about me. Over the past few years, I have shared everything with the three of you." I teared up, but kept going. "You have been there for me, and I would have liked the opportunity to truly be there for you, to try to address what motivates you to purge. And then I blame myself, because now I suspect that there were moments that I should have known. Okay, that's my issue with BJ right now."

I lit BJ's candle, and from that moment, she had to start

talking. BJ sighed heavily, and then looking directly at me, she started talking.

"Where do I start? At first I didn't know why I purged, but it's making sense now. Even though my mother, God bless her heart, tried to make sure I knew I was all she needed, I have never felt good enough. When my mother told me the story of my dad not really wanting to be a part of my life, I didn't think it bothered me at all. I had never met him and never had a relationship with him, so as far as I was concerned, I wasn't missing out on anything. But that trip I took where I ran into him out of the blue, made me resent him for abandoning me and providing for this new family what he should have for my mother. He loved them, provided enough for them. So what was wrong with me? Why couldn't he stick things out with my mother; wasn't she good enough? And if she wasn't, then that meant *I* wasn't good enough.

"These are the personal issues that I have tried to suppress, and for the most part, I do it successfully, but other times I am enraged and my way of controlling that is by eating a lot, almost anything I can get my hands on actually. Then I've got to get it all out of me because I eat myself sick, and the only thing that makes me feel better at the time is to purge everything out. It gives me a rush. I know it might sound sickening, but after I do that, I feel good about myself again, and I am reminded that I don't need him, and I don't want him. And it's not just him. I don't want a guy to provide for me, so I have driven myself mad providing for myself, and my driving force is to outdo my father in almost every respect. It stresses me out, and I go back to my pattern of eating myself sick.

"Take your wedding for example, Rory. I enjoyed every moment, but when you walked down the aisle with your mom and dad on each side, what brought me to tears wasn't how beautiful you looked, even though you looked gorgeous. It was him. No matter what kind of relationship you had with your dad, he was there. My father isn't dead, but dead to me, so he won't be there at my wedding, and my feelings of resentment came over me that day. So when you were looking for me before you threw the bouquet, I was in the bathroom purging because I had again eaten myself sick. I could give you numerous stories, and I didn't know how to tell anyone that.

"I have played in my head what everyone would tell me about me being good enough, and on many days when I step into my six-inch stiletto heels and a killer outfit that gets me the craziest looks, I feel that I am good enough, but those other days are still there and I haven't been able to suppress them yet. I want to say fuck him, and fuck everyone who doesn't think I'm good enough! But one of those people is me, so it's not as simple as saying, 'fuck it.' So I am happy that I am here, being forced to deal with all of this and not fall back to my momentary escapes, because I do know that I have friends who love me and I have a guy who would paint the sky purple for me if he could, but I need to work on being good enough for me.

"I know especially you, Rory, since you've had Bella, you're like this mother hen, and I don't like the fact that you've felt betrayed, because that has never been the intent, so I'm sorry. I'm also sorry that I didn't trust Sierra, who even though she can be a bitch," BJ said with a little laugh, "is a damn good therapist to everyone else, even if not to herself." *Everyone* laughed, which blew her candle out. "I'm done!"

Sierra looked directly at Neekoo, and in the sincerity that made you forget how abrasive Sierra could be, she said, "Neekoo, I just want to hear you talk."

"Do I really have to hold the candle the entire time?" asked Neekoo. Willow nodded yes. "I don't think I can do this," Neekoo said in contemplation.

With Dallas sitting close by, Willow addressed Neekoo directly, and quietly said, "I know you haven't made any big breakthroughs yet. Some people find it easier to have those moments here instead of the one-on-one's. Do you want to give it a try?" Chin pressed to her chest, Neekoo shook her head slowly. Willow squeezed Neekoo's hand. Dallas rubbed Neekoo's back as Willow said,

"Maybe you'll address Sierra's statement later?" It was more of a question-statement that didn't need an answer.

I addressed Sierra. "I just want to hear you talk about youself without you compartmentalizing all your emotions."

Sierra laughed and then talked.

"Okay, I'll do this. I am sure now that with my mother's death, I put that little girl aside who was nice, and she's still there sometimes—but I don't like her. What I started realizing was that my hatred for my father birthed in me this person who could be heartless. I think this realization further propelled using the prescription drugs. Funny enough, when I stop to think about it, that addictive nature probably more closely aligns me with his personality, which is just bullshit. That's why I never went to see a therapist. Don't worry, I know I need one." We all smiled. "I've known I needed one since I was ten, but when something like that happens to you at a young age, sometimes you just shut down and shut out, and that's what I did.

"I know this though, I care about you guys more than I care about myself, and if anything happened to you guys, I would lose it. So knowing that BJ's been purging and not letting any of us in, makes me feel as if I was a failure. Even if she didn't want to talk to me, I could have found someone for her. I know, I know, that sounds backward. I should have found someone for myself, too. The question could be why would she trust me if I couldn't trust myself, but she wasn't aware of my dependency, so selfishly I still feel she should have trusted me.

"There are many times that I don't want to care too deeply for any of us and that includes myself, because most times when I am left to my own thinking, I feel most situations are indeed hopeless. I know this makes for a great therapist who is supposed to help others out," she noted sarcastically. "I am all screwed up, I know."

Willow interjected. "Sierra do you feel your friendship with Neekoo, Rory, and BJ is likened to the relationship you had with your mother?"

"I've thought about that a lot actually, and to a degree, they each fill different aspects of who she was or would have been to me. Even though I lost her at a young age, I remember everything about her. BJ has her bubbly personality that I wish I had. I've always felt something is wrong with Neekoo, because sometimes I see in her the same reactions my mother used to have after suffering abuse at my father's hands—a quiet withdrawal and need to please. But like I couldn't do anything for my mom then, I have never been able to go up to Neekoo and ask her if she was abused and help her, even if just by listening." There was a nonverbal reaction from Neekoo that I couldn't quite place.

"Rory is my solace, and I think she knows that. She is the one I go to talk to, so I guess in a sense, she has been my therapist, but unfairly so because what should I have expected her to do after telling her that I was dependent on prescription drugs? Sometimes being around her comforts me like I was always comforted when my mother was around. So Rory, I know I've forced you into more than a few sleepless nights, but those were my most comfortable times."

Willow again directed her query to Sierra. "Knowing the way you feel about your father, how is your trust with guys?"

Sierra paused. There was no question that she and her brothers cared about each other, even if from a distance. Beyond that, as far as we knew, Sierra generally trusted no man. In college she scared them away, and none had stayed the course to find out the person behind that sometimes harsh exterior. She had often acted as if she was better off, and I was convinced that she actually believed that to be true. And then there was Vernon.

There was a moment when he asked me what I thought about a relationship between the two of them, but as far as I knew, nothing happened there. A part of me wanted to protect Vernon, because I knew that he gave everything to anyone he cared about, and I wasn't sure Sierra wasn't going to ruin that. But on the other hand, he was a grown man. With Sierra, I didn't know how she really felt about him, and I had always felt that one would eventually tire of the other. Whatever it was that they sometimes dabbled in would fade into thin air, and there would be nothing to worry about. This is a thought that I held to be a fact.

In college, Vernon had come to visit almost every month (mostly per my mother's request), and like me, he got to see a different side of Sierra. Out of the blue one day he had said to me, "Your girl Sierra isn't that bad."

I didn't think anything of it. What *I* didn't know was on a few occasions just the two of them had gone to different cafés and bookstores and just hung out, drinking coffee and tea and reading books. He had never come on to her and had never pursued her as a date, but simply spent time with her, and that's when their friendship started. With hundreds of miles between them though, their friendship was marked with sporadic communication and a true lack of commitment from either party to truly pursue whatever it was they saw in each other. Again, I didn't think anything of the two of them while we were in college.

One day however, in the month that I gave birth to Bella, Vernon was visiting and had asked me, "Do you think Sierra will ever get into a relationship with anyone?"

"I'm sure she will when she's ready," I had responded, not quite sure where he was going with his question. "Why do you ask?"

"I like her," he said. "I'm thinking about taking things seriously with her, but I would need to know that it's something that she would even entertain."

Vernon was the wait-and-see kind who would only make a move when he was sure there was going to be a positive response. With Sierra, he would be waiting for a while. Maybe it was the hormones of wanting Bella out of me, maybe I was being protective of Vernon in a subconscious way, but my response wasn't the most encouraging. "No one has seen her in a relationship yet; I can't even be a 100 percent sure she likes guys, so I don't know what to tell you."

He never mentioned anything else about it to me.

Now, before Sierra started responding, she moved to sit directly in front of me.

"I know Vernon asked you about the possibility of us being in a relationship maybe about four years ago, and he probably hasn't told you that shortly after you guys had that conversation, we started dating. I asked him not to tell you, because I wasn't sure, and I didn't want you to think I wasn't going to take him seriously. I also know that if I broke his heart, it might have ruined our relationship, and I couldn't let that happen. I trust him. I trust Vernon, but I'm afraid I don't always trust myself, so it's tough letting a guy in even when you know he cares about you, when you aren't sure you trust yourself." She looked at Willow.

"I can trust a guy not to be my father; I have learned that through Vernon. But I can't trust that one day I won't feel like my mother. I have sometimes wondered if I won't follow my mother's footsteps, and that frightens me. These thoughts plague my mind most days, and when I found that being on my cocktail of prescription drugs often kept these thoughts at bay, it was only a matter of time before I became dependent on them. I don't distrust men. It takes me a while to get to know men, but trusting them isn't the biggest issue I have; trusting myself to trust them, is. Vernon seems to have chosen to wait me out."

I loved Sierra. I loved her so much, and I told her that.

"I think it's good that it's Vernon who has to deal with you. He's got the patience for days, and the only thing he's got more than patience is care, so you're a lucky one. And by gosh, if he's interested in you, he knows exactly what he's getting into, so I'm glad you trust him. I love you, and right now you getting your thoughts together and not being dependent on your pills means the world to me. If Vernon helps you get there and stay there, I'm even happier."

We hugged so tightly, and for the first time, I felt Sierra let go, really let go into the hug and she broke down and cried. Nearing the end of our tears, Sierra abruptly pulled back and asked, "And what the hell is this that Michael says you are not fully comfortable with your weight? I thought you were over that. You are the most beautiful woman I know, well … that I know now. You're only second to my mom, and no offense to you BJ and Neekoo, or Willow and Toni, but you are beautiful all over. I wish *you* could see how you relate with each one of us; only someone with a beautiful spirit gets that impassioned about her friends.

"Who gives a damn that you're not as skinny as we are? Look at us! I have to stay on drugs because I am afraid of my own thoughts, BJ's got a dangerous love-hate relationship with food, and Neekoo's sexed up every guy in sight. Long after you've reached whatever your ideal weight is, we're going to fight to keep our demons at bay. I am not minimizing how you've felt in high school, or issues you've had with your weight, but I need you to know that you are one of the most beautiful people out there, period."

I heard everything that Sierra had said, but I was not sure it was all sinking in. It was true that they all had their issues that they were dealing with, but when people saw them, they didn't see their vices. When people saw me, they saw what I looked like, and what I looked like was what I considered my vice. Gosh, my thoughts were sickening to me. I saw my weight as my vice? Did I really care so much about how everyone else saw me? When was I going to see me, and what would I see? My thoughts were interrupted when I glanced over at Neekoo. She was grinding her teeth really hard; you could see it through her jawline.

Toni also kept glancing over at Neekoo; she was the only one who hadn't expressed how she felt. I was hoping that she would take this opportunity and say something now. Through our time at the spa, it was clear that with Neekoo, the three of us had a feeling at one time or another, that something was up. Over the years, her low-key nature had sometimes exhibited itself in awkward moments and made her seem really distant; however, she stayed almost consistently sweet, so regardless of any signs that we thought we perceived, it was easy to dismiss it by saying, "That's just Neekoo."

When everything went silent, Neekoo lit her own candle and looked down at it. With eyes already glistening with a promise of tears, she started talking.

"I have been caught in between different cultures, and I don't even think I know how I am supposed to feel about anything. My mother sometimes says, 'This is not what we do in our culture,' and in my head I am thinking, *What the hell is she talking about? Is she talking about the Japanese, Spanish, Indian, or American part of me?* She would never be so specific. She is Japanese, my dad is the Indian-Spanish mix, but I have always just seen myself as American. So needless to say, I grew up culturally confused. One thing I was not confused about though was deference to men.

"My mother never worked, and she waited hand and foot on my father. I think a part of my mother has always found a way to make me pay for that. I have three older brothers, and I was the last child. I was supposed to wait hand and foot on them, and I did. I wasn't that spoiled baby of the house that everyone in high school swore I was, even though I desperately desired to be. No, when I got home from school, I did their laundry, I got their sports gear together, I took the backseat to everything they did—so I wrote and wrote and wrote. I was left to my own vices, and that's what my vice was. Alone in my room away from the masculine-dominated spaces in my house, I poured out what I wanted my life to be—in words, in the persona called Saha.

"Saha was liberated and outspoken with no male influences in her life. She had a pet who was her best friend; I wasn't allowed to have pets. She stood up to her mother and questioned things that she did not agree with; I did as I was told, always, even when it went against every fiber of my being.

The first time I was raped, I didn't even know that's what it was. I was fifteen. I had fully developed in all those right places, but had had no conversations with my mother about womanhood or what to expect from it. I was a virgin, and I knew what sex entailed. At least as it had been discussed in sex education classes as well as in girls' locker rooms. It was Thanksgiving, and as was customary, my mother made different Japanese and Indian dishes and invited all our family friends, or more accurately, my father's friends and their families, because that's how my mother made friends."

The color drained from my face as Neekoo revealed that she had been raped. I looked around. Sierra's expression was intense, and BJ looked distraught. Her hands covered her mouth, and the tears continued to trickle down her face. Neekoo hadn't stopped talking.

"On that Thanksgiving Day, there was an uncle who wasn't able to make it for dinner. He called and joked with my mother that she had better save him a dish. She did. He lived less than a five-minute walk away from us, and instead of him coming over, I was sent over to take him his plate the next day. This was a trip that I had made a few times before, so although I made it begrudgingly, it was with no trepidation that I knocked on his door.

"He called out that the door was open. I turned the knob, walked right in and straight to his kitchen to put the plate down. He was behind me, and I only got startled when his hand touched my thigh, lifting up my skirt. I hadn't heard a single step as he walked toward me. I was nervous and breathing heavy, but couldn't even turn round because that's how close his body was as it leaned into mine with a strong, albeit drunk grip. His breath reeked as he was mumbling a response to my greeting. When I greeted him, I expected him to take a step backward to reciprocate my greeting so that I could try to leave. My ploy wasn't successful. Pressing into me even closer, he said into my ear, 'You're looking good, eh.'

"With lips that were wet and cold, he started kissing on my neck, biting into my skin a few times while at the same time roughly caressing my thighs. He managed to muster through, 'You like this right, you like this, right?' as if he were seeking approval for his technique.

"I tried to fight him off, but as clear as day I also kept hearing my mother's voice in my head. *You don't disrespect men in our culture.* So even though I hated this man for what he was doing, and even though I had never had sex and I knew what was happening on this man's kitchen floor was painful and wrong, I didn't fight him off. I don't know how successful I would have been, but I didn't try. I muffled my own tears, tears cried out of agonizing pain. When he was done, he looked at me and smiled. He didn't even tell me not to say anything to anyone. 'You should probably go home now.' He knew my family all too well; I was a girl, who would believe me? This was just something I was supposed to suffer through. Either way, he knew he didn't really have much to worry about.

"I got home that day, and my mother yelled at me for taking too long. I was anguished over whether or not to say anything to her; I chose not to say anything right away, but got into the bathroom and scrubbed my skin. But it just never got clean, so I kept scrubbing. I got yelled at again for wasting water, so I stopped, and after getting dressed I asked my mother if I could talk to her. In fact, we barely talked most of the time. She asked questions and I answered, or she gave instructions and I followed. Whenever we 'talked,' it was me sitting there carrying out a chore and acting as her sounding board as she talked about whatever it was that was going on with her.

"My dad wasn't home, and she was in her room by herself, rearranging her closet. She asked me to take out all her socks and underwear and start refolding and rearranging them back into the wardrobe drawers of her closet. I was so nervous as I was thinking about the best way to say this to my mother, my stomach started hurting. I told her that I thought I was raped. She asked me to repeat myself because she hadn't heard me, and this time I told her that Uncle Armin had raped me. She slapped me. My mother slapped me when I told her that my father's friend had raped me. How dare I speak such ugly things of respectable people, she had said.

"I was in tears, and I knew that unlike my American peers,

I couldn't run out of the room; I had to stay there and listen to a lecture on how rude the young ones were becoming, and I had to remember that I might have been born here, but I shouldn't take on any disrespectful young American teenager traits. I finished my task of folding her underwear and socks and asked if I could go and finish my homework. She dismissed me; also without warning me not to tell anyone, because she knew that she had successfully drilled into me that that would be disrespectful. I went to my room, and I wrote through tears. My entry that day had Saha being the victim of an attempted rape, but unlike me, she was able to stab the guy before she got away.

"That day was the first of quite a few rapes. I didn't report any of them. A couple of them were friends of my eldest brother, but the constant was Uncle Armin. He stopped when I turned seventeen, and since then I have not been able to look him in the face. When he comes over to our house, I am not able to stay in the same room with him and my mother. I lost respect for my mother because she continued waiting on him, feeding him, nullifying the fact that this man, this monster had touched her daughter inappropriately. I hated my parents more than I disliked Mr. Armin; if it weren't for them, he wouldn't have had the comfort to do what he did without fear of any repercussion. She told him everything, so I was convinced that my father knew. How could he still shake this man's hand, how could he? They must have assured themselves that without a shadow of a doubt, I was a liar.

"I was glad to be leaving home when I did, and it's why I almost never went back to visit. I was ruined. They had ruined me. Sex was nothing good to me. It became a product and act to engage with a guy to get what I needed to get from him. It was nothing for me to have sex with multiple guys, and I have never enjoyed a single moment. As long as I get something I can use out of it, I am okay. Guys see me and soon enough they make it clear that they are interested in me. I know what they want, and after I've done my research, I give them what they want without argument. In some cases during the act, I get what I want; and lately it's about a story.

"I don't know what love is, and I feel empty because of it, so normally when you are talking about love, I tune out. I know I should have felt bad when I slept with some of the married men, maybe because of you, Rory, but I've wondered why I should feel bad when it's the guys who come after me and not the other way around. Like in the bathroom at your wedding, the manager of that financial company that worked with Michael, the married one … ? We did it there. And it was there that he told me about the company closing due to insider trading, and he gave up names; I didn't even have to ask. Yes, it led to prosecutions, but that wasn't my fault. I was a journalist getting a story, whose facts happened to be very true; it just happened to be delivered through sex. I want to feel bad, but I don't. I appreciate being here, primarily just to escape, because I think my only cure will be understanding and feeling love. I don't think you can provide that as a therapy solution, so I'm not being skeptical or anything, I just know right now I'm taking a much-needed break from what has become my life, and that's it for me."

I don't know how long Neekoo took; her candle had burned out long before she finished, but none of us had interrupted her. The room was dead silent even as she finished. She looked at us and shrugged her shoulders, and we all just sat there trying to wrap our heads around everything we had just heard. Toni went and got us some tea.

Willow gave some assurances. "Neekoo, I need you to know right now that you are loved. When I look at these girls, they love you with no conditions; you have to let them love you, though. I am not making excuses for your mother. I wouldn't dare. But I am guessing that she was abused in some way when she was young and silenced herself, and she found a need to silence you, even though what she should have done is break the cycle. As strange as it sounds, by getting something out of the act, you have empowered yourself, and if you were to have a daughter, I believe you wouldn't silence her in the same way. What I would like to see, though, is you empowering yourself in a healthier way, and I am hoping you will give us a chance to let you see how it is possible to do so. It is by no mistake that the four of you have ended up as friends."

Willow had us all hold hands as we sat in our circle, and she whispered something in the ear of BJ, who was sitting closest to her; BJ in turn whispered it to Sierra, Sierra to Neekoo, and Neekoo back to me. The phrase was, "I am becoming the best me." I smiled reflectively. Once the phrase had made it around the room, Willow released us with, "We have done a lot for one night and need to rest through some of the revelations we've made. Please drink the chamomile tea that you'll be getting shortly. It will help you settle your racing minds tonight. Make it an early night, ladies." She hugged each of us and exited the room.

ELEVEN — *Me, Myself and You*

We had cried so much during that group session that sleep was a remote idea when we got back to the cabin, even though it really should have been the first thing we did. Instead, at one in the morning, we nursed our cups of tea and just talked.

"Shit! I can't believe I just admitted to you guys that I trust Vernon. You cannot tell him that I said that," exclaimed Sierra, realizing that she had just made a huge revelation to herself and all of us in that moment.

"It's not like you said you loved him, Sierra," said BJ. Sierra was silent.

"Oh my gosh, she loves him," said Neekoo in a calm voice that bore a hint of surprise. We all looked to Sierra for confirmation. She gave none, but looked down into her tea with a smile on face.

"You really think you love him?" I asked her under my breath, still not knowing how to feel about the actual idea of Sierra and Vernon together.

"Yes, I really think I'm in love with him," she confirmed in a whisper that all of us heard. She needed a Vernon in her life, I thought in deep reflection. Vernon was a Michael. He would love without condition.

"For starters, nothing I do bothers him," answered Sierra with a tinge of playful annoyance, and then she said to me, "Doesn't that annoy you?"

"Oh it bothers him, he just doesn't let anything fester. So while you're thinking about how he's going to respond to something you might have done to upset him, he's moved on from it. He won't discuss any of the little stuff because he doesn't see the point—oh, and he's almost always right about the big stuff."

"That's exactly what Sierra needs. Someone who won't sweat all *her* small stuff," said BJ.

"Oh please, I'm not that bad," said Sierra, defending herself.

"Yeah, and you don't have to listen to yourself, Sierra," said Neekoo.

"Whoa." BJ and I reacted in unison to Neekoo's jab. She barely took any jabs at any of us, and definitely not Sierra. Sierra laughed.

"So you guys have been carrying on an unrelationship relationship, long-distance thing for how many years now?" asked BJ.

"It looks like it's been about four years now. I hadn't even paid attention to how long it's been," answered Sierra.

"How did you guys pull this off without Rory suspecting a thing?" asked Neekoo.

"I know, I can't imagine she didn't suspect anything between the two of you," said BJ.

"It has almost slipped a few times," Sierra reflected.

They hadn't bothered lying, for example, about a trip they had both made to Fiji. Sierra had told me she was leaving for a conference at the time and gave me the dates because, between myself and Neekoo, she needed her house watched. Vernon had told me about his trip to Fiji at the same time, and I hadn't even put the two together. I had mentioned Sierra's trip to him: "You know Sierra's going to Fiji as well for some conference. You guys should get together for lunch or something," I said.

"We'll see. I'll be pretty busy," Vernon said. Sierra told of countless more incidents, and we all had a good laugh at how the two of them had been able to pull the wool over our eyes without exactly trying. It was easy not to be suspicious—in my wildest thoughts, I wouldn't have put the two of them together. They were both headstrong and living states away from each other; there was no reason to suspect that they snuck away together every now and then. *Wow*, was all I could think. I made a mental note to find out from Vernon why he thought he couldn't mention his "thing" with Sierra to me.

As if hearing my mental note, Sierra said, "And neither of us thought it was necessary to tell you, Rory. We never knew what to call what we did, and it wasn't always consistent." My response was a shrug and a questioning look in my eye when I asked, "Is it a relationship now?"

"Boy ..." Sierra sighed. "I don't know, but I don't think so."

"You don't—" I started to say, but Sierra cut me off with, "Hold on, moving on from me, Neekoo. Just for my curiosity, a couple of those guys in your past? How was Senator McGuire? He seems too uptight!"

"Sierra! Seriously?" cautioned BJ.

"Forget the last part of what she said," I said, shaking my head. "But seriously, do you want to talk about any of it?"

"I don't even know," said Neekoo, brushing Sierra's statement off with a dismissive wave. "It happened so long ago that I think it has partly defined who I am. It will sound weird, but I learned to find something positive from the rapes."

BJ started shaking her head with subtle defiance and quietly said, "I'm sorry, Neekoo, what was the positive lesson here?"

"Being numb to anything negative," answered Neekoo. She continued explaining how she rationalized her past. "When you are forced against your will to be there, it's tough the first time around, but after a few times, you learn to escape your own body. More importantly, I learned how not to feel."

"Wow," I breathed out. My eyes were tearing again. Long gone were the judgments I held of Neekoo. Not only did her words explain her actions that became the cause of her recent investigation, it really did explain her entire relationship with us as a friend. She was never the one to blow her lid, always the one amicable to any plan we had. It *all* made sense.

"Aren't you in essence invisible?" BJ asked.

Neekoo smiled. "No, not really." And to no one in particular, in an almost distant voice, Sierra said, "There are advantages to being invisible."

Neekoo's past was the primary topic of choice for the rest of our night. It led to her talking about some of the sex-capades that she had had with some very important, and some not so important but information-valuable men in politics and business. We talked till five thirty in the morning, and an hour later we had to join everyone else.

The weekend that marked the end of our second week and the beginning of the third week was a relaxing one. We didn't have to attend any individual sessions and only had group therapy once each day. Our weekend had our regular schedule of early morning yoga and a gym workout, as well as our evening workouts, but a few things were different.

First, on Saturday starting in the earlier half of the day, we got to do an obstacle course on the grounds of the center; most of us were hopeless at it, but we had fun. We were split into teams of five, with the winners getting a prize of their choice of Swedish or hot stone full-body massage therapy for ninety minutes, while the losers would only get foot massages.

Neekoo didn't want to be on our team and almost ditched us as she was so sure that we weren't going to push ourselves athletically to win. She was kind of right, but thankfully she stuck with us, because as sure as she felt about us, we were also sure that having her on our team would be an advantage. Dorothy asked to join us, and with Tim Anderson, one of the fitness instructors as our obstacle course guide, we were ready to go.

Neekoo was a quiet storm drill sergeant, yelling out words or orders of encouragement during the solo tasks. Sierra noticed Tim encouraging Neekoo, which Sierra translated as flirting. When Neekoo went on her solo task, Sierra went to Tim and with a killer smile on her face, all she said was, "If you really do like her, don't try it. Just don't try anything, okay?" and she walked away. I was standing closest to them so I saw it all, and I almost laughed when I saw his face—he was entirely caught off guard.

Not even Neekoo could fault us for coming in second, because she was impressed by how far we pushed ourselves. Thanks to Sierra, Tim—who had been cheering Neekoo on a bit more boisterously than he did the rest of us—gave a more subdued congratulations to Neekoo, who hugged him in return.

"You think she really likes him?" asked BJ.

"*He* looks like he really likes her," I chipped in.

But Sierra said, "Or maybe he just wants to do her. He better leave her alone."

"Well, he seems nice," said BJ.

"I don't think I want her finding someone while in treatment. How about when she gets out, then what?" stated Sierra with disapproval. Neekoo was heading back our way, so we suspended our conversation. Even though we had lost, the smile on her face could have lit a dark room.

"I think he's cute," she gushed slightly, reminiscent of a high school crush.

As the winning team was headed toward the main house to get their prize, we headed back to our cabin to take showers since our foot massages weren't for another hour. Once back in the room, Neekoo filled us in on what had been going on between herself and Tim, that we hadn't even been aware of.

"Okay, I didn't say anything to you guys, because I didn't want you to think it was about sex," started Neekoo.

"Well, have you had sex with him?" asked Sierra bluntly.

I shoved Sierra. "For a therapist who knows how to restrain herself when necessary, to ask the right questions at the right time and listen at the right time, you really do not hold your tongue sometimes!"

Neekoo ignored both of us and kept talking. "See that's just it. He's different. I'm actually hoping he's not just attracted to me for potential sex. Spending time with him has meant something. We've just done the cute stuff, you know?"

"Like what?" pressed BJ, wanting details.

"It's the slight touches when I let him think he's helping me on the machines. The holding of hands when we are on the trail and hoping that nobody can see us. The talks in the café room as I sometimes wait on you guys to finish your solo therapy sessions. I know what his voice sounds like. I know it's little, but it's not something I typically pay attention to," continued Neekoo.

"When did this start?" asked Sierra.

"Only the beginning of this week," answered Neekoo.

"Don't you think it's too soon? You sound like you're falling for him," cautioned Sierra.

"I don't know what it is, but honestly, I like it," responded Neekoo. "I'm not going to have sex with him, Sierra; I'm going to see where it goes."

"You know what you're doing, right Neekoo?" I asked.

"I don't, but it's the first time that I can say that about a guy, and I think that's a good thing for me. And of course, I need you guys to keep this silent for me. I don't want him to lose his job," Neekoo appealed.

BJ had gone back to get ready to take her shower and called out to us, "Guys, we've got a message on our pillows."

We all went back to our rooms to see what was on our beds. There were a number of items. Notepad, pens and pencils, as well as envelopes were neatly tucked by our pillows, together with a handwritten note. All our notes said the same thing:

Hey Ladies,

You are doing an amazing job with your journey. It's been refreshing to observe you experience some of your admissions and revelations with yourselves, as well as the trust you have put in yourselves and others. Our next task for you is a healthy step to get you even closer to your goal here. At the end of your third week here, we hope to have you address some past issues with the person that you feel contributed to a downward turn in connection with that issue.

We are asking you to write three letters over the weekend to help you gather your thoughts and better articulate them at the time of the meeting. The first two letters should be to the people you want to address. We will be bringing in one of these people to a group session at the spa. The third letter is to yourself. Reflect on who you have been and who you hope to grow into after you've shed some of the demons that brought you here or that propelled loved ones to get you here.

Your self-actualization letter should be sealed in the envelope provided and dated for you to open it in no less than five years from now. Please have your two letters ready for your solo therapy sessions on Monday, and in the spirit of cleansing, speak your mind!

Love,
Willow

I think I got the point behind writing the letters, but thinking about what my content would be gave me some anxiety. I needed to know if the other girls were feeling the same way. "Hey, do you know who you'll be writing your letters to?" Sierra and Neekoo were in the living room with me, and BJ was stepping out of the shower.

"Girl, I can't think about those letters right now," said Sierra.

"I know! That's just another heavy assignment right now. Not in the mood," said Neekoo, who got up to get some water in the kitchen area. Still in her towel and blotting her hair, BJ added, "I'm with you on that, Neekoo. I'm not in the mood for anything heavy right now. I think I know who I want to write one of my letters to, and I am not mentally prepared for that."

We had the rest of the weekend to write the letters, so having expressed our immediate feelings about the new assignment, we decided not to give it any more thought. Instead, we showered and headed over to the Commons, where we had been asked to gather for a special group therapy session. When we entered the Commons, we were treated to fresh flowers, and jasmine and lavender-scented candles all through the room. Willow came in dressed in a well-suited cream-and-pink dress and black kitchen apron with the top flap of the apron down. When she turned on the projector and we saw the screen, we couldn't contain our excitement. On the screen was Pink Bailey's logo centered at the top, and right below it was "A Night with Star Chef, Bailey Johnson, Courtesy of Pink Bailey's, Washington, DC."

Everyone was excited. We were making our own dinner that day, a la cooking class with BJ. BJ had actually known about the plan for a couple of days as Willow had planned it with her.

The Commons adjoined the main kitchen, so it was easy to convert it into a cooking-friendly space. There were stations set up in rows of two down the middle of the long room, and we were paired two to a station, with each one of our monogrammed aprons already at the station. The entire cooking session took over two hours, but no one really noticed the time.

BJ took the group through preparations of stuffed Portobello caps, baked chicken, and grilled salmon. Each was presented against penne pasta and garnished with asparagus and yellow and red bell peppers. The secret was in the three sauces that went with our dishes, which were signatures to Pink Bailey's. Our dessert was a large carrot cake designed with the words "Two more to go!" and fourteen candles on it. It was wheeled out after our meal and was greeted with applause when we all saw what was written on the cake.

Sunday, the beginning of week three, we started early morning as usual with what felt like military physical training for some of us—I was one of those. I pushed myself even harder than my trainer pushed me, and my legs didn't like me for it, but I noticed all the firmness. Although they weren't going to take any of my measurements until the second to last day that we were there, I knew I had lost some weight and felt good about my body. For the first time, I actually began to admit that I thought I had sexy legs.

Beyond our early workout, not much was planned for us to do that day so I thought it would be a perfect day to get down to writing my letters. We were still going to engage in one group therapy session in the afternoon, but that was pretty much it. I went walking the grounds, looking for a good spot to write in. I wasn't the only one with this idea; I passed Neekoo, who was sitting against an oak tree with music in her ears and notepad in hand, focused on her task at hand. I didn't disturb her, as she hadn't seen me pass by. I walked a little further and stopped by the two stone benches that were by the creek. I had brought along a blanket and placed it a few feet away from one of the benches and lay down to start writing. Nothing came to me.

The first and only person I thought of writing to was my father, but I didn't know exactly what I wanted to say to him. It was tough; I had a father in my life, but not a relationship, and I had accused myself of being selfish for seeking that out when I knew of too many who didn't even have a father in their lives.

'Aaaggghhh' was the long mental scream that went through my head as I crossed out the many starting lines on my notepad. I had to get this written. I already knew what I wanted from myself in five years so that one, I hoped, would be a breeze. Finally, I started.

Hey Dad,

I'm sitting on the lush grass of the grounds at the Willow Spa and Sanctuary where Michael and Vernon sent me, Neekoo, Sierra, and BJ to "work on ourselves." Part of our treatment required us to write these letters. Why are you getting this? It is probably unfair of me to blame you for anything, but I need to express to you how I have seen our relationship from my end.

It is clear to me that I came into this world knowing I wanted to be a daddy's girl. It's a feeling that has engulfed me from as early as I can remember, but I have always felt that you have always wanted a buddy. Since you had that in Vernon, you had no real time for me unless, of course, I was engaged in any of the buddy activities. Like the time you took Vernon to a pro-football game and let me tag along. I sat between the two of you, but each time your team scored a touchdown, you would reach over me to high-five Vernon. I wasn't really interested in many of the activities, but it was a way for me to get your attention.

Thanks to you, I would do justice to a retelling of the legend of Vince Lombardi, but I wanted my dad to tell me once that I was beautiful, once that he loved me, once that I could do no wrong in his eyes. I still needed to hear it. I believe that not getting that from you influenced what I expected others to think of me through the years.

I'm okay, and there's no blame here. In fact, I probably wouldn't have said anything to you if

I wasn't asked to write this letter, so really it's not something that I harbor inside of me, it was just a desire of what I wanted that turned into feelings of how I later felt.

I love you,
Aurora

The letter that I was supposed to write to myself truly summed up the person I wanted to be celebrating in a few years. Instead, I wrote the letter to Bella. I told her who I was and who I wanted to become, and how I hoped she also would love and be proud of me.

Hey Bella!

I am in the third week of my four-week stay at a place called Willow's Spa and Sanctuary, and I want to first tell you why I am here. No matter how old you are when you are reading this, try to understand that it is hard for me to write this and not see your baby face, as you will always be my baby. Daddy and Uncle Vernon felt that I and your three aunties (who you will come to know as my dearest friends in life) needed some time by ourselves to bond within ourselves and with each other. We are at this treatment center, which means each of us had some "issues" that we needed to address. My issue has been my body image.

I have no idea what body you are going to grow into, but I need you to know now and forever that you are truly beautiful. Your spirit even now as a little girl soars, and your body will emulate your soul. When I was younger, I struggled with my body because I looked nothing like most of the girls that I went to school with, and they teased me because of it. I mostly struggled with it by myself and didn't really express how I was feeling with my parents until my mom stepped in. It was nice of her to do that because it forced me to really start realizing that there was nothing wrong with me. However, it didn't change within me a desire to be slimmer than the size I was.

My greatest resentment at the time, I would say, was wishing I was a daddy's girl and having my dad protect me from all these mean girls and tell me how beautiful he thought I was. As of the time that I am writing this letter, I have written him one as well, expressing to him that I wished we had a better relationship than we did. I believe we'll achieve that relationship or at least a better understanding of each other, and that's a good thing. You, however, are growing up to be the most confident girl I know, and you're only three! You have a father who adores you, and a mother who doesn't mind taking a backseat to you, because I am just so happy that you feel like you are on top of the world, just about every single minute of the day. Until recently, you smile even when you are asleep.

I am already heading in that direction, so I know that by the time you get this letter, if I haven't already done so by then, I'll be falling in love with my body and my image no matter what it is. I was made to realize this past week that I need to focus on all the good things about me. I know that by the time our relationship shifts more into the friendship stage, I will be nothing less than the most positive version of who I am now, and will hopefully instill that positivity in you as well.

> I am so happy, as I write this letter—who knew writing a letter could make you so happy, right?—because I now know I am beautiful because I was able to help make something as beautiful as you.
>
> Thanks for letting me love me,
> Mom

I was actually reading my letter to Bella out loud as I was writing it and wrote it through smiles and tears of joy. I was euphoric. It may have been the feeling that ensued from writing the letter, and the sunny even though slightly cold fall day, didn't hurt. I was skipping on the inside as I walked back toward the cabin. My faults were plenty, but screw them. I felt perfectly "me" right now, and that felt good.

"Did you finish writing your first two letters?" BJ inquired of me as I got back to the cabin.

"Yes, to myself and my dad."

"I wrote both my mom and my sperm donor—"

"Your mom?" I interrupted.

"I don't want *him* to come, but I needed to write it down to get some of that anger toward him out of my system. I am hoping they don't find him, so I wrote to my mother as well, since there are some questions I need to ask her that I haven't had the guts to ask. I just feel she was dealt a bad hand from the beginning, so I didn't feel I had the right to ask her my questions."

I understood her rationale, and I guess this was the safest environment for BJ to get her thoughts across to her mother without burdening herself with guilt for addressing these issues. Something within me just felt that BJ's dad was going to be there, so I asked, "Hypothetically, if your dad shows up …" I paused because she was shaking her head negatively.

"Just think about it, let's say he shows up. We know they've said they're only bringing in one person for us to face. Will you still send the letter to your mom?" I continued.

"I hadn't thought about it," she responded.

"Wouldn't you still want her to see what you wrote?" I pressed. I felt that although BJ reserved her rage for her "father," there was some repressed anger there, and in my newfound sense of being, I thought it would be liberating for her to deal with the questions she had with her mother as well.

"Only if she were hearing it from me face-to-face. I wouldn't want her to misinterpret one word, because I really don't blame her for a single thing. But I don't know, I just want to ask her a few things about how she felt some of her decisions possibly affected me, you know?"

"I know."

"There's nothing like feeling like an unwanted child and not being able to totally shake that. I know *she* wanted me, or she wouldn't have kept me, but I have questions that I just haven't asked her. Can you believe we are just dealing with this stuff now?! Weren't we supposed to deal with all this emotional junk and figuring out who we were at much younger ages, and not when we are around the corner from thirty?" she said through a chuckle and using a tissue to dab the corners of her eyes.

"I know! I was just thinking the same thing myself. I guess you deal with it when you realize you need to, or when you are forced to. In either case, I guess it really happens when you stop lying to yourself." We both smiled at that last statement, I guess because we both knew how true it was and were indirectly admitting that it had been easier to bury ourselves in work, in catering to others, instead of looking within.

It was time to deal with the letters. Normally our emotional-breakdown sessions happened on Fridays, but this one they reserved for Saturday, and my guess was they were trying to accommodate our guests' schedules—who knows. We were in small groups together with our therapists. Toni gave us the rundown.

"Very shortly, we are going to meet one of the persons you wrote to. You are advised to read to them what you have written; however, if you find that you would rather address them directly, feel free to do so. Be genuine with your feelings. They are allowed to respond to anything you say, but we have advised them to refrain from interrupting you until you are done. It is important that a discussion for clarity happens between each pair, so one of us will facilitate that if necessary. So let's start."

I took a deep breath. We were asked to write letters to two people, I had written to one. I knew my guest had to be my father, so why did I feel so nervous? I looked around at Neekoo, Sierra, and BJ, and the least nervous looking among them was Sierra. She was leaning forward, elbows on her thighs with her face in her hands. BJ's left heel was tapping the floor intermittently, and Neekoo didn't know what to do with her hands.

Toni wasted no time. After her short spiel, she moved the divider that was separating us from our guests. They were in a semicircle just as we were and suddenly the level of nervous energy that I had felt in the air increased by a hundred percent. My dad was there. Neekoo's mom was there. Another man sat in the circle, and it was unmistakable who he was. BJ was the spitting image of the man sitting next to my dad. The last guy in the room had to be Sierra's dad.

Neekoo was sitting to my right, and her hands that had been fidgeting all over her body went to her stomach. I looked over to her and mouthed, "Are you okay?" She nodded and took in a deep breath. Sierra, who was sitting on Neekoo's right, managed a half smile.

Toni addressed us with, "At the back of each of your chairs there's a number, and that's the order in which you'll be going." As we each turned around to see the numbers, Toni looked in my direction and smiled. "Of course, I get to go first," I said with a thin smile on my face. I walked over to the podium that was placed at the end of our row of chairs. Walking up there, my head was jumbled with thoughts about how my father would receive what I had written. What if he didn't receive it well and thought that my perception of my relationship with him was totally unfounded? *Oh gosh,* I thought as I breathed in deeply, shrugged my shoulders slowly, and looked at my father. Seeing my father there was a bit tough.

I read my letter to him, looking down at the letter the whole time. I looked at him when I was finished, and in that moment as he shook his head slowly with a sad smile on his face, I knew he too wished we had talked a while back. When I finished the letter, he got up and spoke, and it was the most heartwarming I had ever seen or heard my father.

"When I got the letter from the center telling us that you were here and needed me to come for a visit, I immediately wondered why you hadn't asked for your mom. Then I kept reading, and the wording said you needed me there to close a chapter in your life, and then I felt I had done something wrong. I am so proud of both you and Vernon, but I'm afraid I made the same mistake my father made with me. As you know, your grandfather was a Marine, and he was just one of those men who didn't believe in showing emotions, and it was easy to become less expressive in a house full of boys. Then you came along. I promised myself that I would be more expressive than my dad was with me, and with Vernon that was easy. The truth is, I didn't quite know what to do with you. I'm sorry. Aurora, I have loved you since the day you were born, and I didn't want to ruin you, so I thought you were better served being closer to your mom—and if I must say so, I have always thought it has served you well. I thought I would just ruin you, and now I find I've failed you, I …" He broke down in loud, uncontrollable sobs.

My extremely macho, military-bred father broke down. My eyes widened, my heart was thumping, threatening to burst out of my chest. I tried standing, but my knees were shaking and my legs just wouldn't hold me up. I fell back into my chair. I was shaking my head and crying as I said, "You didn't fail me. I just didn't know how you felt." My dad was by my side, his knees on the floor, as he hugged me tightly and we both cried.

My dad leaned back and asked, "You really didn't think I loved you?" I didn't want to say it, but I did: "I knew it. I didn't feel it." My dad sighed deeply into his palms and in a muffled voice said, "Then I failed you. Wow, how did this all happen?"

Toni came around and crouched in between my dad and me. She was rubbing our backs when she said, "This is good. It's clear you both needed this, and there's a lot more talking that needs to happen here. We're going to take you back for an individualized session once we're done with group, okay?" Then Toni led my dad back to his seat. As I watched him walking back to his seat, I felt guilt ridden. Perhaps if I had found a way to say something to my dad, we'd have sorted this out a long time ago, I thought. I felt I only had myself to blame.

Sierra's number was next. Before Sierra started, as I blotted my eyes with a tissue, I looked to my left where BJ, I suspected, was involved in her own internal dialogue and wasn't entirely present for the occurrences in the room. Her eyes were intense, lips downturned, and her head was shaking slowly. Her eyebrows raised once, and now with legs crossed over each other, her right leg did not stop shaking. My feeling was that BJ definitely didn't want to do hers, and she was angry. I only hoped that her anger would subside enough for her to be able to get through this exercise.

Sierra chose to go to the podium. Her steps were labored, and when she got there, she unfolded her letter, put on her glasses that she wore sparingly, and held on to the podium. I smiled; she actually looked like she was about to deliver a speech or give a lecture. From the moment she started reading, each time she looked up, her eyes were fixed on her dad and never wavered.

Dad,

I normally refer to you as Mr. Snowden, because for a while there, I considered myself

> an orphan. You are, however, the only father I have, take it or leave it. I don't know where you are in your life now, and before coming here, I didn't care. I'm here because I've been addicted to prescription pills for years, and of course, the ironic part is the fact that I am a therapist who listens to others and tries to wean them off their fears and propel them to deal with their issues. I blame you for my mother's death. I think you've known that.

Sierra looked up and tilted her head and gave him a knowing glance. She didn't wait for a response but kept reading her letter.

> I think I will always blame you for that. I hated you and wanted nothing to do with you for years, and as we both know, I have been successful with the latter. However, since having to face my own dependency, I realize that I was just like you, and strangely, I began to understand a little bit, even though I still hate the outcome of your addiction. Many years ago, I heard through Grandma Iris that you were sober, and I just want to know from you, are you still addicted to alcohol?

He started in a slightly crackling voice, and then coughed to clear out his throat to continue his response. "I have been ashamed for so many years and couldn't show my face around you and your brothers. I thought I could beat it on my own initially, but then I got together with a good Alcoholics Anonymous group, and can now say that I have been sober for ten years and nine months, today."

Sierra looked down at her paper, took off her glasses, and walked over to her dad. She said to him in the most loving tone, "Then I forgive you."

It was a reflex action, but I clapped. I was the only one at first, but then others joined me. With all the emotions that I was going through with this exercise, I just felt so much pride for Sierra. Sierra and her dad hugged. Sierra wasn't quite in tears, but no matter how much her dad tried to stifle them, the tears fell down his face. When they stopped hugging, veiled with a smile, Mr. Snowden made a painful admission, "I haven't hugged my only daughter in almost two decades," and with that, they both broke down in tears. When they hugged again, he kept repeating, "Thank you, thank you." It must have been hard for him, I thought. Sierra was a spitting image of her mother and having to look into those eyes and that face that was a stark reminder of what had shaken their family years ago, couldn't have been easy.

I marveled at Sierra; the girl was one of a kind. Her letter was unexpected as there was no trace of the bashful Sierra, but I was even more pleasantly surprised by her reaction to her dad. Her therapist went over to give her a bear hug when she was walking back to her seat, and she quietly said to Sierra, "I am really proud of you."

Neekoo chose not to get up. Her head was down as she started reading her letter in a matter-of-fact tone.

> Mother,
>
> That is not a fair term to call you, but biology outwits semantics here. You have been a glorified legal guardian who has pretty much carried out her duties, nothing more. That is what I knew as a mother, and that's not good enough. You were home; it was the perfect opportunity for us to bond. I was your only girl, yet you had eyes only for my brothers. You made me serve them, cater to their every whim. I pity their wives right now, because they know how to do nothing on their own. I never complained and found out only in college how much I resented that, when I realized

> how much time I was spending cleaning up after them, when in college I spent less than a third of that time cleaning up after myself.
>
> None of that was too bad, but the day I told you what had happened to me … Do you remember you slapped me? How could you slap me? How could you? Where was the mother in you, even if I was lying?

There was anger in Neekoo's voice, and she was in tears. Still she didn't look up once, to see her mother shaking her head continuously and whispering something under her breath as she dabbed the tears from her own eyes.

> I was raped. Your reaction silenced me for the future times that I was raped, and why would I come back to you, when you nonverbally blamed me?

For the first time, Neekoo looked up and directly at her mom.

> Look at me, I am beautiful. But for so many years back then, no matter how good I was in school, no matter how many writing awards I got, I was worthless, and that had to be the only reason why a guy would rape me and my own mother blame me. So that's what I did, I had sex with so many people. I've slept with so many men because I knew that's all a guy wanted from me, and eventually I started using it to get something from them too. I have herpes, Mom, and I don't know who gave it to me. Sadly I probably gave it to a few of them without knowing it, and I'm going to bear that burden for the rest of my life.

Sierra, BJ, and I were frozen. We weren't being judgmental; it just wasn't anything we would have expected to hear in a million years. I clutched my heart and didn't let go. Sierra turned and looked at me with a raised eyebrow and then back at Neekoo. It looked as if this was the only time BJ was fully present in the room, because her fidgeting stopped as she raised her eyebrows at Neekoo's news. It seemed as if the more negative layers Neekoo peeled off, the more there were.

> I have felt empty and devoid of love, and more so, unworthy of love. But I don't want to be me anymore, I don't want to be you, and no matter how long it takes, I'm going to accomplish that goal.
>
> Neekoo

Sierra and Dallas went over to Neekoo, who assured them she was all right. Toni, who was moderating the whole session, looked over to Mrs. Rahul and asked her if she had anything to say. Neekoo's mom, who had been trickling out tears the entire time her daughter was talking, got up. In slightly broken, but understandable English, she held one hand over the other fist and said, "I love my daughter. I love her. How can she say this? How can she say this about me? When did all this stuff happen?"

"Are you kidding me? You don't remember slapping me after I told you what happened with Mr. Armin?" It was the loudest we had ever heard Neekoo's voice.

"I don't remember, I really don't remember," responded Neekoo's mother, shaking her head.

"This is some bullshit!" Neekoo jumped up and walked behind her seat. The Neekoo before our stay at the spa would not have had this type of outburst. With her own self-admission, she would have mentally escaped by now. This time, she stayed in the moment.

Dallas tried calming her down, saying quietly to Neekoo, "She probably remembers things a little differently, that's all."

"How the hell is she remembering things differently? She wasn't the one raped! This woman is crazy! She's acting like none of that stuff happened! Do you know how that makes me feel?"

"I would have done something if I knew my daughter was raped," interrupted Neekoo's mom, and with that, Neekoo who was still standing, briskly walked out of the room. In fact, she was almost running. The door almost slammed in Sierra's face as she followed close behind Neekoo. Dallas went over to Neekoo's mom and accompanied her out to another room.

Toni continued the session. "Bailey, do you want to read your letter now?"

Through dismissive laughter, BJ responded, "I don't even think it's necessary." She continued without being prompted, primarily talking to Toni but referring to the stranger in the room. "I mean, I don't even know who this man is, and unlike Neekoo, I don't mean that figuratively." The sarcasm in BJ's voice was biting.

"I know he looks like me, and that's how I guessed he was my father years ago when I saw him and his family in San Diego, acting all cool. I have a sperm donor, I don't have a father, and I was hoping you would bring my mom here, not him." There were no tears from BJ as she spoke, and her words were sometimes lined with sarcasm.

"Can I say something?" asked Martin Holmes.

Toni gave him the go-ahead with a nod.

"I was young and stupid," he started to explain.

"That's not something you have to admit to anyone in this room," responded BJ.

"I was scared," Mr. Holmes said.

"Don't you mean weak? Scared is pregnant with a baby, being pretty much homeless, and not knowing what would happen," BJ interrupted yet again.

"BJ … can I call you BJ?" Mr. Holmes asked. BJ rolled her eyes but didn't answer.

"I can only imagine how you feel about what happened, but he came here for you, so try to hear him out, unless you still want to address him first," tried Toni.

"I have to hear him out? Oh, how great," said a resigned BJ. She decided instead to read her letter.

> Well, Mr. Martin P. Holmes,
>
> I have fantasized about every negative term that the *P* should stand for. Apart from all the obvious reasons, I hate you because of what you have birthed within me. Your lack of action when it meant the most to my mother has me distrusting every man, but especially when it comes to my romantic partners. I have the most amazing man in my life who has made it clear to me that he wants to spend the rest of his life with me, but I am filled with distrust that one day he will walk away, just like you did. It took you less than six months. I thought even if it took him six years, nonetheless it would happen; he would walk away, even though he has done nothing to make me feel that way. I don't trust men—thank you for that.
>
> That is the legacy you left with me, and I don't want anything to do with you for that reason. I don't want some long-lost father in my life. I don't want to know you, because you didn't want to know me.

It was only then that BJ started crying, but her anger was still clear in her voice when she resumed reading.

> When I was on vacation with a few friends, I saw your daughter and your son, and if I had

> anything to say to them, I would tell them that their father is an impostor. I hope you tell your son not to follow in your footsteps, and your daughter to be wary of men like you. I will learn to trust the man in my life because I know he deserves better, but from you, I don't need or want a single thing.
>
> Yours truly,
> Sabine Johnson's daughter

Holmes's head was in his hands as BJ finished reading her short letter. Toni asked if he had anything to say, and he shook his head, eventually quietly saying, "No." He tried, but he couldn't speak. "Wow," he managed to exclaim. He took off his glasses and pressed his thumb and forefinger into the corner of his eyes. His shoulders quivered as he continued to stifle the tears that were falling, and he couldn't stop shaking his head. It was a sight to see. Perhaps he now saw the damage that he had done and the lifelong consequence of his one dismissive action.

My heart went out to both of them, but my allegiance was with BJ. I wanted to go over to her, but Willow who was already sitting by BJ, asked her if she wouldn't mind them having a one-on-one with her dad. "Don't call him my dad. I'll do it if you need me to, but just don't call him my dad," was the answer she gave.

Willow then went over to Mr. Holmes and asked him the same question, and he was open to it as well. Toni led my dad and me out of the room, and Lola took Sierra and her father. We were taken to other rooms to begin our individualized sessions.

Neekoo did not want to have this session with her mom and Dallas, and she said so: "I think this is a bit pointless. As long as she keeps claiming to not know, I don't want to hear what she has to say about my issues." She stood in the hallway that led to the different therapy rooms, reluctant to follow Dallas. With her hand on Neekoo's back, Dallas said, "Let's go in and see what happens, shall we?" Neekoo shook her head, and reluctantly went into the room.

When Neekoo told us later on at dinner how things went in the room, it was clear that she chose to revert back to escaping her issues mentally if not physically. She fought going back into her routine by resisting having the session with her mom, but she gave in.

Dallas had asked Neekoo's mom to imagine that perhaps she had perceived things differently or even forgotten. She needed Neekoo's mom to allow for the fact when something as victimizing as rape happens to someone and they react in the way Neekoo has, rarely if ever is it made up. Neekoo's mom continued to deny ever knowing. Dallas couldn't get a word out of Neekoo through the rest of the session. Neekoo didn't run out, but mentally, she was no longer there.

Trying to end things as amicably as she could, Dallas had asked if they were open to exploring more therapy sessions somewhere down the road to deal with this issue. Mrs. Rahul said emphatically, "Yes. Yes, anything for my daughter." Neekoo wore a smirk on her face, and that was the extent of her response. As Mrs. Rahul left the room, she motioned to Neekoo for a hug. Neekoo did hug her mother and shook her head afterward.

Dallas wanted to check in with Neekoo after her mother left and asked her to stay.

"How are you feeling about all of this?"

"Disappointed, but not surprised," said Neekoo.

"How important is it to you that your mom admits that she dismissed the initial rape?"

Neekoo took in a deep breath first. "It's tough now, but I can't let it derail the progress I feel I have made here. If I have to make peace with the reality that she may never come to terms with her denial of my rape, I'll deal with it. I'll tell myself that she suffers from dementia or something, but not right now."

"That's good. That's really good," said Dallas, giving her approval. "Now let's join everyone for dinner."

When my father and I met with Toni for our one-on-one, I wished I could have taken my entire letter back. I regretted now that my father felt that he had failed me. Toni addressed him first. "I've got to let you know that in meeting you and even without meeting your wife, I am now sure that Rory gets her determined will from you." My heart leaped, and I thanked her from within. I didn't know why she said it, or how she meant it, but I interpreted it just one way. In likening a trait of mine to my father, there's no way he could have failed me. Her statement also got him talking.

"Yes, she is determined. I remember her mother telling me about her search for a university and how she steered the entire process. I knew she'd get it done." Then he turned to me and said, "Rory, please find it within you to understand that I thought the best thing for you was to stay out of your way, and I now know there's something wrong with that. Maybe I'm the one who needed intervention." I smiled; it was a liberating sentiment to hear from him.

Her ever-bubbly self, Toni offered, "So let's agree that you are not to stay out of the way, Mr. Glazer! Your role is to get right in there, and I'm going to be here to show you how. Trust me, *I'm* not staying out of the way." My dad chuckled and said to me, "We're okay?"

"Yes, Dad, we're okay."

"From now on, don't give me the option not to communicate with you when you need me to. We've got to figure out what our language will be, okay?"

"I will—I promise that I will," I said, nodding my head.

"And Aurora …" He paused. "I never thought I had to say it, but you have always been beautiful to me." I shyly leaned my head into my raised right shoulder, shaking my head to fight back tears and then shared a long, tight hug with my dad. Afterward, we headed to the main room for dinner.

Sierra's session with her dad and Lola was cathartic, she told us. I imagined the meeting between them going very differently, especially knowing how close she was to her mother, but it was clear that becoming an addict herself gave her new perspective.

At dinner, Neekoo joined my dad and me at our table, since we were the first ones there. I noticed Mrs. Rahul was gone, and Neekoo was happier for it. I asked her how she was. She brushed off any deeper inquiries with a quick, "I'm fine," and started talking to my dad about Bella—especially her new best friend, Neekoo's dog. To my surprise, my dad kept a picture of Bella in his wallet, and so did Neekoo, so Bella became the topic of our discussion while we waited for more of the groups to join us.

BJ came back by herself. She had refused to meet with Willow and her dad after the group session; instead she went for a walk.

"You okay?" Sierra inquired.

"I just don't think it's fair that someone can make a decision like that with no real consequences," was BJ's answer.

Sierra's father overheard the discussion and decided to offer BJ a different perspective.

"I know this might not help you much, but that's not true. Just because you don't see the consequences doesn't mean that they aren't there. He's paying for it somehow. If he wasn't, he wouldn't have showed up. If the call he got was anything like mine, there was nothing pretentious about it. They told me that there was opportunity for me to rekindle a relationship with my daughter. And I was told that some of the things I would hear could be hurtful, but they really needed me there to help my daughter complete a needed cleansing exercise. Like me, he still had the option not to show up, so the fact that he did means there's a void in his life too. He's suffering too, that much I can promise."

BJ didn't respond.

TWELVE—*Skinny women ARE*

We were leaving for one day, to be back for our last week at Willow's. BJ was coming home with me again.

"Have you spoken to him at least?" I asked her.

"Yes."

"Seriously BJ, have you spoken to him at all?" I asked again, not convinced she was being entirely truthful.

"I have. Probably not everything I wanted to say, but we've spoken a few times," she continued.

"That's good," I said.

"Yeah, I think so too," she responded.

"But you're not ready to see him yet?"

"No, not yet. I know he loves me, Rory, you know? You can't always tell with guys, but there's no question with him. I'm the one who needs to get with it. I love him—don't get me wrong—I don't think anyone else can tolerate me the way he does," said BJ with a light laugh. "He's the best for me, but I don't know if I'm the best for him."

"All I can say is, just be sure you let him make that decision; don't make it for him. That's only fair, okay?"

Everyone was asleep when we got to the Carter residence. BJ

went to set herself up in the guest room. I walked into our master bedroom, and I guessed that the other two Carters must have had an interesting night. Bella had sauce smeared on her cheek, and she lay against her dad's chest, dead asleep. The dog didn't even bark when I walked into the room, giving neither of my heavy sleepers a reason to get up. I wiped the sauce off her cheek, lifted Bella from her dad's arm, and tucked her in her own bed. I changed into a nightshirt and slipped into bed next to Michael. I wasn't sleepy, so I just lay there, thinking about a variety of things, but mostly how happy I was. I whispered "Thank you" to no one in particular, and Michael responded, "For what?"

"I thought you were asleep," I replied, not really expecting to hear a peep out of him.

"I heard you come into the room. That little girl brought me to my breaking point tonight, so I was too happy to oblige you taking her back to bed."

"Smart one. So what did you guys do that drove you to exhaustion?" I asked.

"Tonight she just wouldn't agree to eat unless I allowed her to eat in our bedroom, and I finally caved. Oh, and that was only after she insisted on helping me prepare dinner, some of which ended up on the floor, or in Tiger's bowl, so we started from scratch at least once. We finally ate around 10 p.m., and after she ate, she conked out, and I must have fallen asleep waiting to see if she was down for the count," Michael explained. "I've missed you," he added.

"Awww, I've missed you too, honey."

"I know we set this up, and I'm glad you guys did this, but I can't wait to have my wife back."

"She's here right now," I teased. That's all he needed. I got my brand of lovemaking from my husband that was reserved for extremely horny moments.

I woke up Sunday afternoon to Bella nestled against my back and the smell of some good cooking through the house. Michael was still in bed with us. BJ was cooking up a storm, and I got up to join her. Bella appeared in the kitchen shortly.

BJ had whipped up different types of eggs, potatoes, French toast, and crepes, together with fruit smoothies—which she knew I loved—and orange juice. I was going to playfully accuse her of destroying all my workouts in one afternoon, until I saw the servings she had for each one of us.

My entire dish could have fit into a small cereal bowl—the same as Bella's and hers. The biggest servings on the table were left for Michael, who hadn't come down yet. "Bella, go and get Daddy and let him know Aunty B made brunch for all of us," I said.

"Nope," she answered, nodding her head. "I'm going to stay here with you," Bella said, without budging. I kissed her on the forehead.

"Okay, I'll go," I said. And without a word, she came right behind me as I walked back up the stairs to get Michael.

"Change into your workout clothes before you come down," BJ called out to me. She was already in hers. I woke Michael up, got changed, and with Bella in tow, joined BJ for brunch. All BJ had was a handful of potatoes and tea.

"Okay, so I'm going to change now," announced Bella, running to her room. Bella came back with her tennis shoes and jogging outfit that we had bought for her that matched Michael's and mine. She was clapping excitedly when she came down the stairs. "I'm going to run, I'm going to run," she repeated over and over again. Fighting her on it would be fruitless. I got out her three-wheel jogger stroller, and we went out for a power walk. I apologized to BJ, who I know wanted to do a jog-run at least, but she dismissed my apology as unnecessary.

"Hey, you've been gone from her for three weeks. She's got the right to be demanding," said BJ. We spent the rest of the afternoon doing whatever Bella wanted to do, and BJ indulged her. That included baking cookies for Tiger, even though we told her the dog couldn't eat the cookies since we didn't feed the dog human food.

"Yes, she does," corrected Bella. "She eats my dinner with me sometimes."

This time we beat Sierra and Neekoo to Willow's, but only by a few minutes. Sierra drove herself there, and we asked where Neekoo was.

"She'll be here soon," was all Sierra said.

"You're not telling us something," pressed BJ, and all Sierra did was smile. Then she changed her mind and broke her silence. "Okay, you're going to find out shortly anyway, so I might as well spill the beans. Tim is going to drop her off, okay?"

"What!" I said excitedly. "I thought you had scared him off forever."

"I know. I thought so too, but literally as Neekoo was dropping me off, she got a call from him and they made plans for today. I could tell in his voice he really wants to get to know her, so I had to tell myself to lay off. I just hope she didn't jump his bones yet because as we now know, that's the sign that she's not that into you!" said Sierra.

Neekoo was coming in just as Sierra finished filling us in about Tim.

"Spill it, what did you guys do?" asked BJ.

"He didn't see the inside of your bedroom?" asked Sierra teasing more so than serious.

"If you knew all the places that I've done it in the past, you would know not to ask that," Neekoo responded with a light jab of her own.

"Oooh!" BJ and I exclaimed in unison.

"No, but seriously, I'm not going there with this one … not anytime soon," said Neekoo. She continued, "I had lived in the Washington, DC, area pretty much all my life, but I didn't realize that I had never even walked the national monuments. When he called last night, initially our plans were just for today, but instead he called back and suggested we take a midnight walk. He brought a flask of hot tea and pastries, and I know you're going to say this is cheesy, but we had a midnight picnic and had the most romantic walk through the national mall. We had our first kiss by the waterfalls at the FDR memorial, and I can still remember exactly how I felt with that first kiss. He has juicy lips." She said the last part slowly.

"Okay, stay away from all the sexual details, I haven't had my ration for months now," cautioned Sierra in a warning tone.

"So where did you spend the night?" asked Sierra.

"I haven't slept," giggled Neekoo.

"I can't believe it. This girl is going through the teenage love in her late twenties!" said BJ, shaking her head.

"We got back to my place around four in the morning, and we just sat in my living room and talked. When we realized that we had been talking through 8 a.m., we showered and then headed out for breakfast at Pink Bailey's."

"Okay, okay," said Sierra slowly, and with a hint of approval in her voice.

"We had been talking about you guys for a moment, so I told him he had to see where we would always go to as our safe haven, and he loved the food. We later went over to Neiman Marcus in Friendship Heights because tomorrow is his mother's birthday and he wanted to pick out a pair of diamond earrings for her. After that we had lunch, did some more walking and talking, and then headed over here. That's it," Neekoo finished.

"I think I like this guy," I said after Neekoo's narration of her date.

"Jumping the gun here, are we, Rory?" asked BJ with a disapproving raised eyebrow.

"I didn't say I love the guy," I said slightly defensively. "He just sounds like a good guy."

"Mmh," BJ responded without looking at me. I just smiled and dropped the subject. The most protective of Neekoo, I assumed BJ's tone showed her need to be even more watchful of

Neekoo's acquaintances since all the recent revelations of Neekoo's liaisons.

Sierra then added, "At least one of us got treated to a first-base-worthy date; now let's get to group, we're running a tad late, chicas." I smiled to myself, knowing I wasn't starving for any intimate relations.

We hadn't had time to unpack before joining the group session that evening since we had been talking, so Neekoo didn't realize until we were unpacking later on that night around ten thirty that the diamond earrings were for her.

"Oh, my gosh!" she exclaimed in genuine shock.

"What?" Sierra and I asked, wondering what the problem was. BJ creased her eyebrows as she looked in Neekoo's direction, nonverbally asking the same question.

"They were for me," she said in a quietly sweet tone, with her eyes glistening. As she put them on, I could see that they were beautiful teardrops. I glanced over at BJ with a raised eyebrow and pursed smile, trying to communicate with her that there just might be something there. We each told Neekoo how beautiful she looked in the earrings. She wore them the whole week.

During our last week at Willow's, we kept our regular schedule of workouts, group sessions, and team-building exercises, but all of it was fun this week. We all knew this was the last lap, and we had an extra burst of energy that fueled all our activities. We were having a ceremony on Friday, and they wanted us to invite as many people as possible to help celebrate our four-week journey. BJ and I were invited to help design our graduation with a limitless budget. We wanted each one of the twenty of us who had been through this journey to have a moment to say what they liked most and least about their stay, and then we just wanted everyone to have a great time. The color for the day was white and pink, so we asked Willow to get as many pink scarves as she could for all the women to accessorize their outfits with, so that we could all have something in common.

The end of the week came fast. Thursday evening we were

finishing our last solo sessions and were told by our therapists that they wanted us to change into bathrobes and meet at the auditorium at around seven in the evening. The auditorium was a multipurpose room where presentations and movies were shown; it had movable couches. When we walked in, it was dimly lit with candles all over, and there were blown-up pictures of us on the walls. I recognized mine from an anniversary dinner with Michael, and then I recognized a photographer from The Look and a few more members of the staff.

"Cynthia?"

"Hey, Rory! We've missed you!" said Cynthia, throwing her arms around me for a tight hug.

"Am I allowed to ask you what you are doing here?" I gave a suspicious look and shake of the head that I meant as *I don't know how I feel about you keeping something like this from me.*

"You have to be surprised with everyone else; sorry, babe, but you're going to love it," she said. She then touched my arm, and I felt her warmth. "We're okay about me not letting you know about Michael plotting your escape from work for an extended period of time, right?"

I wanted to ask questions. I wanted to know *specifically* what he had told her, but instead, with a reflective smile I said, "Of course we are," and I gave her a hug. It started as a light hug, but then she embraced me tighter. Right or wrong, I took that nonverbal reaction as the answer to my unasked questions.

Willow, Toni, and Dallas came in and got our attention. We were asked to go to the section of the auditorium where our names were, and that was the cue for stylists and makeup artists to come in and set up clothes, shoes, makeup, and accessories around us. We were having a makeover photo shoot. It helped to explain why in the past couple of days, they had taken our measurements. It was good enough for all of us just to know that many of us were in healthier shapes with increased flexibility, simply loving our bodies. Little did we know there was more.

Willow had contacted all the boutique owners she knew, as

well as buyers for some of the major fashion houses in Georgetown, and had matched our measurements with numerous outfits. She knew we had photographers at The Look and had called them. Cynthia orchestrated the rest. She contacted stylists she knew who wanted to be involved in giving us the gift of looking "you perfect" as Cynthia termed it.

We had fun playing dress up. The front of the auditorium was set up as the photography studio with lights and different canvasses. There was a documentary crew present, recording how this particular exercise made us feel about the whole program. It led into many of us also talking about our entire experience at Willow's, especially the stories about our first week there and how impossible we all thought this whole thing was going to be. We got to pick our favorite pictures from the shoots, which were going to go up side by side with our previous pictures on the wall. With sparkling cider and water to quench our thirsts through the shoot, many of us felt like full-on divas for one beautiful evening.

The next morning, our last day at the center, our favorite outfit from the night before was hanging right outside our doors, with the note "Because every woman is deserving" attached and a jewelry box that enclosed a diamond tennis bracelet. I had never asked who was footing the bill for the four of us, and I am sure that between Michael, Vernon, and DeLuca, they could afford it, but I said to Sierra, "We need to do something special for our guys."

She agreed. It would be our first joint gathering, once back into our regular lives. Our bags were packed, and our beds made when we realized that we were going to miss being there. We were sitting in the living room of the cabin.

"I'm going to miss it here," said Neekoo in a faraway voice that seemed to address no one in particular. "I know," the rest of us chimed in.

"I've also decided that I'm going to quit my job," Neekoo continued.

"What?" I asked.

"Yeah," she said mostly to herself, in a manner that suggested that she was just now really confirming that decision to herself. "I need to do something different."

"That seems like a leap. Do you know what you're going to do next?" asked Sierra.

"No, not yet, but I'm not going back to the paper."

"Well, you can always help me out until you figure it out," offered BJ.

"Yeah, and you know I'll be more harm than good at Pink Bailey's," answered Neekoo with some sarcasm. This, however, was true.

Our call time for our closing ceremony was two in the afternoon, and we were supposed to line up at the back stage of the auditorium until all the guests were seated. Once that happened, they lined all twenty of us at the front doors for us to make our entrance. There was some music playing in the background as we walked in, and as we made our entrance, all our guests got up to clap. Willow gave the opening remarks, talking about how blessed she was to have run into all of us, and that she knew that we would remain friends and ambassadors of the center, helping other women find their "calm." Then briefly, all of us gave our testimonials and assertions. The last person to go was Dorothy. We expected to hear Willow give closing remarks, but the closing remarks came from DeLuca, standing in the audience with a microphone in his hand and Willow by his side.

"I know you hated me for bringing you here on that first day, but that's how much I love you. To me, you are always perfect. I could have waited until we all got out of here, and we talked about things a little bit more, but I've known from the moment I laid eyes on you that *I will be committed to this woman.* You don't have to say yes, just that you'll think about allowing me to remind you every day that you are the most perfect woman alive to me, by making me your husband."

He wore his signature beautiful, confident smile as he took one step after another toward the stage, and BJ in her baby blue dress and pink scarf around her right wrist, could do no more than gasp. Everyone in the room was waiting for her response, and as DeLuca got to her, with one knee bent and a princess-cut diamond ring in one hand, he asked again, "Will you marry me?" "Yes, yes, yes," was her response, and the kiss was intense amidst all the applause.

"Finally!" I said when I walked up to congratulate DeLuca. He smiled. Looking at BJ, he said, "That was really meant for you, right?" Vernon, and Michael had left their seats. Neekoo and I flanked Michael, and Vernon was next to Sierra. Everyone socializing and meeting each other's family and friends was the way the way our "graduation" ceremony ended. We partook in some of the lite fare provided and then we grabbed our bags and were chauffeured away in a couple of DeLuca's cars to have our own celebration—Pink Bailey's for drinks and dessert.

I was sitting in my office, proofing some storyboards for a new commercial idea we were developing for a client, when my door opened and I heard, "I've got it! I've got it!" from an excited Neekoo barging into my office. We had been out of the center for about a week. Once by my desk, she dialed Sierra and BJ's numbers, put them on speakerphone, and asked them how long it would take them to get to my office. When I heard Sierra ask, "What for?" I couldn't decide if she sounded irritated or distracted.

"Just get here. How long is it going to take you?" was Neekoo's response to Sierra.

"I can be there in twenty minutes," Sierra said, definitely sounding preoccupied. She hung up the phone.

"And you, BJ? When can you get here? I can't start until you guys are both here."

"I can also get there in about twenty," responded BJ, then she couldn't help herself and asked, "You can't give us a clue?"

"No, BJ, just get here," Neekoo said, not giving in.

"Seriously, nothing? I think I'm done with surprises, good and bad, for the rest of the year."

"I'll see you shortly, BJ," Neekoo said in a soft singsong voice with a chuckle. "I'm hanging up now," she added in the same tone.

"Okay! See you soon," BJ said, and they hung up the phone.

She wasn't bouncing off the walls yet, but I had never seen Neekoo this excited. She wanted to use my small conference room and made me promise not to come in until the other two got there, then we were to come in together.

BJ walked into my office with, "Do you know what this is about?" None of us knew.

"We better get in there and find out," I said. Sierra came in after BJ, asking the same question, and BJ was the one who said, "It better not be about that guy from the spa." BJ's protectiveness of Neekoo needed to let up on this guy, I thought.

"You are going to give him a chance," I said to BJ in a demanding tone.

"She doesn't have to give him anything." Sierra chuckled.

"You're agreeing with her about this now," I said in a scolding tone to Sierra.

"Oh no, not at all. I'm just making a point—*she* doesn't have to give him anything. You need to make sure Neekoo only gives him a little." BJ laughed, while I scolded, "Both of you are nuts, period." I opened the door to my conference room.

It was a different, quite professional Neekoo who greeted us when we got there. She had folders with our names on each one, placed in front of three chairs. The three of us wore different quizzical looks on our faces. Standing at the head of the table, Neekoo started her presentation.

"As you three know, I quit my job without knowing what I was going to do next, and gladly so. And then it hit me; it was right there in front of me—*The Look*, a well-being lifestyle magazine for women who aren't seeking to be perfect but to celebrate who they are while enhancing every aspect of their lives in a healthy way." She paused, waiting for our reaction as she had directed us to the first page of the package in front of us that gave the rationale for the magazine. I was totally taken by surprise. As I was taking it all in, my face was reflective. In my peripheral view, I had seen BJ look over my way. Neekoo continued.

"Of course, I could have called it anything, but I felt there couldn't be any other name other than *The Look*, because it was entirely too fitting. I was hoping that you would see the sense behind the name. I want this to be a partnership between us, Rory, with *The Look* magazine housed under the agency. It would eventually become a multimedia powerhouse, you know, with a video arm … okay, I'm getting ahead of myself. Back to the magazine. I would assume duties as editor in chief, and I was hoping Rory would be the publisher, and Sierra and BJ—you could pretty much pick any roles you want. At the least, though, I would like to see you have your own columns in the magazine. So what do you think?"

I didn't respond immediately, as I flipped through the presentation in front on me. "Wow," I started. "This really isn't a bad idea. But …" She must not have heard the hesitation.

"I know, I know, isn't it great?" asked Neekoo, breaking out of presentation mode and going back to being excited as she had before. "BJ? Sierra? What do you think?"

"Well, of course, I think it's great, but are you up to heading an entire staff of people and running the show full-time?" asked BJ.

"I thought about that, and on the editorial side, I've got it covered. I already have in mind those that I would recruit to make up the rest of the editorial team. I plan on offering telecommuting contracts for some of the staff and will use freelancers as much as possible as well. We need to discuss advertising, and I am sure Rory can help with that." She didn't wait for me to answer. "I am not expecting an immediate answer; in fact, if I am being presumptuous and imposing the role of publisher on you, we can revisit that."

"You are really excited about this," I said with a smile. "We are going to make it work. We'll figure out roles later, even if I remain a silent partner of sorts. Maybe as a subsidiary of the agency, we can intertwine aspects of the magazine. We just need to sit down and strategize the plan."

"Cool. Can we meet tomorrow?" asked Neekoo.

"When would you be launching it?" Sierra jumped in, noting that Neekoo seemed to be moving a bit fast with the whole idea.

"I was thinking six to nine months from now? Maybe a year at most, hopefully," answered Neekoo.

"Phew! Okay, you haven't entirely lost your mind yet. With a proposal for a meeting with Rory tomorrow, I was afraid you were trying to do this in three months or something. All right, I'm in," said Sierra.

"Me, too," chimed in BJ.

"I don't think I have to say it, but obviously I'm in, too," I responded. "But, we do have to iron out a few things to make things more seamless and to get the buy-in of my current staff."

"Of course, of course," said Neekoo, nodding her head. Then she started talking a mile a minute about all the ideas she had for the magazine.

Before we left the conference room, BJ told us that she was having a little engagement party at Pink Bailey's and wanted us all there in about two weeks. She suggested that if it was okay with the rest of us, we could use that moment to thank Vernon, Michael, and DeLuca as well.

"Although we wouldn't be thanking *him*, I guess you can invite Tim as well, Neekoo," said BJ in a matter-of-fact tone.

"You're sure?" asked Neekoo as a sister would. With a one-shoulder shrug, BJ said, "Yes. I want us to do something special for the men in our lives, and that's your guy right now, so yes." Neekoo smiled. I smiled and shook my head, knowing BJ was probably still feeling a little reluctant about Tim, but this was her way of showing that she would stand by whatever Neekoo chose.

BJ wanted it to be a midnight party, hoping that I wouldn't mind because I would have to find a sitter for Bella. I was sure my mother would love to have Bella for the night.

BJ was doing really well. She was still seeing Willow, but on an outpatient basis. She hadn't resolved anything with her dad yet, and she didn't really feel the need for a relationship with him, but when Willow had told her that she would still like to continue to see her, to Willow's delight, BJ said yes. They set up weekly sessions, and according to BJ, she hadn't purged since we had started the treatment center. But more importantly, she wasn't getting stressed out as much. It was agreed between the two of them that her handling of stress the way she did was definitely a residual effect of never having dealt with her bottled up resentment for her father. She had also stopped calling him her sperm donor.

Neekoo was the most obviously improved, and it showed in her personality. After leaving Willow's, she was a different person; she was excitable, fun loving, and energetic. Tim had to have something to do with it as well. They were still seeing each other, and they spent a lot of time together. According to Neekoo, they hadn't had sex yet, and he wasn't pushing it. She knew she liked him a lot. She was almost even entirely sure that she probably loved him—her exact words—but she knew that as of right now, she just couldn't' sleep with him because she wanted to make love to him and not have sex with him; that was very important to her.

If she hadn't just mentioned the magazine idea, we were all betting on the fact that she was going to either own her own gym or partner with Tim. He owned his own multiworkout–fitness center in DC, and if she wasn't out with Tim or with BJ at Pink Bailey's or at The Look, she was at the gym. Although it didn't seem like it, it was a healthy dedication to working out that had become her therapy. I joined her about two to three days a week now.

Dallas had wanted Neekoo to also continue outpatient therapy with her, hoping to salvage some kind of communication between Neekoo and her mother, even if they wouldn't build a relationship. All Neekoo said was that she would think about it. Before our time at the center, even if it wasn't too often or for long periods of time, Neekoo called home and communicated with her mother to make sure all in the family were doing well. Since her mother's refusal to acknowledge knowing about Neekoo's rape, Neekoo had settled into comfortable incommunicado with her mother, and she had expressed to us that she felt healthier for it.

The biggest change I noticed about Sierra was hearing her talk about her and Vernon for what seemed like all the time. For all intents and purposes, Sierra seemed as if she was doing fine. I wanted to keep an eye on her because even before we went into treatment, although she was a self-admitted prescription drug abuser, it wasn't even something she did all the time. So it was hard to tell now, whether or not she was still using anything. I chose to believe that she wasn't. She hadn't resumed full work hours yet; she was easing back into her full schedule.

BJ was hard at work planning the midnight engagement party. It was in two weeks, and she wanted all of us to rehearse a dance number for the party. Her theme for the evening was "Private dancer meets Casanova." The night was going to be about BJ and DeLuca, but overall she wanted us to make it about our mates, and us too. Sierra put up a fight when she heard BJ's desire for us to do a dance number.

"No, I am not doing it! You're probably going to want us to wear some skanky outfits, too," Sierra objected.

"And what would be the fun if we didn't get to dress up in some skanky outfits!" rebutted Neekoo.

"We're all doing it, Sierra, *all of us*, whether you like it or not. It's my day, and that's what I want from you," responded BJ.

"Now that's cheap; you're really going to pull the 'it's my day' card and it's not your wedding yet?" fought Sierra.

"Yep, I sure will, since you're choosing to put up a fight," said BJ.

Rehearsals started for us the next day during extended lunch hours so that none of the guys would suspect a thing. BJ had found a dance studio and a private tutor who was going to whip us into a considerably fluid choreography routine by the night of the party. Initially I was anxious, knowing in my heart that I would be the last to pick up most of the steps, and I would be making an absolute fool of myself, but not even that tempted me to stop. I was excited as I drove up to the dance studio, knowing that I would at least have fun with the rehearsals, and on the night of the party, Michael was going to be in shock that I had actually gone through with this.

The rehearsals kicked our butts for the first few days, but then we were really feeling it. Our entire performance was going to be about ten minutes long, with us doing two songs. The first song was a celebration of us being women, and we were going to be fully attired. The second number had us stripping down to our sexy lingerie that BJ, Neekoo, and I were so excited to get, and it intertwined some pole-dancing moves and us teasing the guys with a lap dance.

The big day arrived. BJ wanted us at Pink Bailey's at 9:30 p.m., and she would have the crew set things up for the event before midnight Michael and the guys would join us at midnight. BJ was picking everyone up, and I was the first pick-up at a quarter after eight. I went into my guest room to see my mother, who had graciously driven down from New Jersey to come and spend the night with her grandbaby. Bella was sleeping in my mom's room that night. My mom was making silk pajamas for Bella, who was determined to stay up and help, even though she was primarily just getting in the way by placing the different pieces of material against her body to see how it would look on her. I had a very patient mother, so an outfit that would have easily taken my mother a half hour to get all sewn up, was taking much longer. I kissed them both good night, and assured my mother that she didn't want to wait up. I was gone.

When we got to Pink Bailey's, there was still a crowd. It was Saturday night and normally it didn't close until two in the morning, but there had been signs all week that they would be closed at 10 p.m. this night. We walked into Pink Bailey's around 9:35, and BJ asked for the doors to be locked. It could take those who were already inside dining another hour or so before they left. The last guest finally left around five after eleven, which gave us no time at all to get things together. The cleaning crew had been cleaning and rearranging the restaurant as guests were leaving, so when the last guest left, the crew went into full swing, clearing and cleaning the place out and vacuuming the floors.

The setup was a U-shape seating outlining the dance floor. Five short tables ran parallel along the dance area, with a bit of space between them and one long table that anchored the two parallel lines. The long table was the head table where BJ and DeLuca would be seated. It was draped with a jacquard rose design gold linen cloth; the other tables were draped in white linen. Long-stem fuchsia and pink calla lilies and white draping orchids in clear pilsner vases served as the floral centerpieces. There was pink, teal, and brown chiffon and silk cloth tied strategically around the centerpieces and the lone mic stand in the middle of the dance floor, and that served as the finishing touch to decorating Pink Bailey's for the event.

I was placing the gold party-favor gift boxes containing eucalyptus and mint candles on the tables when the DJ started setting up near the bar. Although the cooks were still back in the kitchen working on the desserts that were going to serve as the finger food, with the background music ready to go, it was time to start.

The attire was cocktail to formal. It was their color, so BJ and DeLuca were complementing each other with elements of teal. She had bought him the teal silk tie he would be wearing against his coral pink shirt and gray tailored suit. She had picked out two dresses for the evening. The first one was a floor-length bustier dress with the gray bustier portion edged in teal to match the flowing, tiered chiffon skirt. Her second outfit was a short teal outfit that flared from the empire waistline with coral pink accessories. I went with a pink number, and had laid out a pink tie for Michael to match my outfit.

People were arriving at exactly midnight, and Sierra, Neekoo, and I were there to greet them at the door, directing them to the bar for drinks. When all twenty guests had arrived, we locked the doors and started the event. I was the unofficial master of ceremonies, as we had totally forgotten to get one. After the initial greeting, I started with showing the picture slide we had created of BJ and DeLuca.

"I would like to thank everyone for joining us for this special moment. As we celebrate the official engagement of Anthony and BJ, Bailey's mom and Anthony's brother will be coming up shortly to say a few words about our guests of honor, and as a backdrop, you will see a visual representation of the BJ–DeLuca story." BJ's eyes grew larger with that last statement; the slide show started early, so I eased out of the way of the projector. Laughter ensued with the first pictures that popped on the screen of BJ as a baby and DeLuca as a baby. Cynthia, who had edited all the images to try and tell a story, had a picture of both of them on each slide at specific stages in their lives. She had also inserted some fun captions that made it seem as if they were searching for each other all their lives. I initiated the well wishes.

"I have known Bailey Irish Kennedy Johnson—phew! Thank goodness she simply goes by "BJ," four names for a tiny thing!" I paused, as there was a ripple of chuckles through the room.

With a beaming smile, I continued, "I've known BJ since she was in college with me, Sierra, and Neekoo, and probably next to her cooking, I would say that love is a close second passion. What I know is when she knows she loves you, she gives you everything."

I looked directly at DeLuca when I said, "I know it has taken her a little while to allow herself to accept how much she loves you, Anthony, but she's there, and I know hers is a commitment you can take to the bank. You may need to open a second account though." I don't know where that second part came from, but thankfully Sierra started laughing and everyone joined in. "She is definitely lucky to have you, and I know you are lucky to have her too. We love you both, and we are too excited for you."

"Here, here," Michael called out, and Sierra and Neekoo started applauding. Everyone else accompanied them.

BJ's mom was next.

"Since Bailey was born, I have known that she is the most precious thing in this world to me. I have never needed anything else but her." Her voice started choking with imminent tears, but she raised her hand to signal that she was okay. I went to stand by her, nonetheless. "When I met Anthony, I was afraid I wasn't going to like him, I was afraid he was going to take my daughter's heart and she wouldn't have enough for me, but then I saw the two of them together and I realized that just like me, he was committed to her. It was in his eyes, and my heart soared because I knew she had something that I didn't, and if I had to share her with him, at least it would be with someone who was committed to her." By now she was speaking through her tears.

"So Anthony," she said and paused to exhale completely, "continue to take care of my baby, even when she acts as if she doesn't need you to take care of her." BJ's mom went over to her table to give her daughter a long hug and a kiss, and then she had a hug for DeLuca.

The entire time her mother spoke, the tears flowed freely down BJ's cheeks as she wore a sweet and loving smile, with eyes just for her mother. When her mother had mentioned that BJ had something that she never had, DeLuca planted a kiss on BJ's wet cheek. BJ took his hand and kissed the back of his palm.

The last speaker was DeLuca's brother and business manager. He was the same guy who had been called in to see BJ the first time she had walked into his dealership and she had pointedly stated that she wanted the owner not the manager.

"BJ, BJ, BJ. The girl is feisty. Classy, but feisty. My introduction to her wasn't the most pleasant," said Joseph to begin his toast. BJ playfully hid her face. "She made it clear that I wasn't the one she was looking for, and it was clear to me that the girl knows exactly what she wants, so I didn't even argue before I got her to Anthony. As I left the room that day, I knew Anthony was hooked. Heck, all we heard from that day onward was Bailey this and Bailey that. Hey, I honestly thought she was a bit high-maintenance for him, but she put a smile on his face and that's all that mattered." BJ treated Joseph to a disapproving look with a raised eyebrow, but it was accompanied with a sly smile. Shaking her head and calling out loud in a teasing tone, Sierra said, "He's not trying to get invited to any of her dinner parties." Everyone laughed. Neekoo gave Sierra's side a dig with her elbow. I shook my head.

Joseph continued, "There was a time I asked about BJ, and he said she was taking a break from the relationship for a while. Anthony never took a break from the relationship."

"Aww," escaped from my lips loud enough for others to hear. I couldn't help it.

"Anthony was sure that one day she would become Mrs. DeLuca. It's pretty much official, and all I can say is BJ, you have our permission to keep him out of the office. Congratulations, guys!"

"Thank you, Joseph," I said with a hug, resuming my pseudo-emcee duties. I turned everyone's attention to the single journals at the center of each table. They were to write down their stories of BJ and DeLuca in it as well as their well wishes toward their journey to becoming Mr. and Mrs.

"See, this is why I shouldn't quit my day job. Before we start writing our well wishes, BJ, Anthony, any words?" They both looked at each other, and DeLuca motioned for BJ to do the honors.

"High maintenance?" BJ started in a feigned exasperated tone and squinted her eyes directed at Joseph. Many of us laughed.

"Seriously, I feel so much love when I look across this room. Mom," she said as she and her mother started choking with tears. She continued through tears and a smile, "There is simply no one better than you. Thank you, thank you for me." BJ's head was tilted to the side with her hands on her heart. Her mom blew her a kiss.

BJ shook her head slightly, calming her tears. Then she threw her head back when she said, "I am the luckiest person in the world to have found Anthony. I can only hope to be there for him as unconditionally as he is for me. Lastly, I know I speak for Anthony when I say we are so lucky to be surrounded by people who love us as dearly as this close circle does. Thank you."

As the applause erupted, I asked for everyone to raise their glasses for a simple toast, "To Anthony and BJ." Several repetitions of the toast went around, and people started chattering as some turned to start writing in the journals. Everyone indulged in the different libations and finger foods that were served.

With that, I handed the microphone to Cynthia. She introduced a singer who was going to buy us some time to get into our performance outfits. The four of us excused ourselves and headed to BJ's back office.

BJ and Neekoo were the first to get ready. We had our lingerie on first, and on top of it we wore tear-off cat suits and clear-heeled dancer's shoes. I was getting ready and needed help zipping up the back of my suit. Neekoo and BJ had already left the room, so I went back to BJ's private restroom, where Sierra was touching up her makeup. With one hand holding the door open and another holding the top of my outfit together, I said, "Hey, I need help." And then I immediately stopped short.

"Pills, Sierra?" I asked in a sinking voice that betrayed my feeling of disappointment.

"I swear, it's my first time since we got out of that place. Actually from before we went to Willow's. But I need it tonight, just this once. I can't perform without it. I really can't. Don't tell BJ, I don't want to upset her," Sierra said in a rushed and desperate tone.

Trying not to sound too exasperated, I answered with concern, "Hasn't that been your problem, always going back to them no matter how long you stay away?" I stopped briefly then added in a stronger tone, "I'd rather you didn't perform." Sierra simply whipped me around to zip me up.

"I can't back out of performing now, Rory. Don't say anything to BJ."

"I won't do that to her, but Sierra …" I started to say.

"I know, Rory, I really do. I promise I do," Sierra assured. "Come on, let's go and make fools of ourselves." She finished as she rubbed my shoulders. I hugged her tightly and let go. At that time, I just didn't feel I could do anything else.

The four of us stepped onto the dance floor to a rousing applause. Cynthia announced, "And here's a special dance number from Bailey, Rory, Sierra, and Neekoo. Dedicated they say, to the special men in their lives."

The reaction to our performance of the first song was met with encouraging cheers; I know I missed a few steps. Accurate dance steps clearly became irrelevant when we ripped off our cat suits at the beginning of the second song. Stripped down to tastefully designed lingerie, we strutted to lead our men from behind their tables to the chairs awaiting them on the dance floor. DeLuca was seated in the first chair that was placed about four feet in front of the other three. Michael and Vernon flanked Tim. It was at that exact moment that the realization set in that my brother was seeing me in my lingerie. I was gripped by performance anxiety for a fleeting second, but I made sure to keep my eyes zoned in on Michael alone. Only DeLuca got a full-on lap dance, but from the look on Michael's face when I was dancing, he enjoyed every minute of my performance for him.

It was worth it all, really it was. But having seen Sierra pop those pills before our performance, I had some mixed feelings. Through the performance, I thought that as far as we had come, this time I needed to really stay on top of Sierra.

Afterward, we changed back into engagement appropriate outfits and joined everyone on the dance floor. As I danced in my husband's arms, with each of my girlfriends in their men's arms, I was happy for how far we had come. The smile that illuminated their faces and the lightness that traveled through their voices seemed to reveal the souls of women at peace with themselves.

One thing was real—in that instance, we were all truly enjoying the moment, savoring the illusions of portraits of our own perfection.

About the Author

T.Richard is a mass media college professor with a passion for women's issues. She founded and currently operates SimpleComplexity, LLC, a nonprofit organization that promotes character and esteem building over physical beauty in young women. Richard blogs and lives in Maryland with her two dogs, AlPacino and PiaDora.